# Pocket Dog

# Pocket Dog

## JIM GARLAND

Boyle
&
Dalton

Book Design & Production:
Boyle & Dalton
www.BoyleandDalton.com

Paperback ISBN: 978-1-63337-750-9
E-book ISBN: 978-1-63337-751-6
LCCN: 2023917162

Printed in the United States of America
1 3 5 7 9 10 8 6 4 2

*Pocket Dog* is dedicated to
Feynman, Kepler, Maxwell, and Newton
for sharing their untiring good humor,
loyalty, and enthusiasm with the author.

# THE LAGOS
# ROYAL COURIER

## LIBRARIAN ANSWERS EMAIL, RECEIVES FORTUNE

BY AKUME NDIGWE

April 7: Mr. Oliphant Allyinphree, 31, a librarian from Boston, MA, USA, yesterday received the surprise of his life. As we reported last week, the renowned Zamfara Wretched Children's Orphanage was on the verge of bankruptcy because its $600 million (USD) endowment had been frozen for months due to the untimely death last year of its transfer agent. The endowment is managed by the First National Bank of Boston and stipulates that the transfer agent must be a US citizen.

"For months, my staff and I emailed inquiries to thousands of US citizens," explained orphanage director, Margaret Kabila. "But even after our irrevocable and generous promise of a ten-percent commission, nobody answered us until we received Mr. Allyinphree's reply."

It seems America is such a virtuous and noble nation that its people have no need for mere financial gratification.

"Mr. Allyinphree saved our children."

Allyinphree is the great-great-nephew of the legendary scholar Gustav Allyinphree. His commission, a lump sum annuity, is valued at $60 million (USD).

Contacted by telephone at his Boston home, Allyinphree said, "I missed the part in the email about the commission. I just wanted to help the orphans." Asked about the flood of marriage proposals he had begun to receive, Allyinphree, who is single, said that for now he hoped his windfall might help him meet a nice woman.

# FAINT HEART, FAIR LADY

**Trocheta intermedia** is a German freshwater leech found under flat rocks in a stream in Freiburg-Herdern. This I remember after nearly two decades, because I can still picture the magazine photo of the tiny leech's swollen red clitellum with its female and male genital pores separated by a mere two annuli. That was heady stuff for a twelve-year-old. I hid the magazine under my mattress, and my adopted parents never knew.

What haunted me about *trocheta* was not so much the oddity of two genders rolled up into one, but rather my belief the slimy little creature was privileged to go through its entire life without ever feeling lonely. Of course, back then, my understanding of hermaphroditic leeches was wrong on many counts, but even today, I can still feel that hollowness deep in my gut.

Ironically, my friends have tried to reassure me the City of Boston, my city, is a near-paradise for unattached men seeking a female companion, and it's true that wherever I turn, I see smart, attractive possibilities. I see them lingering over a foamy cappuccino at Bean So Long, hunched over an elliptical trainer at their gym, skimming *Writer's Digest*, browsing the vegan section of used bookstores, or enjoying an animated tête-à-tête over Grey Goose martinis with their after-work colleagues. In fact, one could plausibly argue that the entire Boston metro area is enveloped in an invisible, enticing fog of pure estrogen. Surely then, one would think any employed, moderately presentable, lonely thirty-one-year-old male should be able to find a suitable companion here. That is, for those of us who aren't lazy, freeloading, oversexed, patriarchal, soul-destroying slobs, which I hope is most of us, including, I also hope, me.

So what is my problem?

That is the question I posed to the universe one crisp Saturday afternoon in early autumn after I had been holed up at my desk sifting through my daily avalanche of marriage proposals. I am a committed rationalist who eschews pseudoscience. I don't believe in astrology, karma, homeopathy, naturopathy, or almost any medical procedure beginning with "holistic." So if the universe was not toying with me because of aligned planets or some unremembered transgression, that left two logical possibilities to explain my troubles, the first being my job.

Please understand, I love my job. That morning, for instance, I'd spent a fascinating two hours in Widener Library helping an MIT emeritus professor research *sepiadarium kochi*, a tiny orange squid that lives at a depth of sixty meters in tropical Pacific waters. The lives of us reference librarians are filled with such adventures, but, alas, they are not adventures easily shared.

However, by far, the bigger culprit was my unexpected sixty-million-dollar windfall. For half a year, the First National Bank of Boston had been sending me a monthly annuity check for $209,136.53 from an irrevocable trust the Nigerian Zamfara Wretched Children's Orphanage set up in my name. I pride myself for living within my means, so I had no desire or need for the money. But the rest of the world certainly did. In the days after my story went viral, I even had to take a leave of absence from work to handle pitches from investment firms, politicians, tax advisors, and salespeople. Why in the world would I want to buy a yacht, a condo in Dubai, or a share of a Bahamian golf resort? I even received invitations to serve on non-profit boards and attend formal fundraisers. As if I owned a tuxedo.

At first, I thought I'd donate my entire newfound fortune to worthy causes, but then I learned I couldn't access my trust fund's principal. I was a transfer agent imprisoned in his own account! I didn't find this dilemma amusing. For the rest of my life, I would receive a huge monthly stipend I had no use for. And I couldn't even give away this stipend, not without first creating a charitable foundation, hiring an investment manager, setting goals, implementing performance reviews, composing a mission statement, and retaining a general counsel, an auditor, and a tax accountant. I knew someday I'd have to cope with all that, but for the time being, I just let the money pile up in my checking account like dirty laundry.

And as if that weren't bad enough, marriage proposals started arriving, at first a trickle, but once my story and home address became public (three million likes on social media sites alone), they poured in by the thousands, some perfectly formatted and spell-checked on laser printers, others composed on ancient typewriters or handwritten in delicate cursive script on perfumed stationery. From across the world came an unstoppable tsunami of entreaties bearing the hopes and dreams of the lonely, the despairing, the miserable, and frequently, the unclothed. My heart ached for these needy souls, but even though I had to reject their overtures, I resolved at least to be civil. So when I wasn't working, I wrote each of them a personal note, knowing every sealed envelope, email, and text message carried an unavoidable burden of disappointment. I had become a purveyor of unhappiness to a loveless and lonely planet.

> *Dear Carla Sue,*
>
> *Thank you very much for your letter, but I must regretfully decline your proposal of marriage. I am so sorry to hear of your mistreatment by the Internal Revenue Service. However, I am sure when you are released from the Danbury Women's Correctional Institution, you will have a full and happy life.*
>
> > *Sincerely,*
> > *Oliphant Allyinphree*

The irony was I had done nothing wrong. The universe had heaped riches on me and flooded me with offers of marriage, but I felt cordoned off from the uncomplicated pleasures of life and love by my own good fortune. People kept asking me if that Nigerian email had changed my life. Yes, of course it had, I wanted to tell them, but for the worse. However, I had to keep my mouth shut. How could I expect understanding from people struggling to keep up with their mortgage payments, student loans, and medical bills—and that was just about everybody I knew. How could they believe I truly didn't want riches and fame? I wanted my life to be simple, orderly, and not muddied up with endless, time-absorbing complexities. Yet I knew what they would think if I tried to explain myself: *Stop whining, you ingrate.* Frankly, I couldn't blame them.

So that afternoon, increasingly despondent and in need of air, I closed the lid on my antique phonograph and slipped its brittle vinyl disk into a paper sleeve. (While working, I had been listening to my collection of Anglo-Saxon fertility chants on the old Mayden Castell label.) I rose, stretched, and lumbered stiffly onto the front porch of my small brick house. Squinting, I rubbed my eyes, took a deep breath, and surveyed the lengthening shadows. The afternoon sky glowed with blousy, pink-tinged clouds, and leaves from my lone maple tree flitted like confused moths onto my tiny front lawn. A quiet breeze had captured the faint, pleasant aroma of hickory smoke, and across the street two young mothers exchanged gossip while their determined toddlers burrowed into an aromatic mountain of cedar mulch. Down the sidewalk my neighbor Annie walked Beatrice, her portly, asthmatic bulldog. Annie is an energetic, no-nonsense journalist for the *Boston Globe* who lives two doors up the street. She has wide brown eyes and an open, friendly smile, and I hoped someday to ask her to join me at a concert or maybe even to dinner. *This could be that day*, I decided, and so why wait? I ratcheted up my courage and, with a reckless wave, called out to her.

"Ollie, I've got the best news," she yelled back. She bounded across the lawn toward me, her face flushed, dragging a reluctant Beatrice. I'd never seen her so ebullient, but before I could say anything, she blurted, "You're not going to believe this. Last night my boyfriend, Bradley, asked me to marry him! I can't wait for you to meet him. He reminds me so much of you." She narrowed her eyes to calibrate my reaction while a drooling Beatrice, exhausted by her six seconds of exertion, collapsed at my feet, looking like a big wheezy meatloaf. Unfortunately, my pretense of untrammeled joy at Annie's news may not have been wholly credible, because a moment later she placed a hand on my arm.

"Ollie, I'd love to see you get out more, to connect with the big world out there," she said in the compassionate voice one uses when addressing the maimed. "You know, faint heart never won fair lady." She knelt on the grass and rubbed Beatrice's ears. Then she looked up at me with a tight frown. "How're you coming with the marriage proposals? Any possibilities?"

Shaking my head, I thought about those I'd answered that afternoon. "Nothing today. Last month one seemed promising, a local musician, a tubist in the Boston John Phillips Sousa Marching Band. But I learned she practices two hours daily, always at home after dark. I didn't think it would work out."

"I see your problem," Annie said, trying unsuccessfully to suppress a smile. Then she stood to face me and was suddenly all business. "Okay, tuba players are out. So who's in, Ollie? Tell me about your dream woman. I'm sure you must have one."

She had caught me off guard, and I struggled to come up with a description. In truth, I didn't have a dream woman. Seeing me flounder, she added, "I'm not talking about her career, or bra size, or whether she's a vegetarian. What about her interests and values? What is she passionate about?"

"I guess I haven't been thinking that way," I said, trying not to sound as clueless as I suddenly felt. "I just want to find somebody who is a good person and who—" I stopped, embarrassed at where the sentence was taking me.

"And who will love you?" Annie said in a soft, cautious voice.

I nodded without speaking, feeling my face redden. I turned my attention to Beatrice, who studiously ignored me, and then I looked up as Annie gently squeezed my forearm. Speaking slowly but firmly, she answered her own question. "That's too low a bar, Ollie. Somewhere out there is a special girl for you. Like you, she is lonely and smart. You just need to find her and let her know you deserve her. Let her see what you can bring to the table."

"I wish it was that easy," I said, provoking Annie to laugh as if the answer to my quandary was self-evident.

"Ollie, for starters, you need to cast your net in a bigger pond. I know you don't like the bar scene, but how about online dating sites? That's how Bradley and I found each other." Glancing down at Beatrice, she added, "Or maybe you should get a pet? Puppies are irresistible to women." She outstretched her arms as the idea firmed, palms outward, a minister exhorting her congregation. "A big, manly dog. Yes, I could definitely see a big, manly dog in your future."

That evening I relaxed on the sofa of my small living room and thought about what I could bring to the table. I took stock of my books organized into categories and subcategories; of back issues of *Ancient Asian Fonts* stacked neatly on the coffee table; of the hand-carved ebony rhinoceros from my Nigerian orphanage perched menacingly on the fireplace hearth; and beside it a Bambuti pygmy blowgun from the Congo, its bore stained gray with Black Mamba venom. Would women find my possessions fascinating? Or would they see through their hints of rugged adventures and exotic travel, as unlinked to reality as evanescent morning dreams? Would they inspect my lovingly arranged bookshelves and see, not the signature of an organized mind, but the mark of frantic desperation?

For me, meeting women has always posed a challenge. There's a historic pub in my neighborhood, The Boiled Hound, a low-ceilinged watering hole with a weathered faux-Tudor façade of gray stucco and dark, rough-hewn oak planks. The pub was founded over a century ago by an ancestor of mine, shortly after the cryptic disappearance of his neighbor's pet bloodhound, who bayed for hours every night. Today, unattached young professionals cluster at the pub after work, and through the building's hazy old windowpanes and pitted black iron mullions, I've watched them chatting and laughing in boisterous groups at wood tables. Sometimes I've seen them go off in pairs and caught snippets of flirty conversations spilling out the open door and leaving me with a tightness in my chest at the thought of soft, nestled fingers in my palm.

But I didn't feel any desire to join them. I couldn't picture myself with a bunch of guys gulping a pitcher of margaritas and preening for the women at adjacent tables. Or worse, sitting alone on a bar stool, nursing a pint of bitter and feigning interest in the Celtics on the pub's big TV screens. So I just stayed away.

A fireplace draft rustled the linen curtains on the large bay window facing the street and rescued me. The fabric billowed, disgorging dust motes that sparkled like tiny jewels in the late afternoon sunlight. Outside on the concrete sidewalk, a man and woman about my age walked their Labrador retriever, the color of milk chocolate. The Lab had the kindly and dignified demeanor of an elderly animal, with a muzzle gone white and a ponderous gait. The woman was pregnant, with long dark hair plaited into a thick braid. Her companion was tall, with wire-rimmed glasses and an air of easy confidence.

A breeze caught a pile of fallen maple leaves on the curb. The woman laughed as the leaves fluttered up around her like monarch butterflies. The man brushed a leaf from her hair, and she turned, smiled at him, and took his arm with the relaxed intimacy of a longtime lover. Their Lab rewarded them with an appreciative wag, and then the three continued their stroll past my window. I wondered if Annie's vision meant that soon there could be a dog in my future. A big, manly dog? An interesting possibility, but it wasn't the sort of decision one should rush into.

# 2

# CHATEAU
# DOM PEDIGREE

*Dear Marija,*

*I'm very touched by your offer of marriage. I've never been to Croatia and thus especially appreciate the snapshots of you at the naturist resort in Valalta. I must say, you have a beautiful tan and appear quite fit, and the surroundings are lovely. However, I'm not really the clubbing type and don't think I'd fit in very well with your social group. Nevertheless, thank you so much for your proposal.*

*Sincerely,*
*Ollie Allyinphree*

**The following Monday,** I drove straight home from work and logged onto the website of Chateau Dom Pedigree, the famous Napa Valley online vineyard and dog breeder. *At Chateau Dom Pedigree, our wines are never dogs, and our dogs never whine.* The kennel's home page featured a sprawling Tuscan-inspired castle made of orange sandstone tiered into the hillside. It had a roof of red tiles and a tall square, crenelated tower with vertical slits, an intimidating defense against marauding hordes of beer drinkers and cat lovers. A trim decorative lake protected the entrance with a hand-operated drawbridge leading to wooden entry doors guarded by two bronze Doberman pinschers. A sign said: *Goldfish! No Swimming!* Orderly rows of carefully manicured grapevines stretched down the valley.

I scanned the pages of awards and listings of the kennel's championship dogs. I read the story of the founder's demise in 1873, when, at ninety-four and in failing health, he plummeted barefoot into a huge oak cask of tawny port. Ignoring pleas from his frantic employees, he floated peacefully for a few minutes until, exhausted, he settled into the sediment at the bottom of the cask. And there he remained, entombed, his grieving family honoring their pledge to him never to disturb the graceful aging of their premier wine. Decades later, the Chateau's 1873 vintage port astounded the wine world by receiving the highest score ever awarded a California winery.

Lastly, I turned to the for-sale puppies, limiting my search to the Ls and XLs. I hadn't been allowed pets as a child, but a large black-and-tan Beauceron named Robespierre lived next door, and we became close friends, exploring the neighborhood together and sharing secrets. I figured an imposing dog like Robespierre would be perfect for me. I eventually settled on a handsome XL German Shepherd puppy with a brownish-gray coat, deep chest, bushy, flowing tail, and gracefully sloping hindquarters.

*Meticulously raised in our exclusive European oak kennels, Scout is a robust, full-bodied puppy, with the trustworthy, loyal, helpful, and friendly demeanor of a 100% German Shepherd varietal. Ever courteous and kind, his lineage has consistently been rated above ninety in competitions. You can expect your new puppy to be obedient, cheerful, and brave. An exceptional value for discerning owners looking for a clean and reverential pet. Three thousand dollars.*

I pressed ORDER NOW, typed my name, address, and Visa number into the shopping cart, and was about to press SEND when I had a premonition of something gone awry. I knew that was crazy thinking, but to be doubly certain, I clicked BACK and reread the description. Scout was a gorgeous puppy. I returned to the shopping cart and tried again to press SEND, but now I couldn't get the cursor to work. Whenever I moved it toward SEND, it slowed down. The closer I got to the button, the more slowly it moved. The cursor was never going to reach the button. How paradoxical.

I leaned forward and browsed again the summary listings, but Scout was still my first choice. I started to return to his listing when I noticed a small blinking button labeled CLEARANCE at the bottom of the screen. I'm always looking for a bargain, so out of curiosity, I clicked it, and up came a photo and description of a single puppy. The text was in an unfamiliar font that had a distinctive Asian feel.

*An unpretentious domestic blend, this unusual XL puppy sparkles with an intelligent head perched enticingly on a sturdy frame, with subtle hints of loyalty and determination. It is his big heart, though, that makes for his attractive and polished finish. His name is Tex. (Sorry, no returns on clearance puppies. Interview required.)*

The description didn't mention price, and the photo showed an ordinary tan shorthaired puppy with black spots, erect ears, and a shortish tail. He was sitting on his haunches, perching, with front paws together and his head turned slightly toward me, as if being auditioned. I tilted my head side to side, and his gaze seemed to follow me, his expression drawing me in with an amused, compelling warmth I hadn't seen in the other photographs. I sat back in my chair and closed my eyes to sort my thoughts. After a short hesitation I straightened, and without knowing quite why, I put my hand on the mouse and clicked ORDER NOW. When the shopping cart appeared, I deleted Scout from the list, added Tex, and moved the cursor toward the SEND button. Now it seemed to speed up, as if drawn by a magnet. Some sort of software glitch, I assumed. Unsure what to expect, I pressed SEND and stared at the acknowledgment screen. *All sales pending until buyers approved by Chateau Dom Pedigree.* It appeared I had bought a dog.

I was about to sign off when my computer ding-a-linged to tell me I had a Zoom invite coming in from Chateau Dom Pedigree. They certainly didn't waste time. I accepted the call, and an attractive woman wearing glasses with thin, dark frames appeared on my monitor. She had a pleasant smile, slightly tousled brown hair that brushed her shoulders, and wide, intelligent eyes. An unusual ivory-colored medallion hung around her neck by a thin gold chain, and on her left hand, I caught a glint of what appeared to be a wedding band. She smiled and adjusted her glasses.

"Good morning from Napa Valley, Mr. Allyinphree," she said. "My name is Regina Malbec. I'm Chateau Dom Pedigree's customer service representative. I've just received your order and want to thank you for it. However, before we fill it, I do have a few questions. I hope this is a good time for your interview?"

I sensed an urgency to her voice, as if interviewing me was, inexplicably, a high company priority.

"Nice to meet you, Mrs. Malbec. Sure, go right ahead." Feeling a little disoriented at the pace at which things were happening, I sat up in my desk chair and ran my fingers through my hair. I hoped a dime-sized coffee stain on my shirt wouldn't show on her screen.

"Oh, it's not Mrs. Malbec," she said quickly. "I mean, I'm not married. I . . . I'm in a relationship, but things aren't . . ."

She looked down and shuffled through the papers on her desk. "Ne to hrædwyrde."

"Excuse me?" I leaned forward, thinking I'd misheard her, and caught a glimpse of her left hand. Wrong finger.

"Oh, sorry," she said, looking up again. "It's an old Anglo-Saxon expression. It means, 'Don't talk so much.'"

"You know Anglo-Saxon?"

"A little, but I'm not fluent." She seemed embarrassed at this disclosure of her linguistic shortcoming.

"Same with me," I said. "I don't practice enough."

She looked at me curiously, maybe thinking I'd made a joke. "Let's see now," she said after a pause. "Where is that list of questions? Ah, here we go." She cleared her throat, leaned forward, and squinted at a printed form on her desk. She looked up at me, and then her brow flickered concern. She held her hand to her mouth. "What's wrong? Do I have something on my—"

"No," I said. I realized I'd been staring. "I was thinking how coincidental it is to talk to somebody named Malbec who works at a winery." That and how cute she looked when she blushed.

"Oh, good," she said, relaxing back into her chair. "My dad was Nepalese, and he changed our family name to Malbec. He was an authority on viniculture, but there aren't that many one-word wine varietals to choose from—"

"Sangiovese, dolcetto, chardonnay, Barbera, viognier," I said, showing off.

She grinned at me. ". . . with only two syllables."

"Okay, uh, merlot, Syrah . . ." I stalled out, having depleted my wine varietal vocabulary.

"Don't forget Riesling," she said. "But Regina Riesling? Too alliterative, don't you think? I'm glad my dad didn't pick Riesling." It was evident I'd met my match in our little game. "Speaking of names," she continued after a moment. She pursed her lips and peered again at the document on her desk. "It says here your name is Oliphant Allyinphree and you live in Boston." She looked up at her monitor. "By any chance are you related to the famous Boston Allyinphree?"

"He was my great-great-uncle. Uncle Gus," I said, surprised she'd made the connection. "Look, here's a picture." I swiveled my webcam and pointed it at a framed black-and-white lithograph on the wall above my desk. "I think he was about ten when this was taken."

Regina leaned forward and studied the child's image. "Oh, how darling! My dad told me your uncle was an inspiration to him when he was growing up in Kathmandu."

"What did he find inspiring? Your father was a scientist?"

"No, I think it was your uncle's rejection of materialism. My dad worried that wealth too often undermines a person's moral core." She hesitated, biting her lower lip, like the conversation was becoming too personal.

I said, "I've heard there's a museum about my uncle in Kathmandu. Someday I'd like to see it."

She waited until I turned the webcam back around. "Um, may I call you Oliphant? And please call me Regina."

"Sure, Regina, but most people call me Ollie."

"Ollie Allyinphree?" she said, suppressing a giggle. "Sorry, I'm being rude."

I laughed too. "Happens all the time. It's a little embarrassing to be named after a children's game."

She didn't answer for a moment, and then, holding my gaze, she said, "Actually, I like it. It means you're free to come out of hiding into the open. I think that's a loving sentiment for parents to bestow on their newborn."

I'd never known my mother and father and had always assumed my nickname was a joke. The thought it was intended as a gift . . . what had she said, a 'loving sentiment'? I swallowed and blinked, feeling sheepish at an unexpected surge of feeling. "I guess I'd never thought of it that way."

Regina watched me without speaking, and then her voice became business-like. "So, Ollie it is. And your age is . . . ?"

I collected myself. "Thirty-one."

"Oh, that's my—Let's see, do you own or rent?"

"Own."

"Good. And your marital status is . . ."

"Single."

"Is that right? Single."

"Is that a problem?"

"Oh no, of course not," she said quickly. "It's that, well, we do worry about something happening to our dog owners who live alone."

"You mean like heart attacks or strokes?"

"Oh, you have no idea. How about choking on fish bones, starving in locked basements, or being electrocuted by frayed lamp cords? Why, we even had a Yorkie owner whose legs were devoured by flesh-eating bacteria, and there was nobody there to help her. But I'm sure your legs are fine," she added after a pause, evidently concerned how I might react to her litany of single-dog-owner calamities. She swept her hair back and flipped to the second page of the form. Glancing up, she said, "Are there close relatives or next of kin who could take care of Tex if, well, worse comes to worst? Maybe you have family living in Boston?"

I said, "No, my parents died in an accident when I was a month old, so I never knew them."

"Oh, I'm sorry. I'm sure you must wonder what they were like, sometimes." She hesitated. "I know I do," she said quietly. Seeing my puzzlement, she added, "I mean, my mother died when I was born, so I never knew her either." We sat silent and then she said, "So who took care of you when you were little, Ollie, if you don't mind me asking?"

"I was adopted and raised by my aunt and uncle."

She looked at me and nodded. "Good. Then, if necessary, they could care for Tex, so long as they aren't destitute, addicted to drugs, or in prison. Or dead, naturally. The kennel has strict rules about that."

"Which part?"

"What? Oh, I see. Everything but the dead part. Dead is okay. I mean, not really, of course, but . . ." She blushed again and held her hand over her mouth. I think we were both feeling a little awkward at the personal sidebars that kept intruding into our interview.

I tried to resurrect the lighter tone. "So far as I know, my aunt and uncle are both retired, substance free, and law-abiding." I didn't tell her they lived in Nevada, I hadn't seen them in five years, and they didn't like dogs. I hoped I'd dodged a bullet.

"Excellent. That's a relief," she said, typing a few characters on her keyboard. I felt a twinge of guilt. "Okay, no other relatives then."

"Actually, I have a twin brother somewhere, but I don't know his name." I was beginning to feel nervous about how my interview was going.

Regina looked up from her desk. "Really? How did that happen?"

"My brother was adopted by a Central American family when we were babies and taken to their home country, but I don't know which country." I felt a little uncomfortable delving this deeply into my family background, but I didn't have any choice.

"And you don't know their surname, either?"

"I know his birth name was Oren, but his adoptive parents changed it. I've searched birth records and interviewed former hospital staff, but no, I don't know anything about him. But I do wonder sometimes how he's doing. Or even if he's still living."

"Of course you do. That's really unfortunate," she said, leaning back in her chair.

I nodded, and then a question occurred to me. "So your dad raised you by himself? Not that it's any of my business."

She bit her lower lip and took a long moment before answering. "Yes, he never remarried," she said finally. "He was a good father." Her voice caught, and I didn't say anything. "I'm sorry," she said. "My dad passed away six months ago. We were very close."

This was not the discussion I thought I'd be having with a woman I'd known for only a few minutes. I wasn't quite sure how things had gotten so personal so quickly. Regina evidently was wondering that also, because she fingered the papers on her desk, looked up at me, and cleared her throat. "Now if you don't mind, Ollie,  I have some financial inquiries. Obviously, we have to make certain our owners can support their new puppy." She adjusted her glasses and consulted the questionnaire again.

"Naturally, but I assure you, that won't be a problem."

"Yes, but rules are rules. Your bank is . . . ?" She pursed her lips, as if she half-expected opposition to her financial inquiries.

"The First National Bank of Boston," I replied, and was relieved to see her relax at this disclosure.

"A good, sound bank. I hear they're pet friendly, too. You can fill in your account numbers in the boxes on the screen, and we'll start our verification process."

"No problem," I said, "but all I have is a checking account and one charge card." I opened a desk side drawer and retrieved my checkbook and a recent Visa statement. I typed the information into the computer, but held my checkbook away from the webcam so she wouldn't see I hadn't recorded my checks or balanced my statements.

Regina looked at her screen and said in a worried voice, "I hope that's going to be enough. Just check 'none' in the boxes on savings, investment, and offshore accounts, foreign stocks, real estate investment trusts, tax-exempt bonds, hedge funds, derivatives, and private equity holdings. Now, excuse me while I give your information to Mr. Milken in our asset verification department. He can be pretty hard-nosed, but I'll put in a good word for you. I'll be back in a jiff."

Regina pushed her chair back, stood, smoothed her blouse, and walked away from her desk. I could hear barking in the background. Chateau Dom Pedigree seemed to be run very professionally, but why did they want so much financial information? Was it because Tex was a clearance dog? I didn't want my skimpy credit history to derail my purchase, but I also didn't want to tell Regina about my monthly orphanage checks. Nothing good had ever come from that money.

While waiting, I thumbed through the October issue of *Ancient Asian Fonts*, which had arrived the day before. The lead article featured newly discovered logograms on a Chinese bronze vessel from the Shang dynasty. I was halfway through the writeup when Regina returned. She sat down and smiled brightly at me. I could see dimples in her cheeks and her eyes sparkled, even in the monitor.

"Good news," she said. "You passed. Mr. Milken assured me you won't have any trouble buying chewy toys for your puppy. Actually, he wanted me to ask if he could contact you with a few investment suggestions. Evidently, a senior vice president at your bank took his call and talked to him about your account. There was something amusing about it, but Mr. Milken was laughing, and I didn't get it all."

"Sure, that would be okay," I said, exhaling. "I've been thinking I should learn more, but I'm not very interested in financial matters."

"Me neither. I've never even balanced my checkbook," she said, pausing while she opened a spiral bound notebook. "Now, if I could get a brief medical history. We need to make sure our owners are healthy. I just have a few routine questions." I sat quietly while she turned to a page in her notebook. "First, do you have tender nipples?"

"What?"

"Oops, never mind, that's the women's page. Silly me." I didn't know why she seemed so flustered. "Okay, here we go. Do you have a history of contagious rashes, Tourette's syndrome, oozing boils and sores, out-of-body experiences, violent fits of rage, strange fevers or palpitations, or uncontrollable flatulence?"

"No, I'm very healthy."

"Good. Do you levitate, speak in tongues, practice voodoo, or talk to God more than five times a day?"

"No to all."

"Are you a witch, and if so, do you conduct ceremonies in a licensed coven? I'm guessing you're probably okay, but I have to ask."

"I'm not a witch, but that's kind of an intrusive question, don't you think?"

"It is, I suppose," she said. "It's just that we had a bad experience a few months ago . . ." She hesitated at the memory and checked a few boxes on her form. Her voice had the slightest accent, Nepalese I assumed. "Now a few final questions, again a formality. Have you ever hijacked a plane, blown up a college dormitory, or shot an elected official who didn't deserve it?"

She was teasing me! "Not that I remember," I said, and she grinned.

"And lastly, do you eat fish at least twice a week, wash your hands after petting goats, and avoid eating garlic before going on a date? Actually, that last one I put in myself," she said with a little laugh.

Was she flirting with me? Now I was the one feeling self-conscious. I said, "To be totally honest, I'm not one hundred percent sure about the goat question. Once, when I was in Canada—"

"Oh, I'm speaking about domestic goats. Sorry, I should have made that clear."

"Then I'm good."

"So let me check . . ." She studied her list again and then set it down on her desk. She looked up at me and exhaled, as if she were the one who had just been interviewed. "Ollie, everything seems to be in order. We'll ship Tex by an overnight animal courier service. We've done business with them for years. The service will hand Tex off to the Boston post office, who will deliver him to your house. You probably won't see him until the end of the week since I want him to have a final check-up by our vet."

She was silent for a moment and then leaned forward. Her voice took on a serious note. "Ollie, I love this puppy. I can't tell you how important he is to me. I'm so glad you're the one who bought him. It seems almost like it's pre-ordained."

"How so?"

She laughed. "Tex and I play this little game together, a variation on hide-and-seek. I call it 'Olly Olly In Free.'"

I laughed too. "Sounds more like coincidence than pre-ordained."

"To tell the truth, I'd planned on keeping Tex for myself but, well, that isn't possible." She looked away from me, momentarily embarrassed, and then turned back. "He's a very special dog, and I'm going to miss him terribly. Please call me when you get him, so I'll know he's arrived safely." She raised her eyebrows and shrugged, as if apologizing for her devotion.

"Of course," I said. I felt like hugging her, but I wasn't sure whether it was to make amends for taking away the puppy she loved, or because she seemed so open and approachable. Whatever, this discussion had not gone like I'd expected.

She fingered her little ivory-colored medallion, weighing a decision. Then, in a voice so soft I had to lean forward to hear her, she said, "Actually, Ollie, there is one more thing, if you don't mind."

"Sure, Regina, anything." I realized I didn't want our conversation to end.

"I was thinking, if you're out this way sometime, perhaps you could meet with Mr. Milken, and afterward, I could show you the kennel and winery. There's a spa up the road in Calistoga, and fun restaurants, and I thought we could get to know each other a little, and maybe have dinner—"

"Oh! That's a great idea, Regina. I'd really like that." I felt my heart thump-thumping.

"Wonderful," she said, relaxing and smiling broadly. "I'll send you an invitation. I mean, I have your address here, and . . . maybe you could even bring Tex."

We signed off, and I sat for a long moment staring at my computer screen, trying to calm myself. Wow. Out of the blue, a smart, pretty woman seemed interested in me. When had that ever happened? I was sure it wasn't my money, and I liked that about her. Then I had a dark thought. Hadn't she said she was already in a relationship? *But things aren't* . . . she'd also said. Aren't what? Going well? Was I reading too much into her words? Maybe she was being friendly only because I was the new owner of her favorite dog. No, best to be positive. Regina Malbec was solidly in my thoughts, along with my new XL light tan spotted puppy, both three thousand miles and three hundred million people distant.

3

# FLYING
# BLIND

*Canus lupus familiaris, population one billion: a furry,
carnivorous scavenger known for drooling, bad breath,
and a preoccupation with bodily functions. Prone to beg-
ging, sniffing crotches, licking its privates, drinking from
toilets, leaving paw prints on bedsheets, chewing fringes
off Asian rugs, and making amorous advances to the
ankles of spinsters.*

**It was inky dark** in my dog crate. I was comfortably warm, with
plenty of water and a soft pad to stretch out on, but even so, the
aircraft vibration and engine noise made it impossible to sleep.
Regina hadn't mentioned my destination, but I'd already been in
the air four hours, so I knew I'd end up far from my kennel.
Unfortunately, when Regina lifted me into my crate and kissed
me on my head, biting her lip to keep from sobbing, I knew then
she wasn't my assignment. It was a bitter kibble to learn it would
be a distant stranger.

I passed my time musing about my future. All of my friends
agree that humans are challenging to work with. Take Zephyr,
for example, a three-year-old Brittany who adores her human,
the kennel receptionist, but is continually frustrated by how long
it takes her to do the simplest things: throwing a tennis ball,
hunting down her iPhone before a walk, opening a package of

liver-flavored treats. Of course, it's not her human's fault that human time runs one-seventh normal speed.

Unfortunately, moving slowly is the least of human problems, and frankly, it's hard to see how the species has survived. Over the centuries, the poor creatures lost their fur, exposing their bodies to frigid nights and bitter winds. They evolved ungainly rear legs and short, useless forelegs, forcing them to lumber around unsteadily. Their tails withered, ruining their sense of balance. Their vision deteriorated, and so did their hearing.

But worst of all, they lost their olfactory sense, most of it anyway, and with it, the ability to communicate. What a terrible handicap, not to mention how awful to be denied forever the bouquet of lovely aromas that envelop other living creatures. That, in itself, should have doomed the species. To their credit, however, humans eventually learned to use vibrations of air molecules to convey their thoughts. Clumsy and inefficient, but better than nothing, I suppose, except in the search for a mate. In that domain, humans are pretty much helpless.

For us dogs, pheromones provide an instant, trouble-free way to perpetuate our bloodlines. One whiff and the procreation instinct becomes irresistible; mating occurs without further thought with whoever is nearby and ready, thus quickly and effortlessly ensuring our species' survival. Humans, tragically, are not only barely able to smell their own pheromones, but they are oblivious to their impact. For them, finding a mate is an angst-ridden nightmare, compounded by their inexplicable cultural preference to restrict the search to people who already know each other. As if that mattered. Of course, that's where we dogs play a role, and it's a good thing.

I was toying with these thoughts as the hours passed. I had no idea where I was going or what challenges I would face. What if my new human didn't keep my water bowl filled, or forced me to eat tasteless dry dog food? So many risks. I was figuratively and literally flying blind. I had no instructions, no briefing, no cautions, no explanation, no context, and no guidance.

I found myself panting and tried to calm down and push away these worries. After all, this was nothing new. That's the way my assignments always began.

# WELCOME TO
# YOUR NEW HOME

*Dear Patricia and Cynthia,*

*Thank you so much for your letter. I laughed when I read about Patricia waking up and finding a Red Sox tattoo on her arm. Quite a jolt for a Yankees fan! I'm sure you must have many other fun stories about sharing the same body. How nice it must be never to feel lonely. However, I must decline your proposal. I'm afraid I'm not much of a base-ball fan, and I've never caught the NASCAR bug, though I'm sure it's my loss. Otherwise, you both sound delightful.*

*Sincerely,*
*Ollie Allyinphree*

**On Saturday morning** the mail truck pulled into my drive-way, its clunky four-cylinder engine rattling my living room windowpanes and spewing oily fumes. It shuddered to a wheezy stop, and the driver's door screeched open. I set down my coffee mug, stepped onto the front porch, and squinted in the sunlight. Modest pre-World War II brick houses line my street, all pretty much the same—two stories, three small upstairs bedrooms, and a rear kitchen. My street is quiet and respectable, with mature maple and chestnut trees. I liked living there.

The air had the freshly scrubbed smell of autumn, and at the street, a tangled mat of leaves from my large maple tree glistened with morning dew. Bart, our mail carrier, had climbed out of the driver's seat and was walking around to the truck's rear cargo door. He glanced at me and scowled. For the past several weeks, Bart has had to make an extra stop at my house because the flood of marriage proposals won't fit through my door's mail slot. He obviously blames me for this intolerable imposition. I stood on my front porch and tried to make nice. "Looks like a fine day, Bart. How're things?"

"Another damn bin of letters," he replied. "Since you're here, you can walk over and pick 'em up yourself." Bart always seemed to be in a bad mood. He had recently transferred to our route from a desk job at the Dead Letter Office, and neighbors had been complaining about misdelivered letters and packages. I walked to the truck, whose red and blue stripes and USPS logo were spattered with dirt and grease, as if the sheet metal suffered an ugly skin disorder.

"Mind giving me a hand?" I said, as I struggled with the overflowing fiberglass bin.

"I would prefer not to," Bart said, his voice overtly sullen.

I stared at him, beginning to feel irritated. "Oh? You feel okay?"

Bart said nothing. His uniform hung loosely on his frame, his shoes were scuffed, and there was egg stain on his collar. From his pasty coloring, I figured the Dead Letter Office was probably in a windowless basement room at the Post Office building. I guessed he was about fifty, though he could have been younger. "Bart, aren't you supposed to deliver the mail to the door?"

"I would prefer not to," he said again, his tone now defiant, as if standing on high principle. He didn't look at me.

So while Bart, the mail carrier who refused to carry the mail, stood impassively, I lugged the container up the steps to the house and struggled to prop open the storm door with my foot. I carried the bin into the kitchen and dumped the pile of envelopes onto the kitchen table. When I returned to hand him the empty bin, he was still standing beside the truck's open cargo door.

"There's an overnight delivery too," he said, gesturing vaguely in the direction of a rectangular wooden box on the truck's bed. It was a bit larger than a shoe box. A glossy red sticker on one side read *Fragile!* "You have to sign for it," he said as he scanned the label.

"Nothing else? I'm expecting a larger crate." I scrawled my name on the scanner.

Bart scowled without speaking, having evidently depleted his inventory of available words. He lowered the truck's cargo door, climbed back into the driver's seat, and started the motor, which belched oily smoke. The truck made a protesting noise as he shifted into reverse and backed out of the driveway. A curious fellow, Bart. Hard man to know.

I carried the box into the house and set it on the kitchen table, pushing aside the envelope pile. It was made from thin plywood, with the cover attached by metal staples, and on the sides was a handful of small perforations. I retrieved a flat-bladed screwdriver from a toolbox in the hall closet and started prying out staples. All went well until my screwdriver slipped on a corner staple and gouged my palm, but I eventually managed to work the stubborn staple loose. Sucking on my bruised palm, I lifted off the box's cover and saw a bottle of white wine lying on its side, nestled in a bed of straw. It had an elegant platinum-colored foil embossed with the vineyard name, and the label featured a stylized line drawing of a Labrador retriever. A small handwritten card looped around the bottle's neck with a gold string:

*Hi, Ollie,*

*I hope you enjoy this complimentary bottle of our finest chardonnay as you become acquainted with your new puppy. It was nice to chat with you. Call anytime. Really, I mean it.*

*Regina*

What puppy? I hoped Bart hadn't delivered my dog to the wrong address. I studied the card and smiled. Regina's handwriting slanted to the left, with open loops in her cursive t's and e's, and a hole between the upstroke and downstroke—the signature of an adventuresome, open-minded temperament.

Distracted, I retrieved an envelope I'd knocked on the floor and noticed my name and address showing through its cellophane window. It was my monthly annuity check from my Nigerian trust account. Always the same: $209,136.53. I tossed the check into the kitchen odds-and-ends drawer beside the refrigerator, where it joined two others, and made a mental note to deposit them in my checking account. I kept forgetting to do that. Then I confronted the pile of unopened letters on the kitchen table and sighed. I had fallen behind in my letter-writing, and there was an even bigger pile on my desktop. Fortunately, I had the weekend to catch up.

I was rereading Regina's note when I heard a squeak like a rusty hinge coming from the box. I pulled out the straw packing and found beneath it a cardboard divider protecting something below. I suspected a wineglass, maybe two, but when I removed the divider, it revealed a small wire cage that was cleverly gimbaled on a metal stand, so it was always right-side up. When the cage swiveled, the bearings squeaked. A small water bottle with a tiny curved nipple extended into the cage's interior, and inside, on a tiny cushion next to a half-eaten dog biscuit, sat a tan-and-black spotted clump of hair with tiny ears and a short tail. Had Chateau Dom Pedigree sent me a hamster by mistake? Something was wrong. I glanced at my watch. In California, it was half past seven; the kennel wouldn't open for another thirty minutes.

No, it definitely wasn't a hamster. The creature was light tan with black spots, short hair, erect ears, a shiny wet nose, and oversized paws. A pink tongue lolled from its mouth, and it panted slightly. I was looking at a tiny, perfectly proportioned puppy. I unfolded the packing slip tucked in the box. It said the dog's name was Tex, aged ten weeks. Instead of an XL puppy, Chateau Dom Pedigree had sent me an XS. Something was more than wrong. This was a disaster. I set the packing slip on the table and studied the tiny dog. He looked up at me and slowly uncurled himself from the floor of the crate until he was standing. He yawned and shook himself from nose to tail, as if shedding rainwater. Then he raised his nose and sniffed the air with short, precise breaths.

After a few seconds, he faced forward, toward the door of the cage, and slowly slid his rear paws backward to stretch out his spine in a succession of small, careful steps. He held his tail perfectly level. With a single motion, he splayed his front legs to each side until his paws formed a triangle with his nose at the vertex. Slowly, he collapsed his forelegs until they rested on the cage bottom with his rump in the air. Keeping his neck level, he turned his head downward to look at the cage floor. He froze in this position, stretching his body lengthwise. Finally, he relaxed, shook himself again, ambled over to the door of the cage, and perched there on his haunches. He looked up at me and wagged his tail.

I could hardly believe what I had seen: a ten-week-old puppy performing *adho mukha svanasana* with the grace and discipline of a yoga master. How had Regina taught that pose to such a young puppy? I remembered her comment about Tex being a very special dog. No kidding. I looked more closely at him, and he returned my gaze, wagged faster, gave a friendly yip, and pawed at the cage door. No question he was the clearance puppy on the website. I moved slightly, and he turned his head to hold my gaze. I had the same feeling I remembered from his website photo, like he was checking me out. So what was going on? I reached in, unlatched the cage door, and he hopped up onto my palm. I lifted him out of the box and scratched behind his ears with my pinky. His tail drooped with pleasure, and the red welt on my palm caught his eye. He turned and licked the sore spot. He was a friendly little rascal.

Still, this tiny dog wasn't what I'd ordered, and I knew I'd look ridiculous walking around Boston with him. I'd exchange him Monday morning for Scout, the XL German Shepherd I'd originally selected. But then I remembered there was a no return policy for clearance dogs. Even so, the kennel would surely make an exception for a simple mistake. The problem was that if I sent Tex back, I knew Regina would be disappointed. To be fair, I needed to talk to her first, so she wouldn't be caught off guard. I was dreading the call.

My watch said it was now after eight in the morning in California, so I sat at my desk and dialed the kennel's 800 number listed on the packing slip. The phone was picked up by voicemail, and I found myself smiling as I listened to Regina's voice. I'd play things by ear:

"Thank you for calling Customer Service at Chateau Dom Pedigree. If you would prefer to hear this message in Acholi, press 1 followed by the pound sign. For Afghani, press two followed by the pound sign. For Afrikaan, press three followed by the pound sign. For Akan, press four followed by the pound sign…"

I set the handset on the desktop, pushed back my chair, walked to the kitchen, washed and dried my breakfast dishes, and replaced them on their shelf. I ground some beans and started a fresh pot of coffee. While waiting for it to finish, I wrote myself a reminder note to take my annuity checks to the bank. I poured myself a mug and took a pint of half-and-half from the refrigerator. I added two tablespoons to the mug, replaced the carton on its shelf, and closed the refrigerator door. Then I returned to my desk and picked up the handset.

"…For Zaghawa, press 348 followed by the pound sign. For Zulu, press 349 followed by the pound sign. For Zuni, press 350 followed by the pound sign. To hear this list again, press zero followed by the pound sign." There was a brief pause, and then, "We're sorry, but the kennel is closed. Our business hours are Monday to Friday 8 a.m. to 5 p.m." Click.

Clearly, I had to wait until Monday to straighten things out. That evening I was planning to attend a lecture on the virtues of platonic love, sponsored by the singles club of the Unitarian Church. The speaker was Professor Lucretia Von Hindenberg, a well-known local scholar who'd written a book on the subject. I hoped Tex was housebroken, but even so, I didn't want him chewing on the woodwork while I was gone. Probably best just to close him in his cage. I looked over at it on my kitchen table, next to the wood shipping box and wine bottle, but it was empty, and its door stood open. I'd forgotten completely about Tex while I was on the phone.

Then I heard a yip and saw him sitting on a stack of unopened letters, staring at my shirt pocket. I lifted him up and he hopped into it, rearranging himself so he could face forward, with his head and forelegs perched on the pocket's upper edge. He seemed so attentive, I left him there and started walking through my house, room by room, explaining each feature aloud, as if I were selling real estate. We toured the three upstairs bedrooms, and I showed him my walk-in closet with shelves on one side and hanging rods on the other.

"I keep my shirts folded on this lower shelf," I said. I noticed he craned his head up to look at my face when I spoke. I gestured to the upper shelf. "And up here are my shirts, sweaters, and T-shirts. I hang my pants, neckties, and sport coat on the rods, arranged by season, and below them on the floor are my shoes, brown on the left, black in the middle, and workout shoes on the right." This was fun. I'd never shown anybody around my house before.

As we completed our inspection, it occurred to me my closet seemed packed full. Could I rearrange it if someday I wanted to squeeze in another person's clothes? On the way back downstairs, I glanced at my double bed, which was also too small for two people. If I slid my dresser over a few inches, I could squeeze another dresser between the two windows facing the rear yard. I looked down at Tex perched in my shirt pocket and noticed he was still studying my face.

Downstairs, we toured my living room, the only room I'd

bothered to furnish properly. I'd covered the hardwood floor with a diamond-pattern Tibetan rug from a consignment store; it had been hand-woven at a monastery during the 1970s from brown and gray wool. I had furnished the rest of the room with a contemporary sofa in beige and brown tweed, a black Chinese coffee table and matching side tables, a Japanese tansu with forged black iron hardware, and a wood Japanese writing desk with bookcases on each side. I was proud of the room's look, though I didn't often get to show it off.

At the end of our tour, I showed Tex my mathematics books, arranged alphabetically—Euler, Gödel, Hilbert, Legendre, Poincaré, and so forth—and then on to physics, the humanities, linguistics, and social sciences. I have a particular interest in Albanian poetry and, of course, medieval fertility chants. I finished by showing Tex my prize possession, a first edition of my great-great-uncle Gus's book on the languages of extinct Polynesian cultures. Bound in leather with gold inlay, its pages yellowed and brittle, the book is only twenty-seven pages, given that there are but a tiny number of extinct Polynesian languages and practically nothing is known about any of them. I cradled the book in both hands and held it so Tex could inspect it. He sniffed the cover respectfully and then cautiously reached out a paw to touch the title page.

After the tour I was ready for lunch and figured Tex would be too. I found half a sandwich in the refrigerator that the owner of a local deli makes for me: roast beef shaved rare, with soft Havarti cheese and horseradish sauce on multigrain bread. Fortunately, I'd thought ahead and also had on hand a bag of puppy chow. I put Tex on the kitchen table and set a few kibbles in a saucer beside him. He glanced at them and looked up at me with an are-you-kidding-me expression, so I tossed the kibbles and rummaged in the refrigerator's lower drawer until I found an open package of smoked turkey slices. I cut a piece into tiny slivers and placed them on the saucer. Tex circled the slivers, sniffed, sighed, and flopped down on the table, facing away from the saucer. He turned his head and looked up at me again.

"Tex, eat," I said. He wasn't interested, so I scraped the turkey into the sink. Now he stared intently at me, his tail motionless. I took a bite of my sandwich, but he didn't drop his gaze, and I felt guilty eating in front of him. "Ahh, I get it," I said finally. I cut off a corner of my sandwich with a paring knife, discarded the crust, and placed it on the saucer. Tex leaned forward and sniffed it cautiously, and with one paw, edged a sliver of onion from between the bread slices onto the saucer rim. Then he looked down at the sandwich and up at me and enthusiastically wagged his tail. I reached over and petted his head. I knew I was being trained.

"Tex, welcome to my home," I said, after we had finished lunch and plopped down on the living room sofa. I'd send him back to the kennel on Monday morning, but we'd be able to hang out together on Sunday. I glanced at my watch and saw I had plenty of time to get ready for my singles club lecture. I placed a sofa pillow on my lap, and Tex hopped onto it. He turned around several times to make a shallow indentation, curled up, yawned, and closed his eyes. The little fellow was exhausted from his long journey. I watched his chest rise and fall. His eyelids fluttered shut, and after a minute or two, he growled and uttered a tiny, muted bark. What could a ten-week-old puppy be dreaming about? Stillness had settled over the room, save for the distant hum of city traffic and the breezes of an early New England autumn. The last thing I remembered before I also drifted off was a feeling of contentment, almost as if some kindly presence had tamed my monkey-mind with an unfamiliar but welcome spirit of serenity.

# IS ELI
# COMING?

*Dear Madison,*

*I know you are angry at your dad for grounding you and taking away your iPhone, but you are far too young to marry me or anyone else. I am sure one day you will find an awesome mate, but that day is years away. For now, you should do as your father says and focus on your science project. Believe me, eighth grade is no cakewalk for anybody, even if she didn't have a teacher as mean and unfair as Mrs. Martinez.*

*Sincerely,*
*Ollie Allyinphree*

**Monday, 11:03 a.m.** I took the day off from work to deal with my Tex problem, sat at my desk, and logged onto the Chateau Dom Pedigree website. As it turned out, I'd stayed home with Tex Saturday evening because my singles group lecture on platonic love was canceled due to lack of interest. Then, yesterday, Tex and I drove to the Boston Common. Unfortunately, my car shuddered and died at the intersection of Beacon and Walnut Streets and I had to call AAA. It was just a short walk from there to Frog Pond, so while waiting for the tow truck, Tex and I went to watch the frogs.

It was just a year ago, the day after Harvard's varsity badminton team trounced the Yale Bulldogs four games to zero, that a thousand tiny white frogs with a blue Y-shaped marking mysteriously appeared in the pond, after two frogless centuries. Subsequently, the frogs doubled in number every month, their croaking soon drowning out the carousel music and shouting children. Local amphibian clubs at first set out large tubs of rancid water filled with mosquito larvae to feed the expanding population, a successful but not terribly popular solution. Then Harvard biologists discovered the frogs were ignoring the mosquitoes in favor of eating each other, thus stabilizing their numbers at four million. Today, the little critters are a favorite draw for Boston frog lovers. And so, while I relaxed on one of the green benches surrounding the reflecting pool (the park staff thoughtfully provide mosquito repellent and paper towels to wipe off frog droppings), Tex frolicked across the lawn surrounding the pond, scattering frogs like clouds of Mexican jumping beans. Tex otherwise seemed older than his ten weeks, and I wondered if he would outgrow this puppy behavior.

But now it was time to act. I looked at the Chateau Dom Pedigree home page, pressed the CONTACT US button and then CUSTOMER SERVICE. I smoothed back my hair and selected the video option. I felt a ripple of nervousness thread up my backbone. *Call anytime. Really, I mean it,* Regina had written. Unfortunately, this was one call I knew she wouldn't want to receive.

But instead of Regina, an older lady with curly shoulder-length brown hair appeared on my screen. She wore a necklace that looked vaguely familiar and had bifocals perched on her nose. She smiled pleasantly but seemed flustered. I could hear barking. "Is this the customer service department?" I said. "I was calling Regina Malbec."

"You've got the right extension," she replied. "My name is Maude Knightsbridge. My husband and I own the kennel, and I'm just substituting for Ms. Malbec, our former customer representative. How may I help you?"

*Former* representative? Had Regina been fired? Was she ill? I introduced myself and explained my problem.

"Oh dear, Mr. Allyinphree," she said, furrowing her brow. "We take pride in sizing our dogs accurately. Let me print out your order, and if there's a problem, we'll make it right. Hold on, and I'll be back shortly." She pushed her chair back and walked away from her desk, and in a few minutes she returned, holding several sheets of paper. "This is puzzling," she said, squinting at the first page. "Ms. Malbec wrote that you did very well in your interview. However, you say you ordered an XL puppy but we sent you an XS?" She set the papers down on her desktop.

"Yes. Is there any chance I could exchange him for a German Shepherd puppy named Scout?" I glanced over at Tex, who was sitting on a paperback book at the edge of my desk. I hated the thought of putting him through another long cross-country flight. He wasn't a too-small sweater or defective toaster oven.

"Scout's still available," Mrs. Knightsbridge said. "He's a fine dog." She adjusted her glasses and looked down at the pages on her desk. "But this definitely says you ordered an XS." She looked up at me. "What breed is your puppy?"

"I think he's part Dalmatian, perhaps a bit of poodle. Hard to say."

"A mixed breed? But we specialize in purebreds." She picked up the second sheet of my file, studied it for a moment and then looked up and smiled. "Now I see what happened, Mr. Allyinphree.

You have one of our *pro bono* puppies." She put the paper down, clasped her hands, and rested them on the desktop.

"Let me explain. Almost every week, somebody drops off an unwanted puppy at the kennel, sometimes an entire litter. Normally we just take the puppies to the Napa County animal shelter. Once or twice a year, however, we make an exception. Those are our pro bono puppies. Our vet checks them out and gives them their shots, and then we place them on our clearance page. We give them away, since most of their owners couldn't afford one of our regular dogs." She grimaced. "Oh, I didn't mean to suggest you couldn't—"

"That's all right," I said. Now I knew why Regina had so many financial questions. I pictured the undeposited checks in my kitchen drawer and felt a pang of guilt for freeloading off the kennel. In less than a year, I'd already accumulated more than a million dollars in my checking account.

Mrs. Knightsbridge continued. "There are no returns on our PBPs, but you thought you were buying an XL, so I'm happy to make an exception."

"So the clearance page just listed the wrong size?"

"That wasn't the problem. Last month we changed fonts on our clearance page so customers wouldn't confuse the listings with our regular listings. Regina—Ms. Malbec—is interested in fonts, and she brought this one to our attention. She thought it had a lovely Asian look. Unfortunately, the XL and XS in the two fonts look nearly alike. Remind me of your puppy's name," she added as she shuffled through my paperwork.

"Tex," I said, and at the sound of his name, Tex perked up, hopped off the paperback, and yipped at the webcam.

"Oh, now I understand," Mrs. Knightsbridge said quickly, looking up at her monitor. "Ms. Malbec spoke to me about you. Oh, there he is. Hi, baby!" she said. Tex's tail wagged furiously. "Look how big you've grown." She leaned forward and squinted at my desk. "My, you certainly receive a lot of mail."

"Long story. You know Tex?" Regina had talked about me to Mrs. Knightsbridge? That was interesting.

"We all loved him. Ms. Malbec wanted to keep him, but I'm afraid her life has been . . . complicated the past few months, and that didn't work out. So we listed him as a clearance dog."

"If you don't mind my asking," I said, "what happened to Ms. Malbec? I…I rather liked her."

"I can see that," she said with a not-so-cryptic smile. "It broke my heart to see Regina leave, but it was for her own good. When she left, she gave me this necklace that belonged to her great-great-grandfather." She held out the ivory-colored pendant up to the webcam. It was about two inches long, shaped like a tiny spoon. "He was one of Kathmandu's leading citizens and a wealthy real estate developer. Regina's his only heir. She's half-Nepalese, you know."

"Yes, she told me that," I said, nodding. "As it turns out, I have an ancestor who also lived in Nepal. But why did she have to leave the kennel?"

Mrs. Knightsbridge didn't answer while she considered my question. Then, looking around the room, she leaned forward and spoke in hushed tones. "Mr. Allyinphree, this is rather personal, and we've never met. Still, I feel Regina wouldn't mind my sharing her story with you, but please keep this in confidence." I nodded again.

"Regina's father died of cancer about six months ago. She had cared for him for two years during his illness and was devastated by his death. The poor man wasn't even sixty. A few months after he passed, Regina tried to combat her loneliness by signing up with an online dating service. None of the proposed matches seemed plausible, however, until she met someone who at first seemed sympathetic and comforting. Unfortunately, this man quickly became possessive and demanding. He wanted her to marry him. Between you and me, I think it was only the inheritance from her great-great-grandfather he was after."

"It sounds like an awkward situation."

"Very awkward. The creep calls himself Eli, but it's just a stage name. His real name is Marion, or something like that."

"Stage name?"

"He's an actor of sorts, but not in the movies or anything. He plays a riverboat gambler on a floating casino. It's an old-fashioned paddle wheel boat, moored near Berkeley. Tourists board it to gamble and drink. The whole operation is pretty sleazy, in my opinion."

I'd only talked to Regina once, but it was hard to picture her with this Eli guy. Reading my doubt, Mrs. Knightsbridge continued. "Mr. Allyinphree, you have to understand. Regina wasn't herself. She was terribly lonely and grief-stricken over losing her father. She knew she should end the relationship, but Eli wouldn't let her. He kept calling and saying he loved her and needed her. Regina's a very compassionate person, and the relationship was tearing her apart.

"Things came to a head three days ago. Eli called from the riverboat and told her to get packed. He said he wanted to take her to Las Vegas, presumably to get married. She told him no, but he wouldn't listen. Then he said he was coming for her. She was confused and desperate. She didn't want to go with him, so she fled just as he was arriving to pick her up. My husband and I drove her to the BART station in Richmond." She sniffled and took a tissue from a box on her desk. She bit her lower lip. "She was like my daughter," she said. Embarrassed, she turned away from me.

"Mrs. Knightsbridge, I apologize for upsetting you," I said, "but do you have Regina's email address or cellphone number? Last week she invited me to come visit and I'd been hoping to do that." I'd never felt so bothered about a woman I'd never met.

She looked at me with a pained expression and sniffled again. Shaking her head, "I'm sorry, but Regina canceled her phone and email accounts. She couldn't even take the chance of telling me her plans. She said she would get in touch with me and my husband later, but I'm afraid she may be gone forever. I'm so sorry."

"Me too," I said. There didn't seem much else to say. I wasn't sure whether I was sorrier for Mrs. Knightsbridge or for myself. I glanced at Tex, who was sitting atop a pile of envelopes watching me, and turned back to the webcam. I took a slow breath and changed the subject.

"So somebody dropped Tex off at the kennel. Why did you keep him as a puppy?"

"That's not what happened," she said, wiping her cheek with a tissue. "Jeb, our groundskeeper, came in one Sunday morning about six weeks ago to check on the dogs. He was filling water bowls when he heard squealing coming from the display room where we keep best-of-show trophies and kennel memorabilia. We're well into our second century, you know."

"Yes, I read the history on your website."

"Jeb followed the sound and found a tiny puppy huddled inside an antique wooden dog crate that had belonged to our founder. Jeb grew up in San Antonio, so he named the puppy Tex."

I had trouble picturing this scenario. "Why would somebody break into the kennel and put a puppy in an antique dog crate?"

Mrs. Knightsbridge sniffled again and reached for another tissue. "What's really strange is that the crate had been padlocked for over a century, and the lock had rusted shut. Jeb had to cut it off to get the puppy out. At first, we figured it must be a prank of some sort, but then we found out Tex was the second puppy to appear inside the crate."

"I don't understand."

"Our founder himself discovered the first puppy there one hundred forty-seven years ago. He had the only key and never found out how the dog got in there. His puppy was larger than Tex, but both were light-colored with black spots."

This was too far-fetched. Puppies appearing in locked dog crates? I just stared at Mrs. Knightsbridge. She didn't seem like the sort who would make up a story like that, and neither did Regina. No rationalist could believe any of this, especially me. There had to be a logical explanation.

She continued. "So we knew there was something special about Tex. Regina wanted to keep him, but when things started to go sour with Eli, she knew that wouldn't be possible. That's when we listed Tex on our clearance page."

"And I bought him," I said.

"And thank goodness you did. Regina was so pleased Tex was going to a good home. For a few days she seemed happier and less anxious, but last week, everything fell apart and she had to flee. "So I guess we're back to square one," she said with a tight smile. She stopped speaking.

I looked over at Tex, who was sitting quietly on my desk, watching me, his head cocked, panting lightly, his tail motionless. I said nothing for a long moment. To Mrs. Knightsbridge my decision was about returning a dog. To me, it was about my future. And Tex's future. The past weekend, Tex and I had walked around Monument Square and I'd watched him frolic around Frog Pond. I showed him my bedroom closet and Uncle Gus's famous book, and we'd shared my sandwich. I had known Tex for only a few days, but Regina was right. He was a special dog. I knew what he wanted.

But what did I want? Just yesterday, I believed a nice woman was attracted to me, and I'd even hoped to fly to California to see her. But now she was gone, and I was starting over. When I was in college, my faculty advisor encouraged me to always have a life plan. That might work in a parallel universe somewhere, but this one was filled with too many detours. Sure, I hoped someday to find love and happiness. Everybody wants that. But all I knew for certain was that turning my back on my tiny new friend wasn't going to improve my odds. I leaned back in my chair and stared out at the maple tree by the street. A leaf fluttered down to the sidewalk, and I remembered the couple I'd seen walking their chocolate Lab.

"Mrs. Knightsbridge," I said, turning toward her, "I'm going to keep Tex. I'm not going to return him." I exhaled and felt a sense of relief in my chest. I'd face whatever the future had in store for me, but I wasn't going to face it by abandoning my friends. Human or otherwise.

Mrs. Knightsbridge let out a sigh, and I realized she'd been holding her breath, too. I saw her eyes glisten. She thanked me and said, "One more thing, Mr. Allyinphree. Please let me know from time to time how Tex is doing. If some day Regina contacts me, I know she'll be anxious to hear about him." And then she added, "If you want, I could suggest you'd like to hear from her as well."

"Thank you," I said, "I'd like that very much."

# 6

# AFTERNOON
# OF A FAWN

*Dear Sarah, Miriam, and Ruth,*

*Thank you so much for your proposal of marriage. Life with eleven toddlers on your Shining Beacon Hog Ranch sounds lovely. Yes, it is hard to understand why the Lord commanded your husband, Shadrach, to hurl himself into the New Year's Eve bonfire, but of course He moves in mysterious ways. Unfortunately, I must decline your proposal. I have never been married and taking on three wives is a bit much for a beginner.*

*Sincerely,*
*Ollie Allyinphree*

**One Saturday morning** in mid-November on the way to my Unitarian singles group, Tex and I stopped by my neighbor Annie's house so Tex could play for a few minutes with Beatrice, her bulldog. The air was still and clammy that morning, with a light fog ghosting the end of our block. While our dogs cavorted, Annie and I sat on her front stoop sipping coffee, and she showed me a follow-up article she'd been writing for the *Boston Globe*. It seemed an unattached professor at Boston University, Ruprecht Somebody, had advertised for an "adventurous female companion" to help him search for rare singing leeches in the Amazon Rainforest. Ruprecht was a runt of a man, with oily hair and a bad complexion, and yet his posting had attracted dozens of applications from women eager to spend two years with him on his expedition. Ruprecht was currently interviewing the top candidates and would make his selection in the next few days.

Three thousand six hundred known species of spiders inhabit the Amazon basin, almost all of them poisonous, some the size of dinner plates, plus untold millions of other ravenous, flesh-eating creatures that swarm, fly, crawl, slither, drop from trees, and pounce. And that's not to mention the mold, the slime, the smothering humidity and oppressive heat, the blood-sucking insects, the filth and decay and putrid water. If living in that hellish place is what it took to find true love, I was in trouble.

"It's not the guy or the Amazon," Annie said, grinning like she always did when she caught me whining. "It's the singing leeches. What girl could resist that siren song?" She had a point, of course, and that did make me feel better.

After leaving Annie, Tex and I headed to my singles group. To take my mind off Regina, I'd been attending more frequently lately and already had seen someone there who appealed to me. Truthfully, I couldn't take my eyes off her. Tall and slender, with high cheekbones and luxurious auburn hair that billowed loosely to her shoulders, she had a spontaneous laugh and a beguiling manner that hinted at unplumbed mysteries. That morning she wore a cream-colored gauzy top over a long fuchsia sarong, a kind of free-wheeling, Asian, hippie-gypsy look.

The problem was how to meet her. A few times over the past weeks I'd tried to introduce myself, but other men were always crowded around her like paparazzi, and I didn't want to be rude. I hoped having Tex along that day might help me break the ice. I slipped him into the side pocket of my windbreaker, and he stood on his hind legs with his head sticking out to see what was going on.

Our group was gathered at Harvard Yard to kick off our month-long festival celebrating the ancient deciduous forests of Middle England. It had drizzled during the night, but the early-morning fog had lifted, leaving glistening droplets of dew on the thin grass and the pungent odor of damp leaves. We all stood in a large, harmonious circle around a massive oak tree, shaded by its spectacular cinnamon-hued canopy, our heads solemnly bowed, eyes closed, seeking peace in our hearts through a moment of silence. Unitarians are forever having moments of silence. At a recent meeting, one of our moments of silence dragged on for nearly an hour, ending only when a participant fainted from low blood sugar.

And so, rather than disrupt the solitude, we stood with our eyes closed and heads bowed, the silence punctuated only by passing traffic and the distant staccato sounds of snare drums from the Harvard marching band's morning practice. Several minutes later, somebody touched my right hand and lightly squeezed my fingers. I'd been musing about Anglo-Saxon fertility chants and impulsively squeezed back, hoping I hadn't crossed some boundary of Unitarian impropriety. I half-opened my eyes to peek at my neighbor, and it was her! Her gorgeous hazel eyes were open wide, and she was looking directly at me and smiling. I swallowed and squeaked out a "hi," which sounded like someone had stepped on a gopher. She leaned toward me until her face was inches away.

"Hello, my name is Fawn," she whispered, releasing my hand and brushing her hair back. "I've been watching you for weeks." Her breath was warm and smelled faintly of cucumbers. I could feel myself blush.

I whispered back. "I'm Ollie. Ollie Allyinphree."

"Meet me afterward so we can talk?" She raised her eyebrows slightly.

"Really? I mean, yes, of course, but where—"

"Shhh . . . later." Fawn turned away and bowed her head. I felt a quiver of excitement at this unexpected turn. Quiver of excitement? No. I felt like the Charles River had just parted.

Our moment of silence ended a few minutes later when a group member started to cough uncontrollably. He had done this once before, and even though I suspected fakery, I was grateful for his outburst. Our circle eventually dispersed after we recited in unison Joyce Kilmer's famous poem about trees. When we got to the part about a hungry mouth pressed against a flowing breast, Fawn stepped closer, smiled, and pressed her arm against mine, almost squishing Tex, whom she evidently hadn't noticed. He squealed, and she recoiled. "Oh," she said quickly, squinting down at the head sticking out of my windbreaker pocket. "You've brought your hamster." Tex growled, but I decided to let it pass. Tex looks nothing like one of those simple-minded furry rodents, except for his size, of course, but I was sure the insult was unintentional.

Afterward, we walked to my favorite coffee shop, the Bean So Long Café on Church Street, known for its unique coffees. Before we entered the café, I set Tex on the ground so he could run behind a bush. "I've just had him a few weeks," I explained while we waited. When he returned, I offered to let her hold him, but she wrinkled her nose, and he scampered back into my pocket. I feared that hamster comment had gotten them off to a rocky start.

We turned to enter the café, when Fawn put a hand on my arm, stopped, and faced me. Just then a dark green sports car drove past, and the driver braked and turned his head to look at her. Before driving on, he glanced at me, grinned, and gave me a thumbs-up.

"Ollie, something's bothering me," Fawn said. There were hints of worry wrinkles across her pale, unblemished forehead. She clasped her arms together. "I've been trying to get your attention for weeks. I usually don't have trouble getting men to notice me. I didn't think you liked me," she pouted, brushing my arm with her fingertips.

"What? No, not at all." I didn't know what else to say.

Bean So Long was mobbed with pale, sleep-deprived Harvard undergraduates, but Mr. Pettigrew, the proprietor, waved to us and gestured toward a rickety oak table under a large chalkboard listing the day's specials. The café was redolent of espresso, fried bacon, and fresh-baked muffins, almost but not entirely masking the pungent odors of stale beer and marijuana permanently infused into the sweatshirts and blue jeans of the students. We sat down, and I took Tex from my pocket and deposited him on the tabletop, where he perched on a napkin. Fawn watched him warily while Mr. Pettigrew wended his way to us through the crowded tables.

"Ollie, how nice to see you and Tex again," he said. Then, noticing Fawn across from me, he segued to, "And who is your charming friend?" He bowed slightly as if addressing minor royalty, wiped his hands on a flour-dusted forest-green apron, and extended an open hand to Fawn, who cringed slightly before accepting it. After introductions, he said, "Ollie, I have again our Kopi Luwak beans for you. Aiyana has been ill, so we've been out of them for a month. Fortunately, she's fully recovered and back in business."

After we placed our order, I explained to Fawn that Aiyana was Mr. Pettigrew's pet Sumatran civet, a paradoxurus hermaphroditus. "Asian civets play an essential role in the processing of Kopi Luwak coffee beans," I said. "The civet's digestive enzymes soak into the beans, making short chains of amino acid monomers"—I noticed Fawn's blank expression—"that give the beans their unique flavor. Then, when the beans are collected—"

"How are they collected?" she asked, squinting narrowly, a note of suspicion in her voice.

"It's an extremely interesting process," I said. "After their natural migration through the civet's digestive track, they—"

"Oh no!" she shrieked, holding both hands to her mouth. Her eyes opened wide. Tex yipped and jumped to his feet. "They eat the beans and then shit them out? You drink coffee made from animal shit?" Fawn shuddered violently and her face paled. She seemed about to gag.

"Technically, I suppose you could say that, but—"

At that moment, the server arrived with our drinks. Fawn had ordered green tea made from wild Tasmanian devil weed, a duodecim size. I had ordered the viginti size of Kopi Luwak coffee but now regretted my decision. Fawn glared at the large mug being placed on the table. As the steam from the menacing black liquid curled lazily in her direction, her eyes darted around the room, suggesting an urge to flee the building.

"So you're a tea drinker," I said, desperate to steer the conversation elsewhere.

"I don't drink coffee," she replied, her nose wrinkled, as if coffee fell in the same category as the effluent from a bus station lavatory. Tex had settled back down on his napkin and was watching us.

"Yes, I know other people who can't tolerate caffeine."

"It's not the caffeine," she said, furrowing her brow and holding her empty teacup up to the light to verify its cleanliness, then filling it from a small chrome teapot. "It's the starving plantation workers. Hour after hour, laboring under the blistering sun, chained and beaten for the slightest infraction." Her voice quivered at the thought.

"Chained and beaten?" I said, unclear about where the conversation was heading. "But—"

"Let's not talk about this anymore," she said sharply. "It's too upsetting. Tell me about yourself." Fawn sat back in her chair, clasped her hands together, and rested her elbows on the table. Her eyes caught mine and held my gaze. I found her directness exciting, but also a bit worrisome, like she was testing me. I didn't want to make any more coffee flubs, so I struggled to organize my thoughts. "Let's see. I'm thirty-one and grew up in Boston. I work as a research librarian for the Widener Library—"

"Really? How interesting. I didn't know people did research on libraries. There's a lot to know about the big Smith library in Washington, but—"

"No, I work *at* a library. But you're right about the Smithsonian Museum. It has a fascinating history that dates from James Smithson's gift—" I sensed myself rambling but couldn't stop.

"You're very smart, aren't you?" she said, rescuing me. She reached out and lightly touched my arm. "Tell me about your family."

I felt myself blush, simultaneously thrilled and disoriented. "I was raised by my aunt and uncle. My birth parents lived on a small New Hampshire farm, but they died in an accident when

I was a month old." I wasn't sure how much detail Fawn wanted, so I plunged ahead. "My mother taught math at a community college and my father was a linguist."

"A linguist? Wow, that's so specialized. Didn't he ever want to study spaghetti or maybe those cute little bow tie pastas?" Fawn relaxed back and crossed her arms.

"He was a language scholar," I explained cautiously, trying to avoid sounding patronizing. "He studied Marycandu, an extinct Polynesian language. I have a great-great-uncle who deciphered it back in the nineteenth century. It's spoken in clicks and chirps."

"Oh," she said in a flat tone implying that Marycandu was on a far lower rung than linguini on the ladder of desirable scholarly specialties. I lifted my mug, but nervously slopped a few drops of coffee on the table. I wiped them up with my napkin.

"What happened to your parents?" Fawn extended her forearms on the table, carefully skirting both the coffee-contaminated area and the portion of the table where Tex was sitting.

"There was a goldfish pond on their farm, and one day, the small dock collapsed while they were feeding the goldfish. They fell into the water."

"And drowned?" Fawn said, her eyes glistening. She leaned forward and placed a hand on mine. Unitarians, as everybody knows, are revered for their emotional sensitivity.

"Worse. The goldfish were ravenous and started swarming, and—"

Fawn sucked in her breath. "Oh no! I had no idea that goldfish were, you know..."

"Only in large numbers," I said, "and only a rare subspecies of the Japanese Ranchu goldfish, the ones without a dorsal fin." Fawn furrowed her brow but said nothing as she wiped her eyes with her napkin and contemplated this familial tragedy. She studied me, as if reading my mind. Seconds passed, and the silence became awkward, so I said, "Now your turn. Tell me about yourself."

"Me?" she said, startled. "Sorry, I was studying your aura." She reached for her teacup, took a sip, and grimaced, as if tasting contaminants in the hot water. She set it on the table.

"My aura?"

"The colored energy vibrations radiating from your head." She pushed her chair back, better to see my vibrations. "Yours are fascinating. Look, there's a fuchsia one. Just like my sarong. Well, isn't that a happy omen?" She giggled and pulled up a corner of her sarong to compare the colors. "I can tell you're lonely," she continued, focusing on my aura in the deliberate manner of a psychic peering into a crystal ball.

"I wouldn't exactly say—"

"You're good at math. And, wait, there's something else." She frowned and stared into the empty space above my head.

Lonely? True, I live alone, but aloneness isn't the same thing as loneliness. I needed to think about how one evaluates loneliness. The coffee shop had filled, and a small crowd of customers hovered around the entrance, awaiting tables. Mr. Pettigrew wiped off an adjacent two-top vacated by two male college students. They threaded their way toward the exit, one hobbling on crutches, a cast on his left ankle. His friend carried his backpack.

"You like animals too," she said, glancing at Tex, who was still perched on his napkin. The tension in her voice gave the impression pet ownership might be a weightier topic for her than my being good at math. "Have you taught him any tricks yet? Can you make him sit for me?"

"He's already sitting."

"Oh, of course. Can he shake hands?" She reached toward him with her pinky, tentatively, as if concerned he might bite it off. Tex appraised her extended finger with marginal interest and then gave me one of his are-you-kidding-me looks. Facing her, he reared up on his hind legs and twirled around like a ballerina. He stopped and slowly lowered his body, keeping his rump in the air and collapsing his forelegs until his nose rested on the tabletop. He held that position for a few seconds, and then sat back up and wagged his tail. Two female students wearing crimson Harvard sweatshirts who had just seated themselves at the vacated two-top applauded his performance, but Fawn seemed unimpressed.

"Is there a problem?" I asked. "Does Tex bother you?"

Fawn swallowed and placed a hand over my wrist. She didn't speak for a long moment, weighing her words. "Ollie, I'm going to tell you something I've never told another soul." She released my wrist, lowered her eyes, and stared at her nearly full teacup. She picked up a spoon and stirred the tea, which did not appear to need stirring, and carefully rested the steaming spoon on the saucer. She took a cautious breath, as if counting to ten, and looked up at me. "Ollie, I had a terrible experience with a small dog when I was a young girl." Her eyes filled with tears as she spoke.

"My God, what happened?" I asked, concerned I had stirred up painful memories. The coffee shop had become noisy. At a nearby table, a scowling man with a black beard and a thick Russian accent was berating a female companion about the mathematics of nine-dimensional Riemannian manifolds. Evidently, she had said something insulting about them that enraged him. I looked back at Fawn. She dabbed at her eyes with a napkin that was beginning to look as soggy as the one I had used to sop up my coffee spill. Then she turned to me and spoke in a voice so soft I had to lean forward to hear her.

"When I was ten, a stray Chihuahua mix we named Sparkle wandered into our commune. After he had been with us about a week, I woke up one night and was horrified to find him crawling on my chest. I just lay there, my muscles frozen, unable to scream. In the dim light, his face looked so . . . evil." She shuddered. "I watched him crawl toward my face, moving closer." Fawn closed her eyes and started to bawl. She buried her head in her arms on the table and wrenched out muffled, choking sobs. The two students wearing Harvard sweatshirts watched us, alarmed. I mouthed okay to them and reached over to cradle her hand. She looked up, gave my fingers an appreciative squeeze, and then pulled away. Gasping, she sat upright and struggled to catch her breath.

"Did Sparkle attack you?" I asked, imagining weeks of painful reconstructive surgery.

"No," she said, twisting strands of her hair into a tight cord. Her hands trembled. "Oh God, no. He licked me, Ollie. On my mouth. Over and over and over. I could taste his saliva."

Fawn could no longer speak. Sobbing, she again rested her face in her hands on the table, and we remained silent. Then she pulled herself together, sat upright and looked at me. Her eyes were red and puffy but now seemed filled with resolve. "Thank you, Ollie," she said, her cheeks streaked with tears. "Thank you, thank you, thank you."

I half-nodded, unable to think of any appropriate words and a bit unsure what I was being thanked for. I made a mental note to send her an article I'd come across recently on the antimicrobial properties of dog saliva enzymes. Once she saw how friendly Tex was, I knew he wouldn't be a problem for her. "How long did you live on your commune?" I asked, thinking a change of subject was called for.

"Until I was twenty-five." She sniffled, smoothed her blouse, and untwisted her hair, pushing it to the side. "I left a year ago and moved to Boston. When I left there were ten of us, and I was the youngest."

"Was it an urban commune?"

"Like in a city? Not unless you think Ugly Otter, North Dakota, is a city. That was about an hour's drive from us. We used to go there in the spring to buy seeds. We actually lived on Cow Lake."

"So you raised beef on the commune?"

"Never! We were vegetarians. Why did you think that?"

"Well, you know, Cow Lake."

"Oh, I see. No, Cow Lake just smelled like cows, but there weren't any there. Mostly just mosquitoes and black flies. There were lots of those, but we didn't eat them."

I tried to think of something polite to say about the commune but stuck with the culinary theme. "You must have many favorite vegetarian dishes."

"We did at first, but then we learned that cooking transforms the nutrients in vegetables to toxins. So five years ago we decided to eat only raw vegetables, mostly carrots and lettuce, but every year or two we would also have a good harvest of cabbages."

"But what about the food pyramid, you know, protein and fat and—"

"You don't believe all that nutrition propaganda, do you?" Her voice took on an edge, and she narrowed her eyes and looked around the room. Satisfied there were no eavesdroppers, she leaned forward and spoke in a half whisper. "Ollie, you can't believe Big Agro. They're killing us with their lies. That's why there's so much cancer in the world, and arthritis and heart attacks and . . . all those other diseases. Scientists know this, but they can't say anything." She gripped the edge of the table, her cheeks flushed pink. She was exquisitely beautiful.

She continued. "After we rejected cooked food, the *Ugly Otter Gazette* published a story about our new healthful lifestyle. That's when the poisoning began. We grew thin and frail. Our bones became brittle, and our skin turned orange. It was horrible. Eventually, we figured out Big Agro was sprinkling poison onto our vegetable garden at night."

I tried to smile sympathetically, but I suspected Fawn's commune family had not immersed itself fully into the world of twenty-first century nutritional science. "So you still eat only raw vegetables?" To me, Fawn appeared well-nourished, if quite slender.

"Sadly no," she said. "If I did, they'd hunt me down and poison me. They never give up. That's why I moved to Boston last year. Nobody can find anything here. I don't have a cell phone because they'd track it. I don't subscribe to magazines or newspapers, or even have a TV. They can find you anywhere." She sighed deeply, as if exhaling toxins. "That's why we disbanded the commune. For protection, we even changed our last names. It was our only chance to escape." She leaned back in her chair and rested her hands nervously in her lap.

"What did you change your name to?" I asked.

"Dew," she said.

"Fawn Dew?" I said, incredulous.

"Yes, like how in the morning the grass sparkles with drops of . . . um, water. It's so pretty."

"Who knows what evil lurks in the hearts of men," I said. We sat in silence for a moment, pondering this insight. A cloud passed in front of the sun, sweeping a shadow across the room.

Fawn now seemed lost in thought. Finally, she spoke. "Ollie, I need to tell you something very important, and then I must go." She leaned toward me and spoke in definite, measured words. Her eyes still glistened from the stories about Sparkle and Big Agro treachery.

"Ollie, you and I are opposites. You are logical and methodical, and I am intuitive and spontaneous. I believe we are destined to be together, and I know you will soon learn to love me. Ollie, we will become one. Our spirits will merge into a single beautiful aura, and together, we will explore the world and its mysteries. Imagine what adventures await us."

As I sat speechless, Fawn touched a finger to one of the tears on her cheek. She reached across the tabletop and, carefully avoiding Tex, who was watching her warily, touched the finger to my lips. Then she stood, turned toward the door, and without looking back, pushed her way to the exit. Three men in business suits awaiting a table smiled and stepped aside as she glided past and then glanced over at me, admiration in their eyes.

I sat for several minutes, trying to focus my thoughts, the saltiness of her tear still on my tongue. Fawn was unlike anyone I'd ever known. And she wanted me. That had never happened. I exhaled and looked around the coffee shop, alive with the banter of happy people, and I realized I was one of them. I felt energized and ready to embrace the big world. Was this the connectedness my neighbor, Annie, was talking about? I looked over at Tex to see how he was taking all this and saw him sitting, watching my face. I caught his gaze, but he looked away, oddly disengaged. It worried me that he and Fawn hadn't hit it off. I just hoped their relationship would improve once they got to know each other.

I thought about what Fawn had said, about me being logical and her being intuitive. I liked that. It really did seem like we might fit together. Okay, so I didn't get all that aura stuff. But then, intuition had never been my strong suit, even though as a child I did show a modest flair for guessing the next digits of irrational numbers. Should I just trust Fawn's instincts, take a chance, and stop trying to analyze everything? A complicated question.

Later that afternoon at home I sank back on my living room sofa with Tex on my lap. I imagined Fawn snuggled beside me during the coming winter. We would be sipping plummy Sangiovese before a cozy fire while I told her about the Congo's giant Ituri Rainforest. (No matter I had never been to the Ituri Rainforest; we research librarians experience the world in more cerebral ways.) I could picture Fawn smoothing back her hair and squeezing my hand as I described the early-morning mist hanging heavy over the rainforest's dense canopy of giant teak trees. I would tell her about the okapi, the strange half-zebra, half-giraffe that inhabits the rainforest, and how it curls its upper lip, better to sniff out pheromones from nearby leopards.

It was a nice dream. I glanced down at Tex in my lap, and he returned my gaze. Yes, Tex would win her over. I shut my eyes, filled with hope and looking forward to the days ahead.

# 7

# DA DOG
# RUN RUN

*Dearest Ollie,*

*I'm sure you have heard the exciting news that I was the winning contestant for the singing leech expedition. Ruprecht called me last night to say he had selected me, and I was so shocked. During my interview I didn't think he even liked me. So for two years I will be searching for rare singing leeches in the Amazon Rainforest. Ruprecht says this is such important science that I owe it to the human race to do my part. What wonderful adventures lie ahead! Our freighter leaves at dawn, so by the time you read this we'll be on our way. Ollie, I am so sorry if I have disappointed you, but I have spent my life on a commune, and now Ruprecht is giving me a chance for something new and exciting. But I promise I'll call you when I return. I think you're a nice man, even though you seem to spend a lot of time reading books.*

*Sincerely,*
*Fawn*

**Fawn's email rocked me** like a kidney punch. What bothered me most wasn't that our relationship ended so soon, although that was disappointing. What I couldn't fathom was how Fawn could proclaim her blossoming love for me and then decide, a day later, to go live in a rainforest with someone named Ruprecht. In my mind, Ruprecht was ruggedly independent and self-confident, and even if he wasn't much to look at, I knew he would be outgoing and charismatic—the kind of man who made friends easily and whom women couldn't resist. Like Regina's boyfriend, that sleazy actor. At least I knew hadn't driven Regina away, because she'd left before I'd met her. I had this uneasy feeling it was my fault Fawn had left, but I didn't know what I'd done. Or hadn't done.

It was unseasonably warm that morning for November, with temperatures in the fifties. My neighbor Annie saw me sitting with Tex on my concrete front steps and asked why I looked so glum, so I showed her Fawn's email. She buttoned her jacket and sat down beside me to read it.

"Getting dumped happens to everybody," she said, handing me back my iPad. Her smile seemed more amused than sympathetic. "You had one coffee date with her, Ollie. Get a grip." She reached over and put a hand on my arm. "Actually, I can see Fawn's point. She grew up cloistered on a commune and now wants to break loose and explore the world. Fawn's adventures don't come from books, Ollie, and you'd never change that about her. I'm afraid most people are like that."

Annie's words made sense but were also unsettling. I got that Fawn was a fantasy, and I couldn't mold her into someone she wasn't. I suppose I was lucky to find that out quickly. Still, it was hard to accept the idea that a woman with a lifetime fear of dogs because a Chihuahua once licked her on the mouth had decided that living with a complete stranger for two years in a bug-infested hellhole was better than being in a relationship with me. What, I wasn't supposed to take that personally?

But there was a bigger issue. Why was I so attracted to women who were clearly unsuitable for me? Would this happen with every woman I met? I posed this question to Annie.

"Ollie, everybody fantasizes about new romantic interests, so don't fret about that. But for now, stop thinking of every woman you meet as a potential marriage partner." She hesitated and looked at me with a sympathetic smile. "I know you wish you'd had a chance to get to know Regina. To me, she sounded pretty good too. However, I promise there are more Reginas out there. Just keep your eyes open, and don't give up." Indeed.

Several weeks passed, but the crisp autumn days had not yet succumbed to the doldrums of the approaching New England winter. My spirits, however, foreshadowed what was to come, and when I wasn't working, I mostly holed up at home and answered marriage proposals. Fortunately, my morning walks with Tex in our neighborhood dog park helped offset my bleak spirits. It's hard to mope around feeling sorry for yourself in the company of frolicking dogs.

Da Dog Run Run is five acres of ryegrass dotted with maples and weeping willows that buffer my street from an elementary school. Our homeowners' association outfitted Da Dog Run Run with red plastic fire hydrants, sand pits, tidy mowed play areas, and winding trails. Tex's arrival there always called for a celebration by the other dogs, who gathered around him in a noisy bout of nose-touching and butt-sniffing. One would think Tex was a visiting senior dignitary and not a four-month-old puppy. The Ls and XLs took care not to bump him, especially Honey, a bear-sized bullmastiff who appeared to be his best friend. After their greeting ceremony, Honey and Tex usually hung out with me while Honey's owner, a nervous blonde named Matilda, jogged around the park.

But there was one crisp Saturday morning in early December, under a bright sun and powdery azure sky, when Honey and Matilda didn't show. Tex and I had stopped at one of the park fire hydrants when an unfamiliar female white poodle approached. Tex greeted the newcomer with a friendly wag, but the poodle responded by growling and baring her teeth. Her tail rigid, she pulled back her ears and slowly advanced toward him, snarling angrily. Flecks of saliva foamed at the corners of her mouth. I had sprawled on a nearby park bench, but jumped up in alarm just as a thin, dark-haired woman in a black spandex track suit sprinted past me toward the hydrant, presumably the dog's owner.

"Stop, stop that," the woman screamed at the poodle, who ignored her and continued to advance. I ran to rescue Tex, but before I got close enough, he turned to appraise the larger dog. Oddly unperturbed, he turned his back on her, eased onto his haunches, and quietly licked a paw. The poodle stopped suddenly, as if colliding with a force field. She circled him, barking and snarling but maintaining her distance. In response, Tex slowly turned his head and stared at her. He caught her eye, and the poodle recoiled and instantly quit barking. She drooped her tail, whimpered, and started to slink away.

Just then, the dark-haired woman reached them, with me close behind. "I'm really sorry," she gasped as she scooped up the poodle. The still-whimpering dog squirmed miserably in her arms. "I don't know what came over her." She glanced down at Tex. "That your dog? I've never seen a dog do anything like that. He's a pretty cool customer. This one belongs to my boss, but I get stuck taking care of her. We just moved here from LA, and to tell the truth, I'm more of a cat person." She leaned forward and frowned.

"Have we met before?" she said, studying my face. "Wait, aren't you that guy who got all the money from Africa? We saw your picture in the *LA Times*."

"I suppose that could have been me," I said. I never know how to respond when strangers recognize me.

"Cool," she said. "My boss said she'd love to meet you. I bet you two would like each other." She took a short leash from a blue nylon fanny pack, clipped it to the poodle's collar, and set her on the ground. The dog leaned against her leg, keeping a wary eye on Tex. "Oh, by any chance do you know a good dog obedience school in the area? We've got to do something before this monster bites somebody."

"Doggie-Do-Rite is just over there," I said, gesturing toward the elementary school at the far end of the park. "They use the school's gym for classes, every Monday evening at seven o'clock. I've checked them out for Tex, and they have a good reputation."

"Thanks, that sounds perfect. I'll tell my boss. I hope we'll see you there. I gotta run now. We're prepping for a big concert this evening, so wish us luck." The woman turned to walk away. The monster snarled at Tex as she was being carried off, but Tex ignored her. I slipped him into my front jacket pocket, and he stuck his head out to look around. What kind of concert? I wondered. The woman never told me her boss's name.

"How'd you do that?" I said to Tex as we walked home, but he just looked up at me and cocked his head. My little dog was filled with surprises. Back at the house, I found a note from Annie pinned to my front door.

*Ollie,*

*Someone in a military uniform knocked on your door while you were out. I called to him and asked if I could help, and he said he'd be out of town all day but would come back tonight. I told him you stayed up late. He seemed friendly. Also, a woman came by and asked about Tex. She seemed nervous and didn't leave her name.*

*Annie*

# 8

# WHAT'S WRONG
# WITH AMERICAN FROGS?

*Dear Misty,*

*Thank you very much for your proposal of marriage, but I am afraid a mistake has been made. I am Oliphant Allyinphree, a Boston research librarian, not Orlando Alessandri, head coach of the Boston Celtics. I have taken the liberty of forwarding your proposal to Coach Alessandri's office, and I am sure he will be very pleased to receive it. May there be wedding bells in your future!*

**That night,** I stayed up until midnight reading a book of forgotten English lore about Herne the Hunter, a ghost in Windsor Forest who had antlers sprouting from his head. I was weary and ready for bed when I heard rapping, rapping on my front door. Tex, who had been dozing on my desk, woke and barked a few times at the interruption. "Hush, Tex," I said, "it's just a visitor wanting a donation. I'm sure it's nothing more." Even though Annie had given me advance notice, this was awfully late.

I grabbed my checkbook, rubbed the fatigue from my eyes, opened the door and peered into the darkness. In the background I heard the muffled hip-hop thump of a distant concert. My visitor stood in the shadows under the dim porch light. He had neatly combed dark hair, a mustache, and short cropped beard. He was wearing jungle camouflage fatigues. I started to say hello, but then saw he carried a military assault rifle slung over his shoulder and crisscrossed ammunition bandoliers. Several gleaming hand grenades dangled from his belt.

"Whoa!" I said, and started to slam the door when Tex yipped, dashed around me, and bounded onto the porch. He jumped up on the visitor's boot and started pawing at his leg, squealing and furiously wagging his tail.

The man looked down at Tex, grinned, and leaned over to pat his head. Then he looked up at me. "Sorry to be so late," he said with a slight Hispanic accent, "but I saw your lights on, and your neighbor said you'd be up. I couldn't get here earlier."

"That's okay. Come in," I said reflexively, stepping back into the front hall so he could enter. A few seconds later, it sank in that I had invited into my urban home at midnight a stranger dressed like a guerrilla fighter who carried hand grenades and an assault rifle. I guess watching Tex's exuberant welcome had neutralized my sense of caution.

The stranger came into the front hall and tossed an olive leather duffel bag on the floor. Saying nothing, he leaned his rifle against the front hall table, removed his crisscrossed ammunition belts and set them on the tabletop, and stepped forward into the light. Tex followed behind him into the front hall and attentively watched us, still wagging his tail. Standing erect, the man stood eye to eye with me and studied my face, just as the woman from the dog park had done. Then he grinned widely, as if I'd just passed inspection. "Oliphant, it's me, Hernando, your brother. It's been a long time." He choked on his words, and I was astonished to see him blink back tears.

"My brother?" I said, feeling suddenly dizzy. "I have a twin brother named Hernando?"

"I just flew in this morning from Nicaragua," he said, as we both struggled to maintain our composure. "Look at me." He tilted his head upwards, posing for a portrait. I studied his features in the hall fixture light. He seemed a little taller than me, but then, I have a tendency to slouch. We had the same Allyinphree nose with close-set nostrils, same dark brown eyes and hair, high forehead, not-quite-rugged chin. Take away the mustache, the beard, the suntan, and the hand grenades, and I was looking at myself. Good God! I steadied myself against the wall.

"Here, suddenly, out of nowhere?" I blurted, my voice quivering.

"It's really me," he said, relaxing his shoulders and slumping to attention in the lackadaisical manner of a Central American guerrilla fighter. He raised his right arm, grinned, and saluted. "Hernando Felipe de Nuestra Señora la Reina de Guevara at your service." He threw his arms around me in a bear hug. I took a breath to calm myself.

"Hernando, how did you find me?" I said a few minutes later, hoping he wouldn't hear the nervousness in my voice. We were still chatting in the hallway by the front door, but I remained uneasy about his odd midnight visit. What did he want? Hernando Guevara. The name seemed vaguely familiar. Maybe I was thinking of Che Guevara, who had pretty much the same look.

Hernando said, "I read about you in *La Prensa,* and when I got back to Boston this morning, I looked you up. You're the only Allyinphree in the city. I couldn't believe your photo. I was looking at myself." His gaze fell on my old worn-out jeans, and he made a half-hearted attempt to suppress a smile. Then he laughed outright. "A less-well-dressed version of myself." I laughed, too, at this brotherly remark.

"Oliphant," he said after a pause, his voice suddenly hesitant, as if he was about to negotiate unfamiliar territory. I looked up and saw an unexpected intensity in his expression. "I think I've wanted to find you my entire life," he said soberly. "You're the only family I've got. Somehow, I knew you were alive . . . and that you wanted to find me also. Maybe it's an identical twin thing. Or maybe karma."

This last comment surprised me, because I knew what he meant. Of course it wasn't karma, but I also sensed a connectedness to my unexpected visitor, and the feeling shocked me. That's probably what Tex had picked up on. I relaxed and glanced down at my blue jeans. Maybe they were looking a bit ratty.

"You live in Nicaragua?" I said as we moved through the living room to the kitchen. Tex followed us as far as the living room sofa, where he hopped up and curled onto a pillow. I carried Hernando's duffel bag and tossed it onto the breakfast table. Hernando propped his rifle against the refrigerator, and we sat at the table facing each other.

"I moved to Boston from New Haven two weeks ago," he explained. "Years ago I lived in Nicaragua, but this was just a quick business trip to pick up a shipment of tiny frogs in Managua. This morning, after my red-eye landed, I dropped by but missed you and then took the frogs to some Princeton professors in New Jersey. Afterward, I turned around and drove back to Boston."

"You took Nicaraguan frogs to Princeton professors? What's wrong with American frogs?"

"These are newly discovered, black with an orange

tiger-shaped marking on their back. The frogs, not the professors. The profs want them for some sort of sporting event."

"That's a lot of driving," I said.

"Nine hours. But that's not all. When I got back to Boston, I had to teach an evening seminar for my writing students. I'm an instructor at Elizabeth Borden College."

Something bothered me. "Hernando, how did they let you into the United States with, you know . . . ?" I gestured toward his assault rifle.

He laughed. "Oliphant, where've you been? This is America. One of the customs agents wanted to buy it for his ten-year-old daughter, but he changed his mind when I told him it was a dummy." He picked up the rifle and pulled back the cocking lever to show me the blocked chamber. "It's for show."

I hoped the grenades were dummies too. "I don't understand. Why do you dress this way—you know, like a commando?"

"A few years ago, I wrote my memoir, and the cover photo shows me as a guerrilla fighter. Truthfully, I was a student, not a soldier, but my editor said I should dress the part for book tours. Turns out students loved the look, so I've kept it."

"What's your memoir's title?" It was becoming apparent Hernando and I had followed very different life trajectories.

"Originally *Madres Lesbianas*, after the rainforest commune where I grew up. My editor made me change it to *Lesbo Mama*s for the US edition. You've read it?"

"No, but I remember the title and thought I recognized your name. It's about a secret lesbian guerrilla commune, right?"

"They're not guerrillas. The commune began fifty years ago as a safe haven for Central American lesbians. Now it's more like a boarding school. They rescue poor and homeless kids from gangs. I lived there for nineteen years." It was hard for me to imagine a path that could have taken Hernando from a New Hampshire adoption agency to a clandestine commune in a Central American rainforest.

"But let's talk about that later," he said. "I brought you a present from the duty-free shop."

He unzipped his duffel bag, pawed around in it, and took out a finely crafted wooden box. Inside was a crystal decanter of tequila shaped like a sunburst, with a smiling mustached sun god engraved on the front and a polished wood stopper. I'd seen a photo of the brand at the library, one of the world's most expensive tequilas. Even with sixty million dollars, it never would have occurred to me to buy such a bottle. "For special occasions," Hernando said, pleased at my admiring gaze. He set the bottle on the table, and I stood to get glasses from a cupboard.

"Was Allyinphree our parents' name?" he asked, as I poured us two glasses. "I don't suppose we're descended from Gustav Allyinphree?"

"He's my—our—great-great-uncle," I said, sliding one of the glasses toward him.

"Really? That's wonderful. Too bad I didn't get his name too. Actually, I suppose Guevara fits me better." Hernando held his glass to his nose and sniffed, as if evaluating rare wine, and then took a large swallow. I heard Tex yip and looked down at my feet to see he had joined us. I let him hop into my hand and set him on the table. He curled up on a pile of unopened letters.

Hernando reached over and scratched his ears. "Handsome beast. Looks like a fighter. You keep him for protection?" He tilted his chair back and laughed, making his face blush.

"No need," I said, laughing too. I glanced at Tex, who didn't seem to appreciate the merriment. He hopped down from his perch to inspect the olive leather duffel bag. "Alligator?"

"Anaconda." Hernando ran his hand over its pebbled surface. "This one slithered into my tent one night when I was camping next to a lake, and it was him or me. I like the big guys, but I didn't have much choice," he added ruefully. "There's a chemical in their skin that keeps scorpions away." He leaned forward and slid the duffel bag to my side of the table. "Here, Brother, you take it. They'll never bother you again." His eyes canvassed the kitchen, seeking hiding places for scorpions. He slouched back and unsheathed two thick cigars from his breast pocket. He clenched one between his teeth and offered me the other.

"Thanks, but I don't smoke."

"Me neither. These are chocolate almond, good with tequila. They make a fashion statement," he said, sitting upright and posing with his palms outstretched. He did cut an impressive figure: black beard, cigar clamped between his teeth, polished black leather boots, neatly pressed camouflage fatigues, and three gleaming hand grenades pinned to his belt. Add in the twin ammo belts and assault rifle . . .

"Not bad," I said. "Not bad at all. I didn't know hand grenades were chrome-plated."

"These are dress grenades."

Later that night I learned Hernando had been adopted in New Hampshire and then taken to Nicaragua by the owners of a large coffee plantation. His adoptive parents disappeared a few years later after refusing to pay extortion to a drug gang, and he was rescued by Madres Lesbianas. "I was barely five, so my madres raised me," he said, refilling our tequila glasses. "When I grew older, they told me I'd been adopted from the States and had a twin brother. They knew my birthday and that I'd been born in New England, but they didn't know who my birth parents were."

"How many madres lived in your commune?" I asked.

"About sixty, mostly couples, and about fifty children and teenagers. Most of us stay until we're twenty-one, but I stayed an extra three years to work on my writing. That was six years ago."

"Graduate work in a rainforest commune?" There was obviously little resemblance between Madres Lesbianas and Fawn's commune of starving lettuce and carrot growers. The tequila tasted silky smooth, with hints of honey and pepper, and I felt it warming my stomach.

"Think of it like an academic convent. The Nicaraguan government knows where we are, but for the students' safety, the location has to be hidden." We sat in silence for a few minutes, sipping tequila and sucking on our chocolate-almond cigars. Hernando was right: they made an excellent pairing. I wondered how one acquired such a taste growing up in a small jungle community.

"What did you do after you left the commune?" I asked.

"I spent two years backpacking around Europe and Africa and working on my memoir. I love nature and the simplicity of life in the rainforest, but I felt stuck. I needed to get out and see the places I'd only read about."

Like me. Stuck like a barnacle on the side of a Boston pier. How could that have happened? My eyes drifted toward the tequila bottle. Hernando took the hint and refilled our glasses. I could swear the sun god winked at me.

He said, "After I published *Lesbo Mamas,* the reviews were good enough to land me a job as a lecturer in the Yale English department."

"That's a top-tier job," I said, genuinely impressed.

"It was at first." He tossed back the contents of his glass, raised his eyebrows, and looked up at me, so I chugged mine too. So much for the subtle honey and pepper overtones.

"Then, a few months ago, I lost my job," he said. "It was my own fault, Oliphant."

I gave him a quizzical look but said nothing while he reached again for the tequila bottle. He went on to describe a Yale English department faculty meeting to vote on whether to accept a ten-million-euro gift from an elderly alumnus to endow a doctoral program on the poetry of Tristan da Cunha. The alumnus had met his future bride there in 1957 while on a world tour with the Duke of Edinburgh, and they had shared a book of poetry borrowed from the royal yacht's library.

The department meeting had begun with the Yale president urging the faculty to accept the gift because of the "enormous reverence" with which Tristan da Cunha was held in the world of arts. This assertion was met with bewildered silence by the professors, which was clarified only after my brother stood and informed the president that he appeared to be confusing Tristan da Cunha with Tristan und Isolde, the latter a Wagnerian opera, and the former a remote lump of volcanic rock in the South Atlantic Ocean with a population of three hundred fishermen who had no discernible interest in poetry; and that so far as he could tell, no islander there had ever written—or most likely, read—any poems. Shortly thereafter, the faculty voted unanimously to reject the ten million euros, an action resulting in the slashing of the department's budget, forcing the elimination of Hernando's position.

"I was actually okay with that," he said while he refilled our glasses. "At Yale, I missed the rainforest and the outdoors and living close to nature. I discovered a sequestered Ivy League life wasn't for me, so I was glad to leave before I got too comfortable." He reached again for the now-half-empty tequila bottle.

I said, "But you left your commune because it was *too* sequestered."

He hesitated before replying. "True, but some day I'd like to raise a family and settle down, but not in a city. I met many brainy, pretty women at Yale, but they weren't what I was looking for." He laughed, but there was a hint of bitterness. "Not easy to find a woman who'd want my kind of life. I may never find one."

I had the opposite problem. I too was surrounded by brainy, pretty women, and it seemed to me many of them would be quite suitable, Annie's admonitions notwithstanding. I just didn't know how to meet them. Or if I did, they'd dump me for someone named Ruprecht. I tried to suppress my nascent feelings of jealousy. "So you decided to come live in the Boston rainforest?" I said, smiling to mask the taint of sarcasm.

Hernando smiled back. "I don't need much money, so I just take work wherever I find it. I flew to Nicaragua just to pick up the frogs. I'd hoped to visit my madres, but time was too short for a trek into the rainforest. I haven't seen them in six years." He topped up our glasses again. My earlier pleasurable buzz was giving way to dizziness. Tex uncurled himself and walked over to Hernando's glass to sniff the contents. He lapped a tiny sip, judging the flavor, and then plopped back on his stack of unopened letters. I couldn't tell if he liked it or not.

Hernando said, "Now I'm teaching writing at Lizzy Borden. It's just a temporary job. The college gives me a little off-campus office, and I tutor students there in the evening. They call it Hernando's Hideaway." He chuckled at the thought and slopped tequila on his shirt. "I mean, that's funny, right? Hernando's Hideaway." He swallowed and rubbed a hand over the tequila splotch. "Oliphant, I think I better go to the bathroom." He scraped his chair back with a screech that startled Tex and rose unsteadily, still holding his glass.

"Here, I'll take that," I said, rescuing the glass and gesturing to the front hall powder room. Hernando steadied himself against the chair back and wobbled toward the hallway. I wasn't quite so disoriented, but then, I hadn't flown all night, driven nine hours, and taught an evening seminar.

"What about you?" he asked when he had returned and collapsed onto his chair. "How do you spend your time, Brother?" He glanced at the pile of letters Tex was curled up on. "Marriage proposals? I read about those in *La Prensa*." My story was considerably shorter and less romantic than Hernando's. Home. College. Job. Rut. "You go away to college?" he asked.

"If five miles is 'away.' I went to UMass, Boston." I really was a barnacle. Then he wanted to know if I was seeing anyone, so I told him about Fawn and Regina. I retrieved Fawn's email from my desktop, where I'd left a hard copy after showing it to Annie. The universe tilted on my way back to the kitchen, but I stopped midway until it realigned. I meticulously lined up the bottom of the printout with the table edge in front of Hernando, and he leaned forward and studied the words carefully, propping his chin on his elbows.

"Singing leeches," he said, leaning back. He pronounced it *leashes*. "What are the odds of coming up against singing leeches? And then this other girl—what's her name, Regina?" He looked at me sympathetically. "She sounded pretty nice. You've had a run of bad luck, Oliphant."

He knew it was more than bad luck, and so did I. I shut my eyes and felt my head tilt downward. I tasted bile in my throat and tried to steady my breathing, but it didn't work. Then I felt something cold and wet on my hand, so I forced my eyelids open and found Tex's nose touching my palm. He looked up at me, wagged, and as he started licking, warmth radiated up my arm and settled in my chest. I exhaled and relaxed. Tex was always looking out for me.

"Two women in ten years?" Hernando said. "And one of them you never met in person and the other one you met only once." He started to shake his head, presumably in disbelief, but caught himself. "What did you like about Fawn, anyway, besides her beauty?"

I tried to remember, but in my alcohol-fogged state came up empty. "Hernando, I'm not sure. Actually, I know now Fawn was wrong for me, but at the time, I couldn't see that." There was more, but I was finding words difficult. I took a breath and plunged forward. "I suppose I felt if a woman that beautiful was drawn to me then I was . . . making progress or something." I looked away, embarrassed by how I sounded.

Hernando chewed on his lower lip and idly fingered the pin on a hand grenade.

"I get that," he said after a minute. "You just need to get out more, Oliphant, get some practice meeting people. This spring semester I'm holding my writing workshop in a coffee house, so come visit me then. You can bring Tex. Everybody knows women go for men with puppies. Who knows, you might meet someone there." He massaged the back of his neck while he collected his thoughts. "I've got another idea. We've got our birthday coming up in March, so let's also throw a party. Maybe a costume party."

In theory, that *was* a good idea, but I wasn't sure I could come up with all that many people to invite. He continued. "Look, Oliphant, you're a smart guy, a little quirky maybe, but women go for that. If you cleaned up and tried to look sharp, you could be spectacularly handsome, like your brother." He laughed at his little joke. "So don't give up. Somewhere, there's a woman for you. Who knows," he said, grinning, "maybe she'll even have a twin sister." Then, yet another possibility occurred to him. "Is that your junky old car parked in the driveway? Does it even run?"

"Most of the time," I said, and he shook his head in mock resignation, leaned forward, and rested his elbows on the table-top. I knew where he was going and tried to ward him off. "It's not a junker, Hernando. It's a vintage—"

"Oliphant, stop," he said. "You need to listen to me. You've got to clean up your act. Buy yourself some new clothes. And a new car. You can afford it. Buy yourself two or three new cars. You need a fresh start, Brother. I'm serious about this. You can start tomorrow."

I looked at my watch and saw it was almost three a.m. My head was throbbing, but I was in a good mood. I looked at the nearly empty four-hundred-dollar bottle of tequila and yawned.

I glanced at Tex, who was sound asleep on his pile of letters. "Hernando, where are you staying tonight?"

He seemed embarrassed by the question. "I have a cot in my office, but just for a little while. I'm fine."

"I've a guest room upstairs. Why don't you stay with me until you find a place to live?" I felt completely comfortable with my newly found brother. Maybe it was that identical twin thing. Or maybe the tequila.

"You mean it? I don't want to impose."

"Don't be ridiculous."

"Of course I'll pay rent."

I laughed. "That isn't necessary, Hernando. I think I can afford it."

"It's necessary for me," he said. He smiled and reached over and squeezed my arm. In three hours, the first hint of dawn would appear over the Atlantic.

# BILLBOARD
# SHOPPING

*Dear Madison,*

*It is so nice to hear from you again, and that is wonderful news about your second-place ribbon on your science project. OMG! Your dad must be so proud. I'm also pleased to hear about Chad, who sounds like a totally awesome boyfriend. Keep in touch and let me know how your midterms turn out. Just remember to get plenty of sleep the night before the tests.*

*Cordially,*
*Ollie Allyinphree*

**A few days later,** following Hernando's urging, Tex and I headed to Meditation Motors, *where car shopping is a restful, transcendental experience that brings quiet joy to the heart of our honored American customers.* I had bought my beloved Zen Buggy there ten years ago, and although I didn't quite get how a new car would improve my love life, Hernando insisted it was an important part of my Fresh Start. Later that afternoon, he was taking me to Drinkwater's in Cambridge to buy clothes. I'd not heard of the place, but Hernando persuaded me a few upscale casual outfits would also go a long way to tone up my image.

I turned off Soldiers Field Road onto the Massachusetts Turnpike and drove cautiously in the right lane, keeping the speedometer to just under forty-five; at higher speeds, a steering wheel vibration serves as the manufacturer's gentle reminder that motoring should be leisurely, soothing, and peaceful. I ramped off Exit 15 onto southbound Interstate 95, toward Providence, and after half an hour, I took Exit 11A onto eastbound Neponset Street.

New England street names often combine vowels and consonants into words that make no sense, other than to form similar meaningless words when read backward. How endearing it would be if drivers turning east would find themselves on Neponset Street, while those turning west would be on Tesnopen Street. A library colleague lives on Nahatan Street, which spelled backward is Natahan—nearly the same! Nahatan Street is probably named after some long-forgotten Boston dignitary. I wonder if the Nahatans ever realized how close their name came to being a perfect palindrome. This is the kind of musing one would never experience in a Tesla roadster or Porsche Carrera, and it is why I've loved my clunky old car.

From Neponset Street we turned onto Blue Jasmine Drive, and the world calmed. Large oak and cypress trees shaded the drive with soft shadows, and through the tangle of dormant gray branches, I caught glimpses of a quiet forest. The road twisted and curved north, and ahead around the bend, Meditation Motors appeared on the left, the morning sunshine sparkling like incandescent blossoms off the building's façade of white river rocks. A large, curved portico supported by graceful columns framed the showroom, and a festive wooden band of red coping enveloped the building like a giant holiday ribbon. A small llama with brown-flecked white wool reclined lazily on the grass in front of the showroom entrance.

I pulled into the customer parking area, switched off the ignition of my tired old friend, eased out of the driver's seat, and gently closed her door for the final time. Setting Tex on the ground, I approached a salesman in a multicolored robe sitting cross-legged before the entrance on a dark wool blanket. The sun glinted off his shaved head as he rose to greet me.

"Howdy," he said, offering me a lotus blossom from a small floral display. He was a roly-poly middle-aged man with a gentle face. "Name's Flint. Rockford Flint, but everybody calls me Rocky." His English betrayed a hint of a two-toned Tibetan dialect on his short syllables.

"I like your lovely little llama, Rocky," I said.

He smiled. "She's our subtle symbol of serenity and savings. Her name is Llulu."

"Of course it is."

"And you are Mr . . . ?"

"Allyinphree. Oliphant Allyinphree, but please call me Ollie."

"Groovy," he said. "I don't believe we've met." He turned his head, peered out at the parking lot. "I've been here two years, but I can see your Zen Buggy is quite a bit older than that." Just then, Llulu reared back on her haunches, hissing and spitting and batting her forelegs in the air. Tex barked and recoiled. "I'm so sorry, Ollie," Rocky said. "She hates male dogs." He glanced discreetly at Tex's underside and wiped a blob of llama spit from his robe as the colors started to run.

"A most unusual robe," I said, hoping a change of subject would spare him further embarrassment.

"I am so glad you noticed," he replied with a modest bow. "I colored it myself. It is a new American process. One twists the garment into knots and takes containers of dye and—no need to bore you with details."

"One becomes so weary of saffron."

"Precisely. Our owner believes we should immerse ourselves in the culture of our honored American customers. He's an older gentleman who lives now in Kathmandu, but he graduated from your University of Harvard in 1971. He is Nepal's most renowned authority on American and British life. Perhaps you have heard of him? He likes to be called Ringo. He took the name from a musician he admires."

"Yes, a brilliant scholar," I said, making the connection. "I heard him lecture once in Boston about how all you need is love."

"Far out!" Rocky replied, clearly pleased. "Have you been to Kathmandu?"

"No, but I collect ceremonial yak horn figurines from there. The best come from a small studio just across the street from—"

"The Nepal Art Council Gallery?" Rocky's eyes widened. "Next to a café that serves dumplings stuffed with goat meat and spicy green peppers?"

"Why, yes. The studio's owner sent me the menu from that café. She hoped I'd come visit someday. You know it?"

Rocky reached out and grasped my hand, squeezing so firmly that Tex growled. Tears welled up in his eyes. "The café has been owned by my family for nine hundred seventy years," he said solemnly. "I was born in the back room, behind the kitchen, next to the noodle machine. Of course, in those days, sanitation regulations were not so . . ." His voice trailed off, as if he felt he had overstepped the bounds of familiarity. Nepalese are by nature a private people.

"Perhaps we should look at some cars," I said, while Rocky regained his composure. I opened the door to the showroom, but he took my arm before I could enter.

"Excuse me, Ollie, this is now the *women's* showroom. We moved the men's showroom last year when we remodeled." He gestured to another entrance near the edge of the building and started toward it.

"Sorry," I said, but I hesitated in front of the open door. Inside, sitting on a papasan, an attractive brown-haired woman wearing glasses and a long floral skirt was sipping wine spritzers with a salesperson. A large wall mural spelled *WOODSTOCK* on a background of small mauve and taupe peace symbols and framed the showroom display of avocado and pink cars. A faint aroma of patchouli lingered in the room. I stared at the customer, who reminded me of Regina, and as the door swung closed, she turned her head and seemed startled to see me watching. Then, my heart thumping, I joined Rocky, and the two of us walked toward the men's entrance. No, it couldn't be. I pushed the thought out of my head and looked around for Tex, but I didn't see him.

"There he is," Rocky said, pointing toward Llulu, who was lolling on the lawn beside a small stone fountain. I shaded my eyes and saw Tex perched on a small teak bench beside her, their noses touching. They seemed to have become friends. Tex noticed us watching, so he scurried to me, and I popped him into my shirt pocket.

We entered the men's showroom, and Rocky gestured to a chair in front of his desk and retrieved a loose-leaf notebook from an adjacent file cabinet. I smelled sausage pizza, as did Tex, who suddenly started sniffing in full detective mode. "We bake the best all-meat pizza in town," Rocky remarked, looking up from the file drawer. "Absolutely no vegetables or fish. We serve it at lunchtime in the men's showroom, but I can get you a piece now if you like."

"Thanks, but we've eaten," I said and noticed Tex glaring at me. "What do you serve in the women's showroom?"

"Today, spinach salad with raspberry vinaigrette and a chocolate truffle."

While Rocky thumbed through his notebook, Tex and I inspected the showroom. The vehicles, all finished in metallic gunmetal enamel with white racing stripes, rested on navy blue shag carpeting. Twin brown Naugahyde recliners separated by a chrome-and-glass table carved out a small waiting area, while back issues of *Car and Driver* in a magazine rack blessed the room with a comforting manly feel. I picked up an advertising brochure from a small stack on the table and was thumbing through it when Tex yipped. The photo in the brochure showed a spectacular blonde leaning against a large black sedan. In her arms, she held a dog who was a ringer for the white poodle from Da Dog Run Run. Wow.

"She's one of our celebrity customers," Rocky said as I lingered over the photo. "I sold her that car last month. She just moved here from the West Coast. Now, give me one more minute so I can call up your record." While his computer loaded, he looked out at the parking lot. "I've always liked your Zen Buggy model. If you're planning to trade her in, we have a decommissioning ceremony every month for elderly cars before they're recycled. It's a lovely event and gives owners a chance to reflect on their relationship with their old friend and to wish her well in her coming life." He turned back toward his computer.

"Let's see," he said, studying the monitor. "You own your home, work as a research librarian, and you bought your car from us ten years ago. That would make you . . . thirty-one?"

"That's right. Everything else is the same."

"So you're still single, then. And that's by choice?"

Here it came again. Everybody seemed concerned about my marital status. Did I have a sign on my chest that said *Weird, Lonely Man?* Rocky was beginning to irritate me.

"I don't see why my marital status matters in the slightest, Rocky. I'm here to buy a car, not to get married, or even find a date." Having blurted those words, I wished I'd left out the last part. Finding a date seemed an awfully low bar, and I didn't want Rocky to brand me as some sort of pathetic, dateless loser. I looked at his face, but I didn't see any hint of judgmental predisposition. Instead, he looked slightly worried.

"Ollie, if you don't mind my asking, why are you here at Meditation Motors, shopping for a new car?"

"I don't mind," I said. "Truthfully, I'm here mostly because my brother told me I needed to buy one." I paused and looked out the window at my old Zen Buggy in the parking lot. "Not that there's anything wrong with my old car," I added.

Rocky followed my gaze and nodded. "Your old Zen Buggy's a fine car," he said, and then stopped, waiting for me to speak. I was beginning to feel nervous, like I was in some bizarre auto dealer therapy session. I glanced down at Tex, who was studying me attentively, his tail motionless. I searched to find words.

"I, um, my brother that is, thinks I need to get out more and meet people." Why was I admitting this to a car salesman? Rocky raised his eyebrows slightly, inviting more. I heard words come out of my mouth. "I guess I do have a little trouble meeting . . . women. And Hernando—that's my brother—thinks a new car could be helpful to me. In that regard."

Rocky slowly rubbed his chin before answering. From his demeanor we could have been analyzing fuel injectors. He said, "I believe you are not completely convinced your brother is right."

I nodded. "Not completely, I suppose."

"However, Hernando is right, Ollie. You have a very astute brother." He paused and straightened in his chair. "At Meditation Motors our credo is that our products are much more than a means of transportation. We believe every aspect of a car—its size, color, price, performance, styling, sound system, reputation, reliability, gas mileage—is a personal expression of the owner's likes and dislikes, political persuasion, social and economic standing, education and environmental and social justice concerns." He paused to let me assimilate his words and then continued. "We want every automobile we sell to reflect the core beliefs of our customers. So yes, if a buyer lives alone but is open to being in a long-term romantic relationship, as I sense you are, then we want that openness to be reflected in the automobile the buyer chooses. Tastefully, of course." Rocky paused again.

"Look at it this way," he said. "Think of your new car as a billboard. When you drive down the road, Ollie, your billboard broadcasts your personality, desires, and values to the world. If an unattached, intelligent woman who lives on the next block sees you drive by, you want her to notice, not just a car, but an equally intelligent, well-educated young man, with a good career, a respect for the environment, and an openness to meeting a like-minded romantic companion." He paused for a moment and then added, smiling, "And perhaps a desire for children and a family. Your new car, Ollie, if carefully selected, will help you reach those life goals. So as we think about the next decade, I believe you should consider a more spacious model, with room for additional passengers."

Had it really been ten years since I'd bought a new car? I'd just started my library job, and the tiny Zen Buggy had been the only automobile I could afford. Some billboard. I wondered how many women had sat in it with me over those years. Complicated question, actually. If the same woman sat in my car, say, five times, it didn't seem right to count those five occurrences the same as five different women, one time each. On the other hand, I should get some credit for multiple seatings, but how much? I'd need an algorithm. Actually, I wasn't sure I wanted to know. One way or the other, it was a very small number.

I looked up and saw Rocky studying me. I sighed and imagined Fawn sitting on a rock outcropping above the broad Amazon, her hiking boots dangling over the brackish water, her kayak tied off on the trunk of a small bombax tree. A large channel-billed toucan watched from above, and Ruprecht sat at her side, his arm draped around her shoulders.

And how about Regina? Was she still on the run from what's-his-name? I pictured her wide brown eyes and the way the corners of her mouth twitched when she tried to suppress a grin. Where was she now? For certain, not in the women's showroom. Wishful thinking wasn't going to get me anywhere.

And where was I? I caught Rocky's eye, and he smiled again at me. He seemed like a kindly man. I was on my fresh start, dammit. "Yes," I said, without waiting for him to speak, "I think I'd like to look at a few larger models."

"Excellent, Ollie," he said, "I think that's the right decision." He placed his hands on the armrest of his chair and levered himself upright. We walked across the showroom floor, and I stopped momentarily to inspect the newest Zen Buggy model. I was slightly dismayed to see that the speedometer now went up to fifty miles per hour. In my old car, it peaked at forty-five. Otherwise, it seemed like a fine automobile.

"So Ollie," Rocky said, as he caught me inspecting the window sticker, "with your interest in Nepal, I'm assuming you speak Nepalese?"

"Only a few words."

He persisted, obviously trying to wean me from the tiny Zen Buggy. "What other languages do you speak? Many of our customers know several. Why, last week I sold a car to a young woman who spoke Marycandu. She traded in an old Zen Buggy like yours, for a new one just like it, only in Cimarron Red. In fact, she was here this morning, completing her paperwork."

I stared at him. No, not a chance. The odds that—I pushed the thought out of my head. "No kidding," I said, "My brother and I both know Marycandu."

"Aha! Then you must be related to Gustav Allyinphree," Rocky said.

"He was my great-great-uncle."

"I am honored to meet one of his ancestors. This is very thrilling to me. Of course, all Kathmandu children know about Gustav Allyinphree. And, naturally, the terrible accident." He gave a slight bow and skillfully steered me toward two larger models. I admired the spacious Sherpa Grand Sedan, which seats six passengers, or four passengers and two goats if one buys the optional goat compartment. He explained how a supplemental oxygen system is also available for driving above eighteen thousand feet. The SGS was elegant and beautiful but didn't seem to match my station in life. Next was the Mini-Pagoda. A sporty hatchback, it sat two comfortably in the front, with two smaller seats in the back. I inspected the window sticker.

"The Mini-P comes with a special feature for drivers with XS dogs," Rocky explained. "Our deluxe dog crate is included at no extra charge." He opened the door of a small cage with polished wooden ribs suspended from the rearview mirror. I took Tex from my shirt pocket, and he hopped into it, wagging his tail as the small crate swayed. I could tell he much preferred it to the cup holder in my Zen Buggy. According to the window sticker, the Mini-P also came standard with a ten-speaker, four-hundred-watt integrated sound system. The only available option was an audio player priced at two hundred dollars.

"That's an accessory for owners with collections of vintage recordings," Rocky explained. "We remove the integrated sound system and replace it with an eight-track tape player and three-inch stereophonic speakers. We hand wire the tape players in our own factory," he added proudly, "although we buy the vacuum tubes from China."

I had to admit that was a plus, and quite reasonably priced. I looked over at Tex, who was still swinging from the rearview mirror in his dog crate. His enthusiastic tail wag made it clear which car he preferred. "We have several Mini-Ps of each color in stock," Rocky said, gesturing to a color chart on the wall. I looked at the chart highlighting a half-dozen choices. "What color do you prefer?"

"I like Tranquil Chocolate," I said reflexively. "It reminds me of an elderly Labrador retriever I saw walking by my house. I suppose that's an odd reason to choose a car's color."

Rocky smiled his encouragement. "Not at all, Ollie. That's a very good reason. Would you like to take a test drive? The Mini-P's handling is particularly soothing and restful." I looked again at Tex, who was watching closely, his head cocked to the side. I realized I'd already made my decision.

"No need," I said. "Let's go with the chocolate one." It occurred to me I was having fun. It had been a long time.

"Excellent choice, Ollie," Rocky said. He beamed and we shook hands. "I know this is the right car for you." Tex now stood in his crate, pumping his tail so hard it seemed at risk of flying off. I was really enjoying my fresh start.

The paperwork took only a few minutes, and afterward, the three of us strolled out of Rocky's office into the sunlight and followed a narrow, flower-lined pebble sidewalk around the side of the building to the New-Car Delivery yurt. The yurt had white canvas sides and a sloping circular roof decorated with a large red symbol whose shape resembled the ace of spades. A short ramp led to double entrance doors of lacquered wood, hand-painted with an intricate red-and-purple pattern. Llulu was still lolling on the lawn, but she raised her head and quietly watched as we walked past. A gentle easterly breeze brought in the humid salt air from the Atlantic Ocean.

We entered through the doors onto a glossy wood floor. A round opening in the center of the high ceiling flooded the interior with sunlight. My new car was already parked under it on a large maroon wool rug, bright reflections glinting off its polished chocolate surfaces. Two employees were still working on it, so Rocky and I spent half an hour together in quiet meditation while Tex played with Llulu. Finally, my car was ready, so I shook hands with Rocky, climbed into the bucket seat, and lifted Tex into his deluxe dog crate. We both sat for a few minutes, inspecting the interior and luxuriating in the new-car smell of oiled leather with a hint of incense. The rear seats were tight, but suitable for small children. I smiled at the thought. It was thrilling to start the engine for the first time, and I was pleased at how quietly it ran, considering the new turbocharged model had sixty-five horsepower. The only sound I heard as I drove down the driveway toward the street was gravel crunching beneath the tires. I couldn't wait to show my new car to Hernando.

We turned right onto Blue Jasmine Drive, past Raging Dragon, the huge Chinese dealership across the road whose hundreds of new cars gleamed in the sun like sparkling gems of cubic zirconium. I picked up speed, and two women walking an Irish setter followed us with their eyes and waved as I drove past. The sun had moved high overhead, and the afternoon promised to be peaceful and fresh. I looked in the rearview mirror and glimpsed Llulu grazing at the Meditation Motors entrance, and Rocky once again sitting cross-legged on his blanket beside a small clump of blue poppies. I was half-hoping I'd catch sight of a red Zen Buggy in the parking lot, but I didn't see anything.

With one hand on the steering wheel, I shuffled through my complimentary package of eight-track tapes: the Nepal national anthem sung by the fourth-grade chorale of a Kathmandu elementary school; a lecture by a professor at Tibet University on the vegetables of the Phagmodrupa dynasty; a collection of Lithuanian protest songs; and an anthology of Beatles music sung in ancient Mandarin. Then I found the perfect tape. I slipped it into the slot in my Mini-P's eight-track player, rolled down the windows, and cranked up the volume.

"Talkin' 'bout hey now, hey now," I sang to the noontime sun as we be-bopped down the road, Tex swinging gaily from the mirror in his new dog crate. "Talkin' 'bout HEY NOW, HEY NOW . . . Gonna set yo tail on fire-oh." At this, Tex gave a little growl, but I glanced up at him and saw his tail wagging, so I knew he didn't mean it.

# 10

# THE LEGEND
# OF UNCLE GUS

**When I was a child,** a faded lithograph of a young boy hung above the small school desk in my bedroom. The boy was about ten years old, with unruly dark hair and a sober and thoughtful countenance. He wore a black coat, buttoned to the top, with a white collar and a satin bow tie. His name was Gustav Allyinphree, and he was my great-great-uncle and most illustrious ancestor.

Uncle Gus was born in Boston in 1817, the only child of Josef and Virginia Allyinphree. Little is known about the Allyinphrees, other than several police complaints they filed against a neighbor whose pet barked throughout the night. Shortly after the barking ceased, the Allyinphrees opened a tavern, the Boiled Hound, which is still a popular area hangout.

Young Gustav quickly became recognized as a prodigy, with extraordinary abilities in mathematics, music, languages, and science. At nine, he composed a duet for tenor and alto sackbut. At fourteen, he astounded his teacher, Miss Prudence Sheppard, at Boston's Ebenezer Lyon School, who had just explained to her students that trisecting an angle was impossible. Gustav, "Goosey" to his friends, raised his hand and announced he had solved the problem the month before while lying in bed. Miss Sheppard reprimanded him for impertinence, handed him a piece of chalk, and commanded him to sketch his construction on the blackboard. After studying his scribblings for thirty minutes, she became overcome with emotion and had to be taken to Massachusetts General Hospital. Unfortunately, a janitor that evening erased the blackboard, and no record remains of young Gustav's construction.

At twenty-two, Gustav read Charles Darwin's newly published *Voyage of the Beagle* and was so captivated by the description of the Pacific islands, he joined the crew of a whaling ship bound for Polynesia and for three years endured the harsh shipboard life of a commercial whaler. At first the other crew members spurned him, thinking him odd, but they reversed themselves after he saved the life of the captain, who had suffered a head trauma caused by a swinging mast. Having read about the practice of trepanning by pre-Incan cultures in southern Peru, Gustav opened the captain's skull to remove shattered pieces of bone and relieve the pressure from the injury.

It was on this voyage that Uncle Gus embarked on his quest to translate the language of the Marycandu people, a tiny extinct race of Polynesian islanders discovered in 1773 by an English seaman, Captain Robert Whipple, who stumbled upon tribal artifacts while harvesting giant tortoises on their island. Captain Whipple christened the tribe the Marycandu, after the legendary bedroom skills of French queen Marie Antoinette, whom the captain revered. Later, learning of this fact, French president Charles de Gaulle became incensed, believing the name cast a slur on the French royal court, and ordered the tribe's island to be blown out of existence during the French atom bomb tests of the 1960s.

Uncle Gus studied the Marycandu for nearly thirty years. At fifty-one, he succeeded in translating their dialect, a challenging language that consists of chirps and clicks. The only extant record of the language is an inscription on a stone tablet said to be from the tomb of Igzotwatlx, the Marycandu's virgin goddess of weather. Legend has it that Uncle Gus, when he translated the inscription, was so inspired by its message that he made a spiritual pilgrimage to Nepal. Accompanied by his beloved dog, Darwin, and his best friend, a Sherpa guide, he spent two weeks climbing Mount Machhapuchhre, one of the most inaccessible peaks of the Himalayas. Uncle Gus stopped just short of Machhapuchhre's summit, in deference to Hindu beliefs that the summit is home to the god Shiva. There he sat on a large stone outcropping for two days and nights, Darwin curled at his feet, both declining food. The legend goes that on the morning of the third day, they were struck by a bolt of lightning from a cloudless sky, leaving no trace of Uncle Gus other than a charred spot and a mysterious ivory-colored fetish in the shape of a traditional Marycandu war club. Darwin was uninjured, although the electrical surge bleached the color from his one hundred seventy-nine spots.

This extraordinary event was later reported by Uncle Gus's distraught Sherpa guide, who, after descending from the mountain with Darwin, became a local celebrity. He married a young, upper-class Nepalese poet, and together, the couple founded and served as curators of Kathmandu's famous Gustav Allyinphree museum. The Sherpa guide wore the mysterious ivory fetish around his neck until he died forty years later, a wealthy man and one of Kathmandu's leading citizens. The couple left one heir, a son, who emigrated to America near the end of the century.

Darwin also lived a long life, and after his passing, his body was preserved by Nepal's finest taxidermist and displayed as an inspiration to the museum's visitors. Coloring books showing Darwin atop Machhapuchhre looking for his master have been distributed to generations of Nepalese children, who delight in coloring Darwin's one hundred seventy-nine missing spots, an exercise thought to explain the Nepalese people's interest in art and mathematics. Of course, the destruction of the Marycandu archaeological sites by the French brought an end to further research. However, the Marycandu spirit perseveres through my great-great-uncle's scholarship and teachings, except in France, where his work continues to be mocked and belittled by historians and scholars.

# 11

# LOVE
# STORIES

*Dear Atsuko,*

*I very much appreciate your proposal, but I'm committed to staying in Boston. Nevertheless, I enjoyed hearing about the Santa Monica Sumo Wrestling Club and want to congratulate you on the dual honor of being elected president and leading the women's heavyweight division. And thanks so much for your recipe for chanko-nabe. I love fish stew, and even though I'm not looking to gain seventy-five pounds, it seems just the ticket for wintry New England evenings.*

*Sincerely,*
*Oliphant Allyinphree*

**One Wednesday afternoon** in early March, after Hernando had been teaching his spring semester writing seminar for several weeks, I took time off from work, changed into the spiffy clothes Hernando had helped me pick out, and sat in on his seminar. It was sweater weather, and although piles of grimy slush still decorated the streets, snowdrops were in full bloom.

That semester, Hernando's seminar met at Damned Spot, a historic coffee house on the edge of the Lizzie-B campus, aimed at the local literary crowd. Adjacent to it was Sack of Woe, a locally owned bookstore catering to English majors (*All Angst, No Plot – Guaranteed!*). Damned Spot is the coffee house once frequented by the nineteenth century poet known as Willow, whose framed sepia-toned countenance hangs above the door to the bakery. Willow's notorious poem on the agony of childbirth, delivered one time only, on March 15, 1892, was so wrenching that upon hearing it an anguished female customer stabbed herself with her marmalade spreader and nearly died. The bloodstains on the floor, protected by brass stanchions and a velvet crimson rope, have been a magnet for generations of poetry lovers.

The coffee house is owned by English department graduate students, April and Marvin Maybee, who have been working on their PhD dissertations for nineteen years. On the afternoon of my visit, Marvin had pushed three wooden four-tops together for the seminar. A dozen other tables, half unoccupied, awaited the after-class crush from the college, and a battered oak stool and rickety microphone stand used for poetry readings were pushed against a side wall. Burlap coffee bean sacks framed a large black-board, with the day's specials written in colored chalk. (*New! All-vegan absinthe smoothies!*) A swinging door behind the service counter at the rear led to a small bakery.

Hernando had briefed me on the five students in his seminar, but looking around the table, I counted six. Susannah, a thin sophomore seated to my right, was easy to identify. She had curly auburn hair, a Louisiana accent, and a blood-red T-shirt from her college chorale, Forty-One Whacks. According to Hernando, Susannah carried her banjo with her everywhere. That afternoon it was balanced precariously on her knees under the table, so I scooted my chair to the left to avoid bumping it.

I quickly identified Lancelot across the table from me, a wiry senior dressed in black with shaggy dark hair and wire-rimmed glasses. To his right sat Arizona, a double major in English and women's studies, fashionably attired in faded blue jeans, a black long-sleeved T-shirt with a lime-green drawing of Gertrude Stein, and a brown bomber jacket.

To Arizona's right sat Jeremy, a smallish sophomore with horn-rimmed glasses who, according to my brother, was shy but obsessed with sex. Jeremy had written mostly alien abduction stories but lately had switched to vampires. Sally, a sophomore with short blonde hair and a well-filled-out pink sweater sat on my side of the table. I confess my eyes never strayed low enough to see what she wore on the lower half of her body. Hernando sat at the far end of the table, with his AK-47 beside him, a pointed reminder to campus lawbreakers that coffee house violence would not be tolerated.

By process of elimination, the pretty, brown-eyed girl with straight dark hair sitting beside me had to be the mystery student. She noticed me checking her out, caught my eye, and whispered, "Hi, I'm Fanny. I love your little dog."

"Hi," I whispered back, sitting up straight and scooting my chair in. I'm not good with women's ages, but Fanny seemed younger than the other students. Hernando drew the class to order.

"Cherished students," he proclaimed, pushing back his chair and standing to face our group. "It is time now for our customary invocation." Hernando believed it essential to instill in his students a respect for other cultures, especially those unencumbered by an excess of history, experience, and knowledge. "Today," he said, raising his arms and outstretching them like a prophet's, "we will begin by expressing our profound gratitude to the gods of the ancient Marycandu with a brief moment of silence." Lifting his gaze toward the room's only skylight, he adjusted his stance so that a shaft of sunlight fell on his face, which now seemed to glow with the light of literary insight. After a minute or so, it appeared the Marycandu gods had been adequately thanked, for what I was unsure, and Hernando continued: "Let me now welcome my twin brother, Ollie, who is visiting us today with his little dog, Tex. And I also want to welcome Fanny Forrester, a first-year student who has just moved here from Santa Fe." He glanced up at Fanny, who raised her hand and smiled shyly. He set down the roster and took a manila folder from his briefcase. "Ollie, I believe you have an announcement?"

I scraped back my chair and stood uneasily to address the group. "Hello, everybody. Two weeks from today Hernando and I turn thirty-two, and we want to invite everybody to our birthday party. The owners of Damned Spot, Marvin and April Maybee, have agreed to open the coffee house for us on Thursday evening, March 15, so plan on coming about seven o'clock. The date is also the Maybees' twentieth wedding anniversary. Their parents met at Woodstock, so in Marvin and April's honor, we'll have a sixties theme with costumes optional. You might want to read up on that era before you come."

"What's Woodstock?" Jeremy muttered to Sally, who shrugged.

"Will there be anything to eat?" Lancelot asked, wary of being imprisoned without sustenance.

"We'll be serving Nicaraguan food provided by Sabores Ricos," Hernando said.

"Really?" Fanny said, cuing in on the discussion. "I work at Sabores Ricos. The catering manager didn't mention that."

"What do you do there?" Hernando asked.

"I work in the back," she said, after a slight hesitation. "I don't see customers."

I picked Tex up from the tabletop and placed him in my shirt pocket. He rustled around with his forepaws perched on the top edge of my pocket so he could watch the goings-on. "What a sweetheart," Fanny whispered, reaching over to stroke Tex's head with her fingertip. Tex rewarded her with a weak tail wag, but he didn't otherwise respond. He seemed out of sorts, presumably because of some mood or sound imperceptible to humans.

Standing, Hernando announced to the group: "Let's begin this afternoon with the short stories you all submitted last week and see how far we get." His eyes fell on Lancelot, across from me. Thumbing through the folder, he selected a few stapled pages. "Since we're working on endings, Lancelot, why don't you read the last paragraph of 'Coltrane, Chicken Train, Rain in Spain.'"

"Sure, Professor, the title just kind of came to me when me and my roommates was sitting around—"

"Go ahead and start." Hernando passed the manuscript to him.

"Okay, let's see." Lancelot turned to the last page of his story and started to read. Tex growled at the sound of his voice, so I took him from my pocket, placed him in my lap, and stroked his ears.

". . . the dogwood flowers like a chianti bottle, so i say to ginger whoa baby where'd you get the stuff and she says like cuddly and all dude you're the greatest so here's to the Queen of Bathsheba wow pow how now i feel so great can i have some more but inside her head i see sparks like fireworks at mom's funeral and flames come out of her ears that turn into little dragons and then she dissolves into a puddle of Drano all green and gushy with little teeth and then she is gone just like Jerry Garcia the end."

"Excellent, Lancelot," said Hernando, looking around the table. "Thank you for sharing. So class, what do you think?"

"Awesome," Jeremy said. "I liked the part about Ginger dissolving into Drano. That is so tragic."

"Yeah," Lancelot replied, "just when they were about to get it on, too. I thought about giving it, you know, a happy ending, but that would be so, like, ordinary."

"I am struck by the Freudian allusion to the mother's funeral," Arizona offered, after a momentary silence. "It tips off the reader that the protagonist's relationship with Ginger is doomed because he feels so sexually inadequate."

"Fuck I do," Lancelot snarled, turning red and glaring at her.

Sally waved her hand, and Hernando motioned to her. "My favorite part is the metaphor about the dogwood flowering like a Chianti bottle. That is so deep. I just keep peeling away the layers, and it goes on and on. How did you ever think of that?"

"Hey, these things just come to me," Lancelot said. "No big deal."

"Well, Lancelot," Hernando said, "I think you've really found your voice. Nice job." He looked around the table. Hearing no other comments, he glanced at his watch. "Oh my, we're almost out of time already," he said, "but I want to give Fanny a chance to participate."

"But we've only been here seventeen minutes," Arizona said.

"Ah, but we are laying the foundation for a literary cathedral, one stone at a time," Hernando said. "One does not measure the creative process with mere minutes." His voice had a reproachful tone that suggested Arizona's remark had needlessly interrupted the construction of a great cathedral. He turned to Fanny. "Fanny, did you bring a story with you?"

She nodded and took out several pages from her backpack.

"Please tell the seminar what it's about and then read the ending."

"Yes, sir, it's my first short story," she said, looking embarrassed at the sudden attention. "I'm not sure I want everybody to hear it."

"Quiet, everybody, let's give her a chance," Hernando said. "Fanny, go ahead and set the stage."

"Yes, sir. It's a simple love story, called 'Too Late for the Learning.' Rachel is a schoolteacher who leads a dull, predictable life in the small Midwestern town she grew up in. On her summer break, she drives out West by herself to visit national parks and think about her future. There she meets Alex, an archaeologist, when she's camping in the Utah desert. At first, she sees Alex as a summer fling, but their relationship turns serious, and they fall in love. He asks her to marry him, but she says no because she's fearful of taking the risk. That's all. I'm afraid it's not very exciting."

"I'll say," Jeremy whispered to Sally across the table. Sally nodded and grinned at him, and Hernando scowled at them both.

"Shut up," Arizona said. "I want to hear this." And so did I. I looked at Fanny as she leaned over to set her backpack on the floor and noticed a slight twist to her mouth, as if she were trying to suppress a smile; she wasn't as shy and embarrassed as she was letting on.

"Go ahead and read us the ending," Hernando said. With an overt worried expression, Fanny flipped to the end of her story and began to read:

Earlier that week they had camped on a high ridge overlooking a broad mesa. The temperature had dropped, and they huddled beside their campfire, talking and listening to the coyotes and night sounds. The sky was a bowl of stars, and the grandeur of the Milky Way stretched from horizon to horizon.

"It takes your breath away," Rachel said as she looked up into the glowing expanse. "It's magical here, isn't it? I had no idea." A meteor flashed in the distant sky north of Sagittarius. It left a momentary bright track and vanished.

"There we are," Alex said. He turned to look at her. "You can stay, you know. You can be a part of this with me." He reached over and took her hand.

She knew she had no good answer. How could she tell this man she was too small for his life? That his world, with its azure skies and rough-hewn, friendly people, and snow-shrouded mountains and arroyos and wildflowers and endless desert, was too expansive to fit into her imagination. Where would she feel safe in this place? And in that instant, sitting quietly under the stars beside the man she loved, listening to the music of the desert, she made her decision to leave him.

Now, she slid onto the dusty seat and quickly closed the car door, her hands trembling. She gripped the steering wheel like it was a life preserver. Alex stood looking at her through the open window, his hand on the window frame. A gust of dry desert wind caught his hair, and he brushed it back with his free hand. She saw him blink away tears, and she struggled to control herself.

"Please don't leave," he said, his face anguished. "Please. This isn't right." He leaned his head through the window to kiss her.

"I can't," she said, pulling back.

"Rachel, you're breaking my heart." He reached through the window and touched her cheek. She met his gaze and looked away. He didn't deserve this. She looked up again at his pale blue eyes and wondered if this was the last time she would see them.

"Goodbye, Alex," she said.

"Maybe—" he started to speak but there was nothing to say.

"Maybe."

She put the car in gear and edged forward, resisting the impulse to look in the rearview mirror. Ahead, the highway stretched before her, waves of heat from the afternoon sun rippling above the scarred asphalt. In the distance she saw a road mirage, two figures, shimmering and indistinct. As she approached, they coalesced, and an instant later were gone. Above, an enormous black raven circled in lazy spirals, riding the air currents. Then the highway veered sharply to the east. As she neared the bend, she allowed herself a glance in the rearview mirror, her heart pounding, but it was too late. Nothing was there but the scorched, empty desert.

# 12

# TOO LATE FOR
# THE LEARNING

**Fanny set her story** on the table, looked up at Hernando, and blushed as if she had just divulged an embarrassing personal secret. The group was silent, all eyes on Hernando, who was looking at Fanny with a quizzical expression. Fanny seemed suddenly intriguing! She held Hernando's gaze, a tight smile crossed her face, and then she averted her eyes. I felt a rustling at my shirt pocket as Tex adjusted his stance to get a better view of the class. The room had grown still, save for the *tick, tick, tick* of an ancient ceiling fan and the hiss of the espresso machine. It appeared Fanny's story had even captured the attention of the other customers. It had certainly captured mine.

Hernando, looking around the table, broke the silence. "Sooo . . . class, what do we think? Lancelot?"

"Me?" Lancelot said, in the voice of the doomed. He slid his chair back from the table, as if preparing to bolt. Tex gave a short, tense growl and repositioned himself in my shirt pocket. "Uhh, let's see. Different. I guess it was different." He looked hopefully around the table, but the absence of affirming nods suggested the class expected a deeper insight.

"All right. Different. That's fine. And in what way, specifically, is it different?" Hernando's patient tone suggested great familiarity with Socratic dialogue.

"Okaaay," Lancelot said. He placed his hands on the edge of the table and took a deep breath. "Well, nothing happens. Rachel says goodbye, gets in her car, and drives away. What kind of story is that? I mean, really, you gotta admit that's pretty boring, right?"

Tex made a low growl that rumbled across the table like faraway thunder, no mean feat for a dog that weighed six ounces. Lancelot glared at him and turned back toward Hernando.

"So you'd have preferred more action?" Hernando said, stroking his beard in the manner of a renowned scholar. Tex squirmed in my pocket, and I patted his head to soothe him.

"Yeah, like take the meteor," Lancelot said, encouraged. "At first, I thought that was kind of exciting, but then it, like, fizzled out. Why couldn't it have landed next to them and made a huge crater, maybe set the desert on fire?" He settled back in his chair to let the class digest this plot inspiration.

"What? No!" Fanny picked up her story and held it out to the class. "You don't understand. I wanted this to be about Alex and Rachel's relationship." She looked at Hernando for support, but he was in a distant universe, and she failed to catch his eye. "My story is about choices and risk-taking,"

I'd been working lately to understand the grammatical structures of Tex's language. Successive barks usually follow a Fibonacci sequence. In addition to the simple bark, there is the yip, the woof, the moan, the squeal, the howl, the whimper, and the whine. And, of course, the nuance-laden growl. Tex had now begun to articulate a guttural and low growl that hinted at impatience, exasperation, and anger, leavened by a hint of malice. His body vibrated like a cellphone, and his ears were erect and canted to the rear.

"What do you think, Mr. Guevara?" Fanny said, interrupting my thoughts. She fixed my brother earnestly with an anxious, determined expression. All heads turned to Hernando, and a hush settled again over the room as the other customers followed the ongoing drama. Hernando remained still for a long moment as he weighed his response. Then he pushed his chair back and stood. He walked behind Fanny's chair, leaned over, picked up her story, and hefted the handwritten pages, as if estimating the weight of the ink. Fanny turned her head and looked up at him with still-anxious eyes.

"Fanny, your story is just words on a page," he said, enunciating each word. "Just . . . words . . . on . . . a . . . page." He gestured with Fanny's pages, as if sprinkling us with words, and then he slowly walked to his chair, sat down, and placed the pages on the table in front of him. He bowed his head in the manner of one saying grace and folded his hands.

There was shocked silence in the room as we weighed this somber pronouncement. I had no idea why my brother was being so dismissive. At an adjacent table, a graduate student wearing a Flannery O'Connor T-shirt whispered something to her friend, who shrugged. Then a low murmur filled the coffee house. Nobody at our table spoke, so I eavesdropped on snatches of conversation.

". . . He said *just* words, as in *justice*."

". . . *Just* is a narrowing adverb, like *only*."

". . . So you think the story is about moral choices?"

". . . Leaving her lover to go back to Dullsville, isn't that a moral choice?"

". . . Not to Alex, nothing moral about that."

". . . What, you want Rachel to follow him around, barefoot and pregnant?"

". . . You're missing the point; it's her decision to make."

". . . But did he like her story or not?"

". . . I dunno."

Now Lancelot spoke, his eyes locked on Hernando's face for any hint of disagreement. "Yeah, that's what it is, words on a page." At this, Arizona wrinkled her brow and frowned with an expression that conveyed simultaneous contempt for Lancelot's blatant sucking up to his teacher and the low intellectual bar of the discussion. I was pretty much in her camp, but the other students evidently felt differently, their expressions affirming the majority view that Fanny's story was indeed just words on a page.

"But what should I do now?" Fanny said as she took back her word-filled pages, her eyes flashing desperation. "Do you have office hours, sir? Maybe I could meet with you one-on-one? Please, I really want to learn to write, and your writing is so powerful. It . . . it reminds me of Hemingway," she blurted.

"Oh, Hemingway you say? Really?" Hernando looked up at this interesting new thread.

"Yes. Your prose is so hard and lean. Your words take no prisoners," Fanny added, with a slight smile and a quick glance at the AK-47 propped against the table. I looked at the other students. Lancelot appeared mystified by this exchange. He whispered something to Jeremy, who shrugged about who this Hemingway character might be.

"So, you've read my memoir?" Hernando said to Fanny, in a nudge at centering the discussion back into desirable territory.

"Yes, I loved every page. It was inspirational, so very inspirational." Although Fanny spoke with evident sincerity, Arizona rolled her eyes, provoking a quick shadow of uncertainty across Fanny's brow. Fortunately, Hernando's beaming face dispelled any concern she might have had that her praise could appear a tad fulsome. "So will you help me, Mr. Guevara?" she asked again, pleading.

"Of *course*," Hernando said, his voice warm with reassurance. "My tutoring sessions are in the evenings, after my classes. I have this little spot, a hideaway." He took out a business card from his shirt pocket and passed it to Fanny. "If you like, we can start tonight, say eight o'clock."

"Wait a minute," Susannah said, raising her hand. "You were supposed to tutor me tonight at your hideaway. Can't you tutor her tomorrow night?"

"Tomorrow night's taken," Sally said. "That's *my* regular time. Get your own time."

Sensing conflict, Tex began to bark, first two short barks, then three barks in succession, a short pause, and five more. In stressful moments, Tex sometimes abandons the Fibonacci sequence in favor of prime numbers.

"Can't somebody shut that dog up?" Lancelot snarled. "What kind of dumb animal is that, anyway? He doesn't even look like a dog. He looks like a hamster." I felt Tex shudder violently in my pocket and took him out of my shirt to calm him. I could feel his body shake. I'd never seen him so agitated. The room hushed. I ignored Lancelot and said a few soothing words to Tex, but to no effect. His ears were pinned, his body rigid, and his tail quivered with fury. Suddenly, he snarled and jumped from my hand. He stormed across the table, and in fifteen or twenty steps reached Lancelot, reared back on his haunches, and then, to my astonishment, leaped at his throat.

"Hey!" Lancelot yelled, surprised by this unhamster-like behavior. He yanked his chair sideways to dodge Tex's attack, but a chair leg caught on a floorboard, tipping the chair and spilling him onto Susannah, who lost her balance and crashed into the side of the table. She and Lancelot tumbled into a heap on the floor. Her banjo landed beside them with a loud twang.

Then I heard an angry growl, and Lancelot cried, "Ow, oww! Get that beast off me." He emerged from under the table and wildly swatted at his ear, which Tex was hanging onto with the tenacity of a pit bull. An eternity passed: Lancelot screamed and flailed his head like a madman, Tex swung back and forth like a pirate's earring, and Susannah, who had ducked under the table, saw a thin stream of blood trickling onto her banjo and began to wail, a mournful keening that alarmed the other coffee shop patrons. The proprietor, Marvin Maybee, raced from the kitchen and collided with an elderly professor of Romance languages, who slopped his absinthe smoothie on the floor and down the front of his black turtleneck. Marvin lost his balance on the slippery floorboards and toppled into a heap.

I pushed my way to Lancelot and tried to detach Tex from his ear, but the more I tugged, the harder he bit down. Then, over all the commotion, I heard Hernando's booming voice. "Stop! Everybody halt *now*." I looked toward the far end of the table and there stood Hernando, his legs apart, knees slightly bent, his assault rifle held across his chest. Tex released his grip on Lancelot's ear, gave a shocked whimper, and leapt into my hand. I put him back into my pocket. Susannah muffled her mouth with both hands, tears streaming down her face, while Lancelot, moaning like he'd been attacked by a grizzly bear, climbed back into his chair and gingerly nursed his bleeding earlobe.

"Tex, what did you do?" I said, as order was being restored. Although Lancelot's hamster insult was a cheap shot, it didn't seem a provocation worthy of open combat. Tex looked up at me from my shirt pocket but appeared unrepentant. April Maybee wiped up the spilled smoothie and helped her husband to his feet. "We can't have this, Tex," I said. "You can't go around biting people." I reminded myself Tex's Doggie-Do-Rite classes began the following Monday.

Evidently, coffee house brawls were not unknown to Damned Spot's customers, because within ten minutes the incident seemed forgotten. I didn't know what to think about Fanny, except her story seemed precocious for a freshman. So why had Hernando reacted so strangely to it? And why did she seem so anxious and insecure around him?

We gathered our papers while the students stood to put on their sweaters and jackets. Hernando moved over to the kitchen door to discuss party arrangements with the Maybees. I was still irritated with Tex for biting Lancelot, so I kept him in my shirt pocket and ignored him. Late afternoon customers were already filtering in, and Arizona and Fanny sat at a vacant table to chat while I meandered around the room,

"Rachel shouldn't have left him," Jeremy was saying to Sally as they put on their jackets. "She loved Alex but was afraid to take a risk."

"But the risk was too big. Her destiny was her other life."

"I don't buy that," Jeremy said. "Opportunities have to be seized or they go away. Isn't that what the meteor is all about?"

"Maybe. I have to think about it."

"Me too," Jeremy said as he opened the door and they walked together into the late afternoon sun. Hernando came over and I grabbed my jacket. Just then, someone tapped my shoulder, and I turned to face Fanny.

"Hey, Ollie," she said. "I love your darling little dog. It was so nice to meet both of you. I think your party sounds like great fun." She glanced at Hernando, who smiled his agreement.

"Fanny. I was wondering . . ." I found myself blushing as I hesitated. Fanny raised her eyebrows. "I was wondering if you'd like to get a cup of coffee sometime, you know, to get acquainted?"

"Sure, I'd like that," she said. "Why don't you meet me at Sabores Ricos this Saturday? Say around noon. We'll have lunch, and I can show you the restaurant."

"You don't have to work?"

"I can get away," she said with an amused smile. "Anyway, we'll call that work, since we're catering your party for you." Now that the seminar had ended, Fanny struck me as surprisingly self-assured. She returned to her table, while Hernando and I headed for the exit. As we walked out, he turned to me.

"She's a little young for you, don't you think?" I sensed irritation in his voice.

"I'm just doing what you said and trying to be more social," I replied, striving to sound indignant. The day had turned breezy, and mottled gray clouds drifted westward, intermittently blocking the wan sunlight. The air held a clammy chill, and the whisper of distant thunder foreshadowed an approaching cold front. We stopped to watch two feuding squirrels chase each other along a telephone wire. They hopped onto the branch of a large chestnut tree, skittered down the trunk, and vanished around the battered dumpsters that lined the alley beside the coffee house. Tex barked, so I set him on the ground. He dashed after the squirrels for a few yards but quickly gave up. Tex seemed to know he ought to act like a dog sometimes, but I often suspected he was just going through the motions.

"So you're having lunch with her?" Hernando said, feigning nonchalance as we resumed walking. It sounded more like an accusation than a question. He shifted his AK-47 to his other shoulder.

I parried. "She's interesting, don't you think?"

"To put it mildly. I don't get her at all."

"Hernando, why didn't you want to give your opinion about her story?"

He stopped and looked at me, resting the stock of his rifle on the sidewalk. "I did give my opinion. I loved the story." He seemed truly puzzled, which puzzled me.

"But you said it was just words on a page."

He said, "To evoke love, to touch the heart of a person using just words. My God, that's magic, Oliphant."

"So why are you acting so strangely about her?"

He hesitated a moment before confessing and spoke in a low voice. "Because I don't think she wrote that story. Do you remember the metaphor about the two road mirages merging and then vanishing? Oliphant, that was my metaphor. I used it in a short story for my tutor, Isabella, back in Nicaragua. I never published the story, and there's no way Fanny could have known about it. She couldn't have dreamed that up. It's too big a coincidence."

I stared at him, surprised at how upset he seemed. "You're right, Hernando, that doesn't seem possible. But Fanny's writing doesn't sound like yours, and it's nothing like Hemingway's, either."

Hernando looked confused for an instant and then laughed, "Oh, you mean *Lesbo Mamas*. That's memoir, not fiction. I wrote it to mimic Hemingway because Isabella said it would sell better. You know, the rough jungle life of an insurgent band, the wild animals . . ."

The sun hung low in the sky, and long shadows flitted on the sidewalks like anxious ghosts. Ahead, a small cluster of backpack-laden students shuffled from their afternoon classes toward their dorms and fraternity houses. We came upon a fire hydrant, stopped for Tex's benefit, and moved on in silence. Hernando had a faraway look, and I wondered if he was thinking about Isabella. Or Fanny. Or the stone he had just placed in the foundation of a great cathedral. Okay, a pebble maybe.

A bicycle bell tinkled behind us. "On your right," a woman said, her words melodic with a hint of an accent. We stepped to the curb to let her pass. As her bicycle wobbled past, I got a glimpse of the rider in the mottled sunlight. She had a trim figure, honey complexion, and dark shoulder-length hair that showed under her bicycle helmet. I felt a pang of familiarity.

"Regina?" I called as she moved past, but she didn't hear and kept peddling. "Regina?" I said loudly, but this time her name caught in my throat, and I choked. Still, she didn't pause. Hernando glanced over at me curiously, then looked at the retreating bicycle. "Wait!" he called in a loud bark. The rider turned her head and almost lost her balance. She steadied her bicycle, stopped, and twisted toward us.

"Oh, it's *you*," she said, and her face broke into a delighted grin. Just then a cloud moved from the sun and its light fell on her face. She was speaking to Hernando. I supposed I shouldn't have been surprised.

# 13

# LUNCHTIME
# LESSON

*Dear Mr. Badami,*

*Thank you for your inquiry, but I have never posted a bride-wanted advertisement on the Bangalore Craigslist. Somebody must have been playing a joke, although I do not find it very funny. I can assure you there is no tradition in my country of the groom pledging a million-dollar dowry to the bride's family. Nevertheless, your daughter, Aboli, sounds like a charming and interesting young woman, and I am sure there must be many hard-working, single men in Bangalore who would like to meet her.*

*Sincerely,*
*Ollie Allyinphree*

**I arrived a few minutes early** at Sabores Ricos for my lunch date with Fanny. Filled with nervous excitement, I squeezed my Mini-P between a black BMW and a silver Lexus in the crowded adjacent lot and crunched along a pebble walkway to the large front entrance. The building was imposing, with a tan stucco exterior, large portico with three arched openings, and a roof of curved red tiles. I'd heard *Sabores Ricos* had recently changed ownership, and the crammed parking lot suggested it was a good investment for the new owners. I hoped Fanny and I wouldn't have to wait too long for a table.

At the hostess stand, I gave my name to an exotic Hispanic woman in a black silk pantsuit and surveyed the room. The customers were well-dressed, probably from the high-rise offices a few blocks over. I'd come from my distinctly low-rise office at the library and was relieved I'd worn a coat and tie. Even so, I was pretty sure I anchored the bottom rung of the restaurant's sartorial ladder. The hostess pretended not to notice when I brushed at a white smudge on my sports coat where I'd leaned against a chalkboard. I was glad I'd left Tex at home; Sabores Ricos didn't look like the sort of place that welcomed pets.

"Oh yes, Mr. Allyinphree," the hostess said with a gracious smile. "We've been expecting you." She escorted me around a Spanish-style fountain to a secluded table near the rear, under a large antique mirror. "Ms. Forrester will be here presently," she said as she seated me.

My table had a gray linen tablecloth decorated by a small crystal vase of alstroemeria. I sat and fiddled with a silver table knife, and after a few minutes, Fanny walked through the door from the kitchen. "Hi Ollie," she said warmly as I stood to greet her. "Welcome to Sabores Ricos. Oh, you didn't bring Tex. That's too bad. I was hoping to see him." I almost didn't recognize her in heels and a charcoal business suit. She looked gorgeous. We took our seats, and I did my best to cover the sports coat smudge with my arm. A server appeared holding a pitcher of a cream-colored liquid with a large chunk of pineapple floating in it.

"Good afternoon, Ms. Forrester," he said to Fanny in a suavely cheerful voice, and to me, "Hello, sir. Try a glass of our chicha de maíz. It's made from red corn."

"I hope you like shrimp," Fanny said, once the waiter had gone. "I asked Chef Analucia to prepare camarones a la diabla. I thought we might serve it at your birthday party. We don't have our liquor license yet, so we'll arrange bartending by an independent wine merchant."

I took a sip of my chicha, which was fruity with a hint of vanilla. Even in her business suit Fanny looked no older than nineteen, which meant she was twelve years younger than me. It seemed like she should be running errands or clearing tables. "Fanny, what exactly do you do for Sabores Ricos?"

"I guess you'd say I'm a manager." She appeared embarrassed by the question.

"What do you manage?" I looked around at the servers and busboys, who seemed at least twice her age.

She hesitated. "The staff, mostly. Hiring, firing, among other things," she confessed, now obviously uneasy. I knew I should let the subject drop.

"Like what other things, for instance?"

Her face reddened. "Ollie," she said, "your skepticism is showing. I'm older than I look." I was sure that was true. The part about my skepticism showing. I studied her smooth chin and perfect complexion. "Really, I'm not a kid." She laughed. "I'm almost twenty-six. Do you want to check my driver's license?"

I gaped at her. "Twenty-six? But how . . . ?" I spread my hands to encompass the posh surroundings. I now felt totally confused.

She gave a resigned shrug. "I suppose you were going to find out eventually. Ollie, I own Sabores Ricos. Well, actually, my folks own it. They bought it when I moved to Boston in January, and I run it for them." Just then the waiter returned carrying two rectangular bone-white plates. Camarones a la diabla appeared to be shrimp grilled with tomatoes and onions over white rice. Fanny looked down at her plate and took a small taste, as if evaluating wine. She looked up and nodded, and he departed.

"What brought you to Boston?" I asked, not so much because I wanted to know, but because I needed time to process all these disclosures.

She laughed again and said, "I should have printed out my résumé for you. I grew up here. My dad was CEO at the First National Bank, and my mom was his chief loan officer. Five years ago they retired and moved to Santa Fe." She picked up her glass of chicha and took a swallow. "So that's my story," she said, sitting back and relaxing into her chair. "Not much to tell."

That wasn't her *whole* story. For starters, how did she know so much about Nicaraguan food? Where had she learned to write? And then the biggie: Why was she pretending to be a freshman? I tried to absorb the idea Fanny was a grown woman and eminently dateable. She was pretty, ambitious, smart, and so far as I knew, unattached. I was ramping up my courage to ask her out, when some inner voice cautioned me to go slow.

At an adjacent table, a man about my age sat across from a striking Asian woman with black hair pulled back in a sleek chignon. He wore an impeccably tailored navy wool suit. There were no smudges on it. I looked back at Fanny and found her assessing my face. She set down her fork and looked at me with a sober expression that suggested we'd already used up all the fun stuff and it was time now to move on to business. She said, "Ollie, I need to tell you why I asked to see you today, but you've got to promise to keep it secret."

"Keep it secret from whom?" I thought *I* was the one who asked to see *her.*

"First, you've got to promise. Really, I'm serious about this."

"Okay, sure," I said, as if I had some idea what was happening.

She turned her head to make certain the waiter wasn't nearby. "Ollie, I'm in love with your brother," she said in a low voice, her lips trembling.

I was too stunned to speak. I stared down at my plate of camarones. My first thought was that I was glad I'd listened to my inner voice and not asked her out. My second thought was to wonder how to respond sensitively to this disclosure.

"Are you nuts?" I said finally, looking up. "You hardly know him. You've been in his seminar, what, less than a semester?"

She sat there looking wounded, saying nothing, and I decided I might have been a bit harsh. Then she raised her head. "I've made a terrible mistake," she said, her voice catching. She turned toward the wall so our waiter wouldn't see and wiped her eyes with a linen napkin.

I steadied my hands on the table to get my bearings. "What mistake? You have a crush on your professor. That happens all the time." Out of the corner of my eye, I saw our waiter approaching. He looked at us, did an about-face, and returned to the kitchen.

She said, "Ollie, I owe you an explanation, but please, please don't say anything to Hernando. It's not a crush." She looked up, took a breath, and exhaled. "Hernando is the love of my life. I've loved him for almost eight years."

I just stared at her. None of this made sense, so I held my tongue and let her tell her story. It turned out that eight years ago she had been a college freshman, at Harvard nonetheless, and had read Hernando's memoir in a literature class. "I loved reading about his childhood," she said. "His description of the rainforest as 'an ancient, verdant place, teeming with life, vast and primordial' made me know I belonged there." Her eyes had a distant, muted look.

*Teeming with bugs and snakes,* I thought. I couldn't imagine myself living in a jungle, sleeping under mosquito netting, no libraries, museums, internet, good coffee. I shivered at the thought of Hernando's creepy story of a giant anaconda slithering into his tent.

"What about that life appealed to you?" I asked as the waiter returned to clear our plates. Fanny ordered a carajillo for each of us. She said it was a Spanish coffee drink made with espresso, sugar, and cognac.

"Since we don't have our liquor license yet," she said with a weak smile, "we hide cognac in the kitchen for cooking. Don't tell anyone." Shortly, the waiter returned with dos carajillos. Fanny took a sip and looked up at me. "Look around us, Ollie. We've surrounded ourselves with cities, highways, shopping malls . . . We're trying to force nature to live by our rules. I hate that, and I felt like your brother and I shared those beliefs."

Actually, most of that sounded pretty good to me. I said, "The jungle sounds like a lonely place, though."

"You should check out Harvard sometime. I remember sitting in my Expos 20 class and reading about Isabella, Hernando's tutor. None of my Harvard profs even knew my name. I didn't fit in there, so I dropped out at the end of my freshman year." She took another sip. "I flew to Nicaragua and joined a tour of the Bosawás Biosphere Reserve. One day I met a woman who said she knew where Hernando's madres were camped. She said she delivered supplies there and I could tag along if I'd keep its location secret. Not that I ever could have found it again. When I got there, Hernando had been gone for three years, but everybody still remembered him, especially Isabella, his tutor."

"Hernando told me Isabella was old enough to be his mother."

"There's no way to know," Fanny said. "She looked like a young woman. The Mayangna Indians gave us a skin cream that reverses the appearance of aging. They make it from strange, moaning leeches that lived in our lake." She laughed. "Everybody here thinks I'm a teenager."

"But Hernando doesn't look any younger than me."

"The effect wears off in a year or so. I brought some back with me, but I'm about out." Before I could ask the obvious question, she said, "And I can't get any more. A fungus killed all the leeches. That is, unless they're also in another lake somewhere. I know there are expeditions searching for them."

I didn't tell her about Fawn and Ruprecht. Instead, I said, "So how long did you stay there?"

"Seven years. Isabella tutored me in writing and showed me Hernando's stories and essays. Hernando and I had so much in common I couldn't imagine being with any other man. That's why I came back to Boston."

I said, "Fanny, why the subterfuge? Why didn't you just tell him the truth?"

"I wanted to, but I couldn't. At the time, Hernando was just a fantasy. What if I didn't like him? What if he was physically repulsive? For all I knew he was in love with somebody else. Or married. Or gay. Or he could have grown up to be really strange. I couldn't just walk up to a man I'd never met and tell him I'd been in love with him for eight years and had traveled from Central America to track him down."

"Point taken," I said.

"So I enrolled in his seminar to check him out. I knew I looked like a freshman, but I've worried my writing might give me away. I may have even used a metaphor from one of his stories in an assignment. I stayed awake all night worrying about that. If I did, Hernando must really be puzzled."

To put it mildly. I decided not to tell her about his suspicions. Instead, I just said, "He thinks you're eighteen."

"I hoped there would be a spark between us, Ollie, but there's nothing there. He has no interest in me," she said, struggling to keep her composure. She sniffled and reached for her napkin.

"Fanny, why are you telling me all this?"

"Because you're his brother. I need to know how Hernando would respond if I told him the truth. Do you think I'd have any chance with him? Any chance at all?"

We sat in silence while I mulled over her question. I'd only seen the two of them together once, and I knew Hernando was confused and suspicious about Fanny. It was obvious she was in love with him, but I also knew Hernando was skeptical about romantic entanglements. I doubted he could ever trust her.

"Fanny," I said finally, "I don't see a way this could work out. I'm really sorry." I had to tell her the truth, but I hated myself. I'd never seen anyone look so miserable.

She bit her lower lip and her voice caught. "That's what I thought you'd say, but I needed to hear it. Ollie, please, you can't say any of this to Hernando. Swear to me that you won't."

"I won't say anything, but what are you going to do?"

"I'll probably just finish my seminar and go back to running my restaurant." She reached across the table and squeezed my hand. "Ollie, you're really easy to talk to. Thank you for listening to me. I wish we could be friends. Maybe someday, but . . . I hope you understand."

"I do," I said. There was nothing else to say. We stood and Fanny hugged me. Her face looked feverish, her eyes puffy. She turned quickly toward the door to the kitchen.

Lunch hour had ended, and busboys were busy clearing dirty dishes and silverware. As I walked toward the exit the hostess thanked me for coming. The BMW and Lexus had gone from the parking lot, which was now nearly empty. I sat in my car for a few minutes without starting the engine and thought about the promise I'd made to honor Fanny's secret. I felt slightly guilty at the deception but decided I was doing the right thing. Fanny had taken a gamble that Hernando would fall in love with her, and it hadn't worked out. There was no chemistry between them and that was all there was to it.

I hesitated again before turning the ignition key. This lunch had not turned out the way I had hoped. Fawn, Regina, and now Fanny; I was batting zero for three. So much for my fresh start. I started the engine and backed out of the parking spot. Tex was waiting for me at home, and I decided the two of us needed a long walk. I wanted to be with my little dog.

# 14

## TEX GOES TO OBEDIENCE SCHOOL

**Doggie-Do-Rite** is a short stroll from home. According to my dog park buddies, the owner is a small, kindly woman named Nell. Her caretaker, a cute Pomeranian named Shannon, trotted over when she saw me and Ollie walk into the school. We touched noses, and she courteously lifted a rear leg so I could sniff out her past week.

Doggie-Do-Rite is sparsely furnished with metal folding chairs and a podium, since during the day the room is the school's gym. The floor is polished wood, stained with the scents of sweat and old tennis shoes from generations of students. Our class was maybe thirty dogs and their humans, mostly women and a few teenagers. I recognized several dogs from my walks with Ollie.

I looked around for Honey, my bullmastiff friend from the dog park, but she hadn't arrived yet. Honey and I had cooked up our plan a month ago. Honey says her human, Matilda, is an accountant—a bit shy, with a good heart—and we thought she and Ollie might hit it off. One problem is Matilda plays snare drums and practices every day after work. Ollie had a bad experience once with a tuba player, so we knew from the start Matilda was a long shot. Getting them together at Doggie-Do-Rite had been Honey's idea. I was still feeling guilty about nipping that student, Lancelot, on the ear last week, but I hadn't come up with a better scheme to get Ollie here.

I didn't know most of the dogs, but I recognized Cipher, a three–year-old basset hound who, by reputation, is the best mathematician in the city. The human species' lack of math skills is a continuing frustration to us dogs. It's not that humans lack native ability, although they don't exactly excel in that department, but since their brains work at one-seventh speed, they have trouble focusing long enough to follow complex chains of logic. So many burdens.

I heard a whooshing noise, and the metal door from the parking lot swung open, letting in a rush of chilly air and the sounds of street traffic. It was Matilda and Honey, and Honey had a worried look in her eyes. I jogged over, pulling Ollie behind me. We touched noses, and I learned Matilda had fallen in love with her snare drum instructor. We were too late. Ollie greeted Matilda, scratched Honey's ears, lifted me into his shirt pocket, and we headed back to the center of the room. Oh well.

Just then I heard a high-pitched squeal from the PA system that humans couldn't hear. That's another problem. I looked over and saw Nell fiddling with the button on the podium microphone.

"We'll get started shortly," she announced, "but first, I want to introduce a new student. She's a celebrity from the West Coast who's just moved here with her poodle, Little Squeegee. She'll be here in a few minutes." I wondered why Nell didn't introduce Ollie and me. We were new here too.

At the mention of Little Squeegee, there was an outburst of

applause, mostly from the younger humans. "Yes, that's right," Nell continued, her voice beginning to rise. She was obviously excited about this new student. "The LA hip-hop music sensation QTπ is joining us, and we're thrilled to have her and Little Squeegee in our class." More applause and cheering. Ollie clapped politely, but I could tell he hadn't recognized our new classmate's name, and neither had I. Cute Tea Pie? How odd.

"I know you'll find QTπ warm and approachable," Nell continued once the applause faded. "Even though she's a famous celebrity, she's not stuck-up like so many of them. In fact, she tells me she's bashful when meeting new friends, so to break the ice, she gave me this little card to read."

*That is so sweet,* I thought. I knew we dogs would do our best to make QTπ feel comfortable. Nell put on reading glasses hanging from a cord around her neck and squinted at the words on a pink sheet of card stock.

"The Los Angeles hip-hop superstar and humanitarian QTπ began her career at fifteen with her breakout album, *Bitchin' in the Kitchen,* exposing cockroaches in Los Angeles school cafeteria lunchrooms. Many fans have compared her rap lyrics to the sonnets of Bill Shakespeare. Others say they resemble the teachings of Jesus.

"QTπ grew up in South LA, where she spent her weekends handing out food to homeless people. Her mother, Brandi, was a talented dancer who used a metal pole to glorify the beauty of the female form and to collect money for charity. Her father, known fondly by his associates as Squeegee, ran a successful business cleaning car windshields at Los Angeles intersections. QTπ named her precious poodle Little Squeegee in his honor.

Today, QTπ and her backup group, The Tarts (Peach, Lemon, and Mango), tour the country with their music. QTπ devotes her spare time to working for world peace and giving to the poor."

From the wild screaming and clapping at this introduction, one would think the class was being introduced to Mother Teresa. Nell started to turn away but then changed her mind and returned to the microphone. "One other thing. I know many of you heard QTπ's latest smash hits at her amazing outdoor concert, so you'll be thrilled that her T-shirts and posters will be on sale by the entrance after class. And yes, for a nominal handling charge of only $9.95, QTπ will be happy to autograph your purchase."

A minute later, the parking lot door screeched open, and a woman clutching an enormous boom box stepped into the room. The boom box blocked her face until she leaned over and plugged it into an outlet, but then I saw it was the woman from the dog park with the nasty poodle. That monster was Little Squeegee? I was getting a bad feeling. We waited. A moment later the door opened again, sending a knife edge of sunlight into the room. Immediately, the tails of dogs nearest the door began to twitch, and I heard a worried whimpering as an invisible cloud of anxiety drifted into the gym. The cloud moved in our direction, and I gave an involuntary yip when it reached Ollie and me. It was the human female mating pheromone, but not like any I'd ever experienced.

Human mating pheromones have a pleasant, inoffensive aroma, not terribly strong, reminiscent of dog biscuits. But this one had a raw, nasty smell. I started to pant and felt a nauseating taste in my mouth, like I'd been forced to eat stale bargain-basement kibble.

I canted my eyes toward Ollie's face, and even though he

seemed oblivious to it, I could tell the smell was affecting him. He seemed preoccupied and dazed, his eyes fixed on the open door, his pupils dilated. I canvassed the room and saw all the men were acting like that. The women, however, were unaffected; the older women stood politely with their dogs, while the younger ones jumped and squealed with excitement, as if somebody was about to throw a tennis ball. I looked back at the door just as QTπ entered. She was tall, pale, and underfed, sporting masses of wavy pink hair with green highlights. One arm cradled Little Squeegee, now dyed pink to match. She beamed at the crowd and raised her other arm to cheers and applause.

"Settle down, everybody," Nell yelled over the loudspeaker. "Give her some room." The crowd parted, creating a corridor toward the podium. Waving, QTπ ran up to Nell and took the microphone. Just then the boom box started up with the beat of a huge electronic drum. After a few seconds, I heard three female voices, the Tarts presumably, chanting "yeah, yeah, yeah," their amplified wailing synchronized with the drumbeat. They sounded like they were giving birth.

QTπ handed Little Squeegee to the dog park woman and stood at the podium, bare arms outstretched, dark tattoos of large treble and base clefs surrounded by grace notes visible up to her shoulders. She held that pose, feet spread, knees bent, the jarring drumbeat reverberating off the gym walls. The audience stood transfixed. Then she started to move. Her hips twitched to the rhythm, and her knees flexed with each beat. Her arms moved up and down, the microphone in her hand tracing a small ellipse. The ellipse grew as her arms writhed, their motion amplified by the drumbeat. Now her shoulders joined the beat, and her head swiveled side to side. Her hair whipped back and forth in ferocious pink and green waves. Her hips twisted and thrust, and her arms flailed as if she were having a seizure. The men watched silently, dazed, but the women screamed and pumped their arms with her. I looked up again at Ollie and saw his lips silently mouthing "yeah, yeah, yeah." He seemed to be dreaming, his breathing labored and shallow.

QTπ jammed the microphone against her mouth as sweat ran down her forehead and she began to rap. Her voice was raw and erotic and very loud. I wondered if she could carry a tune, not that it mattered much. Bill Shakespeare indeed.

*Hey, hey, I'm QTπ*
*Don't know why, but I wanna say hi*
*I'm from LA*
*And I ain't goin' back*
*I missed that flight*
*Don't gimme no flack*
*Hey, hey, this is your show*
*Let's all hang low, be rarin' to go*
*So fake it, shake it*
*Watch those fleas*
*Sit, stand, heel*
*Whatever you please*
*Hey, hey, all hands on deck*
*Throw off your leash, get off my neck*
*Keep your paws to yourself*
*I know your face*
*I wanna get movin'*

*That's my ace*
*Hey, hey, I'm QTπ*
*Don't know why, but I wanna say hi*
*I'm from LA*
*And I ain't goin' back*
*I missed that flight*
*Don't gimme no flack*
*Don't gimme no flack*
*Don't gimme no flack*
*Yeah, yeah*

The drumbeat stopped to wild applause. QTπ dropped her microphone and bowed deeply, her hair brushing the floor, her arms hanging limply. She straightened and bowed again. There was bedlam in the room, people cheering, clapping, screaming, dogs barking, cellphone cameras flashing. She straightened and blew kisses at us. "Thank you, thank you, thank you so much, thank you, thank you so much." I looked at Ollie, who still seemed dazed. His eyes never left her face as young women mobbed her. I needed him to get away from there—away from her!—as soon as possible.

Nell's voice came over the loudspeaker. "Attention," she announced, "I know we're all thrilled to have QTπ join us today. However, the dogs are too excited now to focus on their lessons, so I'm canceling the rest of the class, and we'll pick up next week at our regular time." The dogs are too excited? Oh, please. Still, canceling the class solved my immediate problem: I could get Ollie out of this place.

By now, the commotion had mostly subsided, and people milled about, gathering coats and chatting. QTπ had moved to the banquet table to autograph T-shirts, and I saw her whispering to the dog park woman. They turned and looked at Ollie and me, and then QTπ started walking over to us. As she approached, her mating scent became even stronger, and Ollie's face took on a confused, unfocused quality, as if he were inhaling a narcotic. This was very worrisome.

"Well, hello, Ollie, who's this?" QTπ purred, touching his arm and eying me with feigned interest. "Is this itsy little sweetie yours?" Ollie nodded, tongue-tied, his face flushed. His eyes had become even more dilated, and he seemed droopy and disoriented. QTπ held Little Squeegee, who bared her teeth and snarled at me. What a nasty bitch. "Hush, baby," QTπ said to her, stroking her ears. "Be nice to the little dog." She looked at Ollie. "What's its name?" Little Squeegee glared at me, and I glared back. There was no way I would ever like that dog. Or her human.

"His name is Tex," Ollie said, struggling to find his voice. He scrunched up his brow, as if trying to jump-start his brain. "How do you know my name?"

"Because I came here to meet you," she said, placing her free hand on his arm and smiling affectionately. "Calista said she met you at the dog park, and you recommended this school. She said we would see you here. I've been wanting to meet you for ages. You rescued all those children from that Algerian orphanage. I love orphans, you know."

Ollie looked puzzled for a moment and said, "It's a Nigerian orphanage."

"Nigeria, Algeria, same thing. I read about you in the *Enquirer*. They really gave you sixty million dollars?" Ollie stood, glassy-eyed, still struggling for words. She didn't wait for an answer. "So I bet you've been living it up. You know, a new house, cars, that sort of thing?"

"I bought a new car, but that's all. I'm happy where I live."

"What kind of car? Where'd you get it?"

"A Mini-Pagoda. From Meditation Motors."

"Why, just last week I bought a new car there. A Sherpa Grand Sedan. I got it loaded, except for the goat compartment. I don't like smelly animals. Oh, I don't mean you, baby," she said, looking down at Little Squeegee. She turned to Ollie, leaving her hand on his arm. "Ollie, I think you and me have got a lot in common." Little Squeegee caught my eye and snarled again.

"We do?"

"We've both got that humanitarian thing going. That's why I bought an SGS. I wanted to get a Beemer, but my agent said humanitarians like that Hindu stuff."

Ollie nodded and grinned, but I couldn't tell if he was just being polite or if QTπ's inability to distinguish Hinduism from Buddhism amused him. This was appalling. I hoped the pheromones would wear off once I got him away from her.

"I read about all your marriage proposals," she continued. "It said you answer each one personally." She shook her head in dismay at Ollie's frivolous waste of time. "I can give you the name of an outfit that'll answer them for you. They hire people to write them out longhand. That's what I do for all my fan mail. I never read the stuff."

"I don't know if I'd be comfortable doing—"

She outstretched a hand, palm out, like a stop sign. "There's no reason for you to waste your time writing to a bunch of, well, I don't want to sound mean, but I'm sure they're just nobodies."

Ollie stood passively, saying nothing, and she said, "So, you seeing anyone now?"

"Not right this—"

"Great!" she said. She studied him, narrowing her eyes. "How tall are you, anyway? I bet you're at least six feet."

"About," he said. "How come?"

"And how old?"

"I'm thirty-one. But I'll be thirty-two next week. My brother and I are having a birthday party for some of our—"

"Really? I love parties," she said, smiling, a lioness stalking an injured wildebeest. She raised her eyebrows expectantly.

"You do? You're probably busy, but, of course—"

"I'd *love* to come. I'll have Calista set it up. You already met her, right?" She reached over, took Ollie's hand, and squeezed it. "You know, Ollie, I have a good feeling about this. About us, I mean. I think we're going to get along great."

"Going to get along great," he said. His words came slowly, without expression.

"I've got to bug off," she said. "Can't wait to see you at your party." She cruised briskly toward the door, the dog park woman in tow. Ollie followed her with his eyes, his mouth half open. The door closed, and a young nobody with matted brown hair wearing a QTπ T-shirt and faded jeans walked up to him towing a small black-and-gray mixed breed. The man looked up at Ollie, his eyes filled with admiration.

"Dude," he said. "You are one lucky guy."

I try to be a kind and forgiving dog, and the last thing I'd want to do is hurt anybody, particularly a human. But as I stood there thinking about QTπ and her despicable dog, I felt this desire to bite someone. But then the desire passed and was replaced by a terrible sense of guilt. All of this was because of me. It started when I bit that student on the ear. I knew I shouldn't have done that, even for a good cause. So now what was I going to do? How was I going to get Ollie away from that awful woman?

# Party! Party! Party!
## Thursday! Thursday! Thursday!
# Ides of March!

Remember the Summer of Love?
Well, neither do we.
So come check it out,
With my brother and me.
We'll make love not war,
Maybe smoke some grass.
If you think we're kidding,
Yes, we are, alas.
Damned Spot is the spot,
Time is seven-thirty.
Don't forget your ID,
In case you get thirsty.

(Please check large-caliber firearms at the door, teachers exempted.)

# 15

# HAPPY BIRTHDAY, DEAR OLLIE

**A half-hour before our party,** Hernando and I turned into the alley behind Damned Spot, edged past a green dumpster, and pulled into the coffee house's small parking lot. A narrow loading dock lined the rear of the building. It wasn't dark yet, but I could see light from the rear kitchen entrance. Hernando went inside while I stayed in the car to review remarks I'd be making for the open mic talent session. I needed to make a good impression with QT$\pi$, that is if she showed up. After a few minutes, I slipped Tex into my shirt pocket and started up the concrete steps to the loading dock when a catering van from Sabores Ricos pulled in beside us. Two women in uniforms began unloading foil-covered food trays, so I held the door to the kitchen for them.

"Ollie," I heard when I entered the kitchen, which smelled of chocolate. "Great to see you." Marvin Maybee, holding a tray of brownies, grinned at me. He was wearing open-toed sandals, a black T-shirt, and denim bell bottoms with a peace-sign insignia stitched onto one leg. His pupils were dilated. "Whaddya think?" He giggled. "I'm Jerry Garcia, right? How about a brownie? They're my special recipe." I noticed Hernando munching a brownie, and he winked at me and held up two fingers in a V, so I decided to try one. We squeezed past the caterers into the main room, which was empty except for Marvin's wife, April, who was inserting candles into empty raffia-wrapped Chianti bottles. April came over and gave us a hug. Hernando wiped brown crumbs off his face with his sleeve and grinned at her.

"Who are you tonight?" he asked. April had let her hair down, which hung almost to her waist and was secured with a tan headband. She wore aviator glasses and several strands of multi-colored plastic beads around her neck.

"Why, Gloria, of course," she said, pointing to a half-century-old framed poster of an identically clad Gloria Steinem. Given April's portly frame and gray hair, the resemblance struck me as somewhat aspirational. I set Tex on a tabletop so he wouldn't get stepped on, and Hernando and I spent the next twenty minutes erecting the folding banquet tables, lighting candles and cans of Sterno, and setting out napkins. I wanted to sneak a glass of wine before guests showed up, but the bar table was empty.

"We're not doing the drinks," a caterer said. "That's somebody else. One bartender is here now, and the other will arrive soon." Within a few minutes, guests began filtering in. Fanny arrived with several other students from Hernando's seminar, and the group bee-lined toward the bar. By then, a bartender had set out a plastic tub filled with beer bottles and ice and was filling wineglasses. I grabbed a glass of white wine from him and greeted Fanny, who seemed nervous until I assured her I'd said nothing to Hernando about her secret.

After a few minutes, we all drifted off to other parts of the room, which was now rapidly filling. Hernando had invited most of the guests, and there were many I hadn't met. It was disconcerting to think Hernando had lived in Boston only three months and already knew more people than I did. My neighbor, Annie, was on special assignment for her newspaper, and I was particularly sorry she couldn't come. I wandered around introducing myself but didn't see QTπ anywhere. Our conversation at Doggy-Do-Rite seemed like a blurry dream, but Calista, the assistant I'd met at the dog park, had called to check on the party's time and place. I glanced at my watch. Forty-five minutes had already passed.

For the most part, our guests didn't wear costumes, although Jeremy, the sophomore from the writing seminar, came as John Lennon, wearing wire-rimmed sunglasses with round lenses, faded jeans, and a sleeveless white T-shirt that said *New York City*. Susannah, the banjo player, came as Dolly Parton. She wore a curly blonde wig and a red-checkered blouse preposterously enhanced with twin balloons. She perched with her banjo on a rickety wooden stool near the espresso machine to rehearse her song for the open mic session, while John Lennon sat at her feet, leering up at her balloons. I felt pleasantly loose and disoriented. People crowded the bar, milled in groups, and clustered at the tables, laughing and shouting. The second bartender had arrived, a woman, and the two of them frantically filled wineglasses. Empty bottles had already piled up on the floor behind the bar. The din increased, and I leaned against the back of a chair to steady myself. Evidently, the brownie was kicking in. April cruised by with a wine bottle and refilled my glass.

I followed an outburst of laughter to Tex's table, where he was entertaining a boisterous group of faculty members from the college. "If I were a rich man," they sang. Tex stood on his hind legs on the tabletop and twirled like a poodle to the melody. He was having a good time. Then a mild disturbance at the entrance caught my attention. Through the bodies, I caught sight of a furry brown head with dark eyes and erect ears hovering above the crowd, staring at me. It was attached to a long, woolly neck.

"There's a Mr. Flint from Meditation Motors to see you," one of the caterers called from over by the door. I pushed my way through the crowd.

"Rocky," I said, "I'm so glad you could come. And you brought your llama, too. Hi, Llulu!"

"I'm sorry we're late," he said as we shook hands. "I hope we've not missed the open mic event. We've been practicing our throat singing. Look, there's Gloria Steinem," he said as April caught his eye and waved. "And here comes Jerry Garcia." Marvin pushed his way toward us. He was wobbling but seemed very happy. "This is so groovy," Rocky said, pumping Marvin's hand.

"Nice robe," Marvin said. "Fits right in."

Rocky beamed and held out a fold of the multicolored fabric. "It's a new American process," he said. "I twisted the fabric into—Oops, Llulu's run off, and I better go find her."

I followed Rocky across the room in pursuit of Llulu, who had headed for the table with Tex and the college faculty members. I picked Tex up off the tabletop and slipped him into my shirt. I stroked his head and looked around the room. Fanny was standing alone beside the cappuccino machine. She seemed disturbed about something, so I pushed my way over to her. "Everything okay?" I said.

She looked up at me with a grim smile. "Hernando's ignoring me, Ollie. I went up to him, and he walked away. I don't know what to do."

"He didn't say anything?"

"He said hello, thanks for coming, something like that, but he was distant and cold."

"Fanny, I'm sorry," I said. "That doesn't sound like my brother. I don't know what's going on with him."

"I better go now," she said. "I don't think I can take this much longer."

"What are you going to do?" I asked.

She sniffled, leaned over, and kissed my cheek. "I don't know yet. I may just drop out of his seminar early. Bye, Ollie, and happy birthday." I watched her thread her way to the exit. I couldn't see any reason why Hernando was being such a jerk. I found myself holding an empty wineglass, so I headed toward the bar. I'd lost track of my refills. There was a short line ahead of me, but I was glad to wait. When my turn came, I held out my wineglass and motioned toward a bottle of pinot noir. I glanced at the bartender, who reminded me a little of Regina. These days, it seemed like a lot of people reminded me of Regina. The bartender picked up the bottle and started filling my glass. I studied her face as she poured and then felt wine running down onto my hand.

"Oops, I'm really sorry," she said, looking up at me and wincing. "My mind was elsewhere."

"No problem," I said, as I shook the drops off onto the floor. She handed me a bar towel. "Everything okay?" It occurred to me I'd asked Fanny the same question only a minute before.

"Sure, everything's fine. Are you okay?"

"Yes, I'm okay."

"That's good. Are you sure I didn't stain your shirt?"

"No, my shirt's fine."

"And you're fine?"

"Right."

Our survival of the wine spillage having been thoroughly explored, we stood awkwardly for a few seconds saying nothing. I sensed impatience welling in the line behind me, but I couldn't think of anything else to say. All I knew was that I couldn't walk away. I'd only seen Regina once, months before on my video call from Tex's kennel, and I'm not very good at faces, and yet . . . my brain was in conflict. Part of me said, 'yes, this is Regina, you idiot, in person, standing before you, looking adorable,' but the other part couldn't accept the odds: Chateau Dom Pedigree's customer service representative turning up three thousand miles away as the bartender at my birthday party. No way, José.

She finally broke the silence. "I, um, it's just that you kind of reminded me of someone."

Oh my God! I felt my hand quiver and almost slopped wine again. "That's funny," I blurted, though there was nothing funny being said. "You reminded *me* of someone. That's a coincidence, isn't it?"

She had turned pale. "Yes, it is a coincidence. I guess these things happen."

"They do. Coincidences in general, I mean."

"Of course. Not this particular coincidence, but the general category of—"

An outbreak of yipping interrupted her. I felt Tex scrambling to jump from my shirt pocket, his rear legs scraping against my chest to gain traction. She gasped and almost dropped the wine bottle. She put her free hand over her mouth. "Oh my God. Tex, my baby, it's really you." She set down the wine bottle and reached out to my shirt to let him scramble into her hand. She clutched him to her chest as he squealed. "I was afraid I'd never see you again," she said to him, sobbing, while he furiously licked her hand. She looked up at me, tears on both cheeks. She struggled to compose herself.

"Ollie?"

"Regina?"

"You remember me?" She seemed about to faint, which is how I felt. The other bartender arrived with a case of beer he'd lugged from the parking lot. He set it behind the table and looked at us.

"Maybe I'd better take over," he said, to affirming nods from the people in line.

Regina and I stepped to the side. For a moment we were both too stunned to speak. I leaned a hand on the bar table to stabilize myself. "What are you doing here?" she asked finally, not in an accusing way.

"It's my party," I said, confused by the question. My heart was pounding.

"Your party? This is *your* birthday?"

"Me and my brother's. You didn't know?"

"No. The caterers hired me." She hesitated as my words sank in. "Your *baby twin brother?* You mean you *found* each other?" She shook her head, as if overloaded by the coincidences.

I felt the same way. Finally, I blurted, "What are you doing here in Boston?"

She opened her mouth but seemed unsure how to answer. Before she could speak, Hernando appeared at my side and grabbed my arm. He seemed out of sorts. "Oliphant," he said, irritation bubbling. "Come on. You've got to announce the open mic event. Everybody's waiting." He looked over curiously at Regina, who was still clutching Tex, her expression incredulous. Her gaze shifted back and forth between us, comparing features.

"Hold on, Hernando, I'll be there in a minute," I said, shaking him off. "I'm sorry, Regina," I said, turning to her. "I really, really want to talk to you, but I have to go." Still speechless, she nodded, then kissed Tex on his head and handed him back to me. I slipped him into my shirt pocket.

"Ollie, now!" Hernando said in his command presence voice.

I glared at him. "Damn it, chill, Hernando."

"Ollie, please, I've got to see him again," Regina said, gripping my arm, her voice desperate.

"Of course, Regina. Can you come by my house? Would tomorrow be okay? In the morning? Say nine?"

"Oh yes, great!" she said, exhaling with relief as Hernando pulled me away. "Thank you, Ollie, and, oh, happy birthday," she called behind me. I wondered if she'd brought my address with her from California, but either way, I'd make sure the caterers gave it to her.

I followed Hernando over to the podium used for poetry readings. My glass of pinot noir was mostly full, but I abandoned it on a tabletop. I needed to calm down. What were the odds of Regina Malbec ending up in Boston pouring wine at my party? I couldn't explain that, but maybe I'd figure it out when I talked to her the next morning. My heart was still hammering, so I tried to slow down and pull myself together. I turned and looked back at the bar table. Regina stood watching us, one hand holding a wine bottle, the other clasped to her chest, like she was dazed also. I caught her eye and she smiled. I remembered first seeing that lovely smile on my computer screen, but it didn't do justice to the real thing. I hoped it wasn't just Tex she was glad to see.

Then I thought of QTπ. Had she decided not to come? It would be okay if she didn't, actually, since it might be awkward for her and Regina to be here together. I glanced again at Regina, who was pouring wine. I didn't want to wait until tomorrow morning to talk to her. It was odd to have the possibility of two women in my life, but there was no law against it. I wondered what Hernando would say. Best not to get ahead of myself. I set Tex on the podium, steadied myself behind it, and flipped on the microphone switch. I tried to push through the fog in my head and remember the remarks I'd rehearsed.

"Attention, everybody, let's gather around. It's time for the Hernando and Ollie Birthday Talent Show. I know you've all been waiting for this moment." There was a scattering of cheers and a last-minute dash to the bar. Guests pulled chairs over to face the podium, others sat on tables and lined the walls. Jeremy and Lancelot from the writing seminar lugged chairs up to the front row and collapsed into them. They both held wineglasses and appeared to be having difficulty sitting upright. I didn't recognize anybody else sitting nearby.

Hernando turned up the lights and handed me the sign-up sheet. I began by introducing Rocky, who'd asked to go first. He stepped up to the microphone and announced a polyphonic duet for human and llama, written by himself to celebrate the upcoming mid-summer sale at Meditation Motors, where the deals couldn't be beat in this or any other lifetime. He explained in considerable detail that he would be the chant master, intoning three notes in the jok-kay low-tone tradition. He said Llulu hadn't yet learned to control the muscles of her vocal cavity, so that her overtones, in the bar-day high-tone tradition, were weaker than he had hoped. For disappointing us, he apologized. His explanation and apology took fifteen minutes. Then he and Llulu leaned their heads together to chant. It was a moving performance and the hit of the talent show.

The other skits also went well. Hernando demonstrated how to field-strip an AK-47 assault rifle in ninety seconds while blindfolded. I had seen him do this before and knew it was a crowd-pleaser. Dolly Parton, aka Susannah from our writing seminar, sang a folk ballad with great feeling. All went well until she got to, *He held a knife against my breast, as into my arms he pressed.* She gestured with a marmalade spreader to illustrate the scene and accidentally punctured her left balloon, which deflated with a loud hiss. Jeremy, who sat directly in front of her, jumped up and screamed, "Oh no, no!" and passed out. Leaving Tex on the podium, I announced a brief intermission to help Hernando lug Jeremy to the exit, so Hernando could revive him and walk him around the block.

I had just returned to the podium when I heard an automobile door open and slam shut, and a moment later Calista, QTπ's assistant, appeared at the still-open entrance. She looked around the room, grimaced slightly, and turned to somebody behind her. I heard the car door open and close again, and QTπ made her grand entrance. There was a collective gasp in the room, followed by stunned silence.

And for good reason. QTπ had donned a platinum blonde wig and an astonishing floor-length skin-tight dress made of a flesh-colored fabric decorated with hundreds of rhinestones. She shimmered and sparkled in the candlelight like an apparition. I gaped at her and couldn't breathe, overwhelmed by the same vertigo I'd felt at Doggy-Do-Rite. It was a strongly erotic feeling, verging on unpleasant. QTπ smiled radiantly, outstretched her left arm, and with her right hand, blew kisses to the guests. She slowly advanced toward the podium, her hips swaying with each tiny step. The crowd parted, as if nobody wanted to soil her path with their humdrum earthly presence. I could feel myself becoming aroused and decided it best to remain behind the podium. I glanced over at Regina, hoping she hadn't noticed, and found her standing, unsmiling, beside the bar table. QTπ had taken about a dozen steps when Rocky's voice broke the silence.

"Marilyn, Marilyn," he said, his voice shaky. "It's you, it's really you. Oh, I love this country." His words were followed by a strange *meeping*, like the sound of the flutophone my aunt and uncle gave me before I started sackbut lessons. I turned and saw Llulu standing beside Rocky, below the poster of Gloria Steinem. Llulu stamped her feet, her neck rigid, the whites of her eyes showing. As QTπ minced past, she crouched, extended her head forward, and moved her ears back against her head. She uttered a loud *ptew* and *horked* an enormous glob of llama spit. It spattered on the floor behind QTπ, who was blowing kisses to the opposite side of the room and didn't notice. "Llulu, what are you doing?" Rocky shrieked. He yanked on Llulu's leash, whose upper lip was curled in what appeared to be a llama expression of self-satisfaction.

QTπ finally made it to the podium. I stood there, mute, dizzy, still embarrassingly aroused, and wishing I'd not abandoned my wineglass. She looked at me, puckered her bright red lips, and placed her hand on my hand. She took the microphone and glanced at Tex standing on the podium. A quick frown flashed across her face, and then she smiled with heartfelt affection and turned to her audience. "Hello, everyone," she said, in a low, sultry voice. "I was driving by and thought I'd stop in and wish my baby happy birthday." She turned and looked at me. Her *baby?* I glanced at Hernando, who was watching us with astonishment. The crowd cheered and applauded.

"Can't a girl get a glass of wine around here?" she sulked, looking toward the bar, where Regina stood, still unsmiling. "Bring me something interesting, dear," she called to her, as her gaze shifted back to the audience. Regina picked up a mostly empty bottle of red wine, dumped the remains into a wineglass, set it on the table, and then turned her back to speak to the other bartender. Calista scowled, walked from the entrance to the bar table, retrieved the wine, smelled it, and frowned, then carried it to the podium. QTπ ignored it.

"I have a birthday surprise for my baby," QTπ whispered into the microphone, as if divulging nuclear secrets. "I know you've all heard about my show opening next week at the new Valhalla Casino in Las Vegas." There was polite applause in the room, although I suspected the English department crowd didn't hang out much at Las Vegas casinos. "Well, I want my birthday boy to come with me to my opening performance as my very special guest. I know we'll have a fun time." She reached out and lightly brushed my cheek with her fingertips. "A *really* fun time," she added, winking at the audience. The women in the crowd laughed, but the men sat transfixed and mute. "You'd like that, wouldn't you, baby?" she said, in a voice as smooth as four-hundred-dollar tequila. I opened my mouth but couldn't speak. I steadied myself on the podium and picked up the wineglass Calista had set there. There were dark particles of cork floating on top and red sludge in the bottom, and it tasted warm, but I drank it anyway. QTπ laughed and said, "I'll take that as a yes."

Holding the microphone she stepped away from the podium. She turned to the crowd and said, "I have one more little present for my baby." She turned back toward me and started to sing Happy Birthday. She looked into my eyes as she sang and slowly moved toward me. She held the microphone against her lips, and I could hear her breathing. I blinked but couldn't look away. "Dearest Oliphant," she crooned, her voice low and sultry. She finished, and carefully placed the microphone in its holder. She put her arms around my neck and drew my face to hers. There wasn't a sound in the room. Then she kissed me, long and passion-ately. The room swayed, and I felt my legs give way. I grabbed the edges of the podium, and Tex yipped in alarm. QTπ laughed, and everybody in the room applauded. Someone brought me a chair and I thudded onto it. I inhaled deeply but it didn't help. After that, everything was pretty much a blank. The last thing I remem-ber was looking around the room. I saw Rocky standing next to Llulu and Tex still perched on the podium. Hernando was staring at me and frowning. Regina had vanished.

# 16

# REGINA

*Dear Ollie,*

*I bet you're surprised to hear from me after ten years, but I still remember our great time together on your 21st birthday. I read the USA Today story about the orphanage email. Wow, sixty million dollars! You must be on cloud nine!*

*After Northwestern, I became an analyst for North Shore Investment Analytics. We manage high net worth portfolios, and last year beat all our benchmarks! (Of course, past performance is no guarantee of future results.) So my life is great, although Charles and I split up a few months ago over a stupid insider trading thing. Oh well.*

*I'd love to get together and catch up. I know we'd have fun like the old days, and I might even have a few mutually beneficial recommendations for you.*

*XOXO,*
*Julie Chen*

**The next morning,** a Thursday, with sun glaring and clothes scattered, I stumbled to the bathroom for Advil and water. A fearsome creature inside my head was hammering my temples to escape. I massaged the bridge of my nose to relieve the pressure behind my eyes and limped back to bed for an hour, hoping to make sense of the previous evening. Everything in my head seemed foggy, but when I held my fingers to my lips, I could feel

QTπ's steamy breath on my face and taste her waxy red lipstick. She'd left me visibly aroused, and I suspected everybody in the room had noticed. Why had I reacted that way? I remembered having the same response at the obedience school when I first met her. Both times it was a reflexive and disturbing feeling.

I lay there with my eyes closed and tried to reconstruct the evening. After the party ended and I was able to focus, I looked around for Regina, but she'd gone, leaving the other bartender to clean up. Meeting her after all these months was a puzzling coincidence. She had been living in Boston all this time, so why hadn't she called? I didn't know what that meant, but it wasn't a good sign. Regina had seemed pleased to see me, but mostly she'd wanted to see Tex. Was I just along for the ride? If so, that still didn't explain why she hadn't contacted us.

To make matters worse, I was sure I'd offended her with my drunken display with QTπ. I felt a knot building in my stomach and had almost convinced myself she wouldn't show, when promptly at nine, Tex barked, hopped off the kitchen table, and raced squealing to the front door. I followed, pausing to toss some fallen newspapers on the kitchen counter. Through the living room window I saw a glossy red Zen Buggy pull into the driveway. A car door shut, and a minute later the doorbell rang. Whew.

"Hi, Ollie," Regina said, sounding relieved, as if she wasn't sure she'd found the right address. She followed me into the front hall and looked down at Tex, who was madly thump-thumping. She squatted and held him to her face. "I've really missed you, sweetheart." She looked up at me and grinned as they slobbered each other. They were very cute together.

She eased Tex to the floor, straightened, and faced me. Some sort of physical contact seemed called for, but we didn't know each other well enough to hug, so we shook hands. I mumbled something like, "It's good to see you," but was unsure what to say next, and evidently so was she, because we just stood there. "Come into the kitchen," I said, as I struggled to fill the silence. "I've made coffee." Regina seemed taller than I remembered, an inch or so taller than QT$\pi$. She had on blue jeans with a turtleneck and tan blazer and looked terrific. I wondered if she'd dressed up for me. I took some half-and-half out of the refrigerator. I said, "So you've moved to Boston and work at a wine store. When did you move here?"

"I'm the manager," she said. "It's a small specialty store, but we have a good reputation." Glancing at the newspapers piled on the countertop, she added, "Did you see our nice writeup last Sunday in the *Globe Magazine*?" I nodded to pretend I'd read it. She hadn't answered my question. She stirred her coffee and set the spoon on the counter. "The job doesn't pay much, but I inherited my great-great-grandfather's estate from my dad, so I don't need much money. Someday I'd like to have my own store, but first, I need to learn the business."

I nodded, and we moved to the living room sofa. Tex sprinted to her lap, and I said, "Mrs. Knightsbridge mentioned your great-great-grandfather owned real estate in Nepal."

"She told you that?" Regina said, looking up at me in surprise. "Yes, it's in a trust, but I've never seen any of the buildings. In fact, I've never been to Nepal. I guess I'm uncomfortable thinking of myself as an heiress. It's embarrassing."

"Believe me, I understand," I said with a little laugh.

"How so? You're a trust fund baby?" She stroked Tex with her index finger while I told her about my Nigerian email. I finished and pointed to the stack of unopened marriage proposals on my desk. "It's nice of you to answer the women personally, but aren't most of them gold diggers?"

"Some are, some aren't. Many just seem to lead sad, lonely lives and are grasping at straws. I'm sure they don't want me because of my rugged good looks."

Regina smiled as if I'd been joking. "I guess we have the same problem. I was dating a man who seemed charming at first, but . . . it didn't turn out well."

"Mrs. Knightsbridge mentioned him to me. Someone named Eli. She said she didn't like him." Regina's eyes widened, and I thought maybe I'd said too much.

She said, "I didn't even tell her I'd moved to Boston because I was afraid he'd find me. I wish that newspaper story hadn't mentioned my name." She rested her mug on the coffee table and looked away. A lot of baggage there, but I didn't want to press her. She'd tell me if she wanted to. All of a sudden, our conversation had again turned personal. That always seemed to happen with the two of us, and I liked that.

After a moment's silence, she turned back toward me. "Actually, Ollie, I have a little confession to make." I raised my eyebrows but said nothing. She took a worried breath, as if about to confess a crime. "Early last December I emailed Mrs. Knightsbridge to tell her I'd moved to Boston and asked for your address. The next morning, I dropped by your house, but a neighbor said you and Tex had gone to a dog park."

"We go there every Saturday. I'm sorry I missed you." To put it mildly.

"Then she told me a man had also come by to see you, so I suspected Mrs. Knightsbridge had given Eli your address. As much as I love her, she can be a chatterbox. I'm afraid I got cold feet and never went back. I'm sorry, Ollie. I should have called you."

"I wish you had, Regina. That was just my brother, Hernando. But I don't understand. If you were so frightened of Eli, why didn't you end the relationship?" She looked at me and shrugged.

"I wasn't exactly frightened, Ollie. I tried to break it off, but he begged me to stay. He said he loved me and if I left, I would ruin his life, and I believed him. I suppose at some level I still do, but I had to escape. He made me feel terribly guilty. It was a sick, controlling relationship." She gave a tight smile but held my gaze, and my pulse quickened. I was startled to realize how badly I had wanted to see her. We hardly knew each other, but there was so much to talk about. She felt it too. "Ollie, I don't know why I'm telling you about my love life." She gave an embarrassed little laugh.

"My fault. I'm being nosy. I don't know how we got into all this."

She swept her hair to the side, behind an ear. "Because you're easy to talk to," she said quietly. "I could tell that when you bought Tex last October. I felt like we'd already known each other." She looked down at Tex, then up. "I was in a bad way, Ollie. I was desperate to find Tex a good home, and you seemed so kind and . . . I've thought about you a lot." She blushed and looked down at the tabletop, suddenly aware of her words. "Sorry."

I wasn't sorry. I was about to say I felt the same way when she said, "So tell me about your twin brother. I thought you were separated as babies." I took a breath to change direction and explained that Hernando had read about my Nigerian email in the news and tracked me down. When I finished, she said, "You never would have found each other, Ollie, except for the Nigerian email. Maybe it wasn't such an awful thing after all." I hadn't made that connection; it reminded me of her saying my nickname was a gift from my birth parents. Before I could say anything, she said, "Now I'd love to hear about QTπ. How did you two meet? How long have you been seeing her?"

Right then QTπ was far from my thoughts, so it took a moment to get my bearings. "We met a couple of weeks ago at a local obedience school." In response to her puzzled look, I added, "For dogs, that is." I didn't tell her I'd taken Tex to the school because he had bitten a student.

"She's very talented and beautiful. It must be exciting to go out with a celebrity."

"I suppose, but we've not gone out yet," I said, trying to shift gears. I also tried not to think about my previous night's arousal problem. "Actually, I hardly know her."

She laughed, sort of. "It didn't quite seem that way at the party. And you two are going to Las Vegas for her performance? You'll have fun there."

"She wants me to go with her next week to shop for an outfit for the trip. That's the only time she has free. I guess that'll be our first date."

Regina bit her lower lip, as if unsure whether to say something. Finally, she said, "I hope things work out for you, Ollie, with her I mean." Her voice seemed sincere, but part of me wished it wasn't.

"How about you?" I said. "You seeing anyone? After Eli, that is?"

She shook her head. "I don't have time. Our catered events

are mostly in the evenings and on weekends. Anyway, after Eli, I think it's best to swear off men, for now at least. He almost ruined my life, Ollie, and I need to regroup."

"I'd think you'd be lonely, though, living by yourself in an unfamiliar city." I was unabashedly fishing.

She responded quickly. "Me? No, I'm not worried about that at all. I hang out with friends, and I have my job and . . . I'm always busy." I nodded, even though none of this rang true. "How about you?" she said. "You also live by yourself."

"Well no, I don't feel a need—" She gave me a sudden, doubtful look, narrowing her eyes. I wasn't being straight with her and was shocked to be so transparent. I forced myself to slow down. "Actually, Regina, I do feel lonely sometimes. I've just lately realized that." I felt my voice catch and hoped she wouldn't notice. I didn't know why I was being so forthcoming, but I wasn't sorry. "Tex is a big help, but at other times, I wish there was—it's been kind of a long time." A long time in this case being never. I felt myself blush.

Her voice turned soft. "Now I'm the one being too personal." She started to place her hand on my arm but thought better of it and returned it to her lap. We sat there without speaking.

"Did you grow up in California?" I asked finally.

She seemed relieved at the new topic. "I was born in Davis. My dad taught viniculture at the university there, but I went to Berkeley and majored in ancient Polynesian languages."

"Then you must know Marycandu," I said.

"Of course," she said, surprised at the comment. "Do you know it, too? Oh wait, I remember. Your relative was Gustav Allyinphree."

"Let me show you something," I said, motioning her to the bookshelves that line one wall of my living room. I pulled out Uncle Gus's book on the languages of extinct Polynesian tribes and handed it to her. "He wrote this while living in Kathmandu."

"Wow, this is a first edition," she said, cautiously opening the cover with her fingertips to the first page. Pressing her lips together, she inspected the gold inlay and leather binding. "It's lovely." She looked up at me and smiled. "Did you find this in Nepal?"

I shook my head. "I've never been to Nepal. I bought it at an auction in New York." She handed the book back to me, and I slid it onto the shelf. "Want to see the rest of my house?"

"Sure. I love your living room." She walked to the table and inspected the carved rhino from my Nigerian orphanage. "This is a gorgeous piece. Ebony, isn't it?"

I left Tex on the sofa and took Regina on the same tour I'd taken Tex on during our first afternoon. She stood in the doorway of my bedroom and looked at it thoughtfully, but I couldn't read her reaction. Then I showed her my walk-in closet. "You're really well-organized," she said, smiling and running her hand over the shelf filled with sweaters. "I like that."

After the tour, we sat on the sofa with Tex, and Regina showed me Olly, Olly in Free, the trick she had taught him at the kennel. "It's kind of like reverse hide-and-seek." She retrieved the bag of dog treats from the hall table and popped one in Tex's mouth. He held it without chewing. "Hide," she said, and he bounced onto the floor. She reached over and covered my eyes with her hands. After he hopped back up on the sofa, she said, "Now you look for the treat." I looked around the room. There were a hundred possible hiding places.

"Just pick any direction, and with every step, Tex will yip. The more yips the closer you are. If he doesn't yip, change direction." I took a step toward my desk, but Tex didn't yip, so I stopped. "Okay, now turn in some other direction." I turned toward the bookshelves, and Tex yipped once. I moved forward and he yipped again. Then I turned until he yipped twice. I headed toward a table lamp, and he yipped three times. After a few more turns, I ended up at the wooden rhino. I touched its tail, and he yipped repeatedly. I counted eight yips. There tucked under the rhino's belly was the dog treat.

"Hmm," I said as I played back the game in my head. "Two single barks, then two barks, then three, five, eight . . . Why, isn't that—"

"A Fibonacci sequence." Regina laughed. "Now you have to give him the treat."

I nodded my head in amazement and sat back down beside her. "I heard him bark that sequence last week. How could a dog—"

"What time is it?" Regina said abruptly, looking at her watch. "Oh my God, I've got to run. I'm sorry, but my shop opens in fifteen minutes. Ollie, this has been really nice." We rose, hurried to the door, and stepped onto the front porch. I didn't want her to leave. She glanced at the spring daffodils blooming under my bay windows and started toward her car, but then her step slowed, and she turned back to the porch. She faced me and looked down at the concrete step. The morning had turned cloudy and gusty, with rain in the afternoon forecast. Humidity hung heavy in the air, and I felt the spritz of raindrops on my face.

"Ollie, I didn't quite tell you the truth before," she said, looking up. "You know, about not feeling lonely. I want to be honest with you." I waited, feeling a tightness in my throat. "I do get lonely," she said, measuring her words. "Not always, but sure, it would be wonderful to share my life with someone. It's just that all my relationships end badly. There were others before Eli, but he was by far the worst. I didn't even like the man, but I was obsessed with pleasing him. I can't go through that again." She shrugged and touched my hand. "Ollie, I wanted you to know that about me. In case . . . maybe you had other thoughts, or something. I don't want to mislead you. I just need to stand on my own feet and not feel like a failure without a man to depend on. Or take care of. I'm thirty-one years old, and my life isn't where I wanted it to be. I've got to fix that. Until then . . ."

"I understand," I said, though I didn't really. I tried to smile, unsure what else to say. "But can we still be friends. I really like talking to you. I'd hate to give that up." Damn it all. This was happening to me again.

"Me too," she said, brightening. "*Of course* we can be friends. Let's get together soon. I'd like that. But now, I've really got to go." She reached out and we hugged. She nestled her cheek against my shoulder, and through my shirt, I could feel her body's warmth. Then, too soon, she drew away and looked up at me with an openness in her expression that hinted at unforeseen fragility.

I stood staring after her, listening to the whine of a big passenger jet banking west out of Logan Airport, and trying to resurrect the feeling of her body against my chest. I glanced up but couldn't see through the mist, and after a minute, the sound faded. Why did I let myself be smitten by a woman I'd barely met, who had just made it absolutely clear she was unavailable? Maybe it wasn't Regina, but the *idea* of Regina. An image of QTπ linked into this thought, and then Fawn, and then a disturbing third possibility: Did I become infatuated with every woman who paid attention to me? Was I that desperate? I took a long, sorry breath, looked down at Tex, who didn't seem to have any answers, and the two of us turned back into the house.

# 17

# FIRST
# DATE

**Buying an outfit for** QTπ's cast party wasn't my notion of fun, but at least they let me come along. That way I could keep an eye on Ollie, not that there was a lot I could do if something went wrong. Some first date. Mostly, though, I wanted to understand her appeal. I couldn't imagine he actually liked the woman.

QTπ's black Sherpa Grand Sedan reeked of unpleasant odors. QTπ sat next to Ollie and me in the rear with that nasty Little Squeegee in her lap. QTπ's mating scent almost overpowered the cloying cologne that the driver, a huge dour man named Carlos, was doused in. Calista, QTπ's assistant, sat beside him in the passenger seat. Calista wasn't a warm person, probably because she always seemed stressed, but she was better than the others. Today, I also got a faint but distinct whiff of fearfulness from her, which puzzled me.

The atmosphere in the car oozed tension, but Ollie hadn't cued in on it. He had the same glassy-eyed look I'd seen at the obedience school and the birthday party. He and I never seemed able to connect when he was with her. QTπ had cozied over to him and put her hand on his knee. A large cooler that said *Bon Vivant Catering* rested on the seat to our left, next to the door. I couldn't sniff out the contents because the other odors were too strong.

"It's crowded back here," QTπ said, as she snuggled closer to Ollie and caressed his knee. He smiled nervously but seemed to enjoy the attention. Her fingernails were decorated with tiny red lobsters. It wasn't crowded at all; the Sherpa Grand Sedan could easily have held another person and maybe a goat or two. "Baby," she cooed, "you don't mind if we make a quick stop at Captain Pattycake's, do you, so I can drop off some food for the toddlers? You and what's-its-name can wait in the car while Calista takes a few photos. It'll only take a minute." Little Squeegee growled quietly and bared her teeth at me, but QTπ didn't notice. I bared my teeth back at her.

Ollie said, "Sure, I like toddlers." Calista turned toward QTπ and rolled her eyes. I felt like Ollie and I were in an enemy camp. "What are we taking them?" he added, looking over at the large cooler.

QTπ seemed surprised by the question. "I don't know. Calista, what are we taking?"

"Let me check the invoice," Calista said. She rummaged through her purse and pulled out a sheet of paper. "A gross of deviled quail eggs, six pints of foie gras, a hundred raw oysters on the half shell, ten pounds of Belgian chocolates. Oh, and we have a hundred carrots carved like tiny snowmen, with little mushroom hats. For our vegetarian demographic."

"That seems like unusual food for toddlers," Ollie said with a frown.

Calista turned around toward the backseat and sighed, as if speaking to a schoolchild. "It's our new image," she said. "We're going upscale, you know, bringing hip-hop to the Ivy League. We've changed the name of our group. Now, we're the Cultured Pearls." She laughed.

"You mean, like Ivy rap?" Ollie said. The two women stared at him. I was startled, too. How did he ever come up with that?

"Yeah, exactly," Calista said. "Ivy rap. I like that. And QTπ will be the Queen of Ivy. We're announcing our group's new name in Las Vegas, along with the release of *Lobster Clasp*."

"Lobster clasp?" Ollie said, still seeming bewildered.

"Our new album. It's a New England theme," Calista replied. "The lead song is 'Crack that Tail,' though my favorites are 'Hot Tamale' and 'Drawn Butter.' We can't have photos of QTπ serving beans. We have a message of hope. Today's street toddlers are tomorrow's debutantes. Isn't that what America's all about?"

Carlos pulled up in front of Captain Pattycake's Kitchen, a one-story building in an industrial part of South Boston whose red bricks had been discolored by decades of factory smoke and city grime. Small children laughed and shouted through the building's open windows. He double-parked in a handicap zone but left the motor running while he opened the rear door for QTπ. Then he retrieved the cooler and escorted her and Calista up a short flight of stained concrete steps to the entrance. Ollie slid over to the window so he could watch QTπ as she moved away from the car. He put his hand on the car's door handle and seemed suddenly ill at ease. I felt his knee jiggle restlessly when the entrance door closed behind her.

I shut my eyes and stretched out on the leather seat. QTπ's scent was still infused throughout the car's interior, but it had diminished enough for me to inventory the neighborhood: diesel fumes, rodent droppings, hairspray, sanitary napkins, cat urine, stale beer, paint remover, and the unmistakable aroma of soiled diapers. Pretty good smells, actually, except for the cat urine. We XS dogs have to be a little careful around cats.

I dozed for a few minutes but was awakened by children crying and screaming "No, no, I won't!" from an open window, followed by a female voice shouting, "Stupid urchins." It appeared the photo-op wasn't going as smoothly as planned. A minute later the door opened, and Carlos struggled down the concrete steps lugging the large cooler. His face was impassive, but he had pâté smeared on his silver-colored suit. QTπ followed, and then Calista, tight-lipped, wiping at a yellowish stain on the front of her gray skirt. I suspected deviled quail egg. QTπ, her face flushed, whispered something to Calista as they came down the steps. Carlos put the heavy container in the rear seat, and the three climbed back in the car.

"How'd things go?" Ollie inquired cluelessly once everybody had settled into the car.

"Wonderful," QTπ said, beaming. "It couldn't have gone better." Calista turned around and looked at her but said nothing. The mood in the car was poisonous but, again, Ollie didn't notice. His passivity around QTπ was driving me crazy.

"Leftovers?" he said, looking at the food container.

"We'll give them to the dress shop," QTπ said. "They'll never know." She leaned toward the front of the car. "Carlos, get a move on. Our appointment was an hour and a half ago." She turned to Ollie. "They're so sweet at Chez Charmante. I know they won't mind us being a few minutes late." I found it interesting that Carlos seemed unaffected by QTπ's mating scent. Did that mean he had developed a tolerance for it? That was encouraging, if it didn't take too long.

The boutique fronted a cobblestone street lined with brick sidewalks. A black front awning stretched over the sidewalk, with the store name above it in large, polished brass letters. Parked cars lined the streets, but two yellow traffic cones protected the parking spot nearest the door. As we pulled into it, a hunched, elderly man in a gray uniform hobbled out of the entrance. He cautiously stepped down onto the pavement and moved the traffic cones. He took short, unsteady steps to our car and held the door for QTπ. "Welcome, Miss Pi," he said in a thin, wheezy voice, breathing heavily. "It's so nice to see you again."

"Hello, Henry," she said to him. "Be an angel and bring in that cooler from the back seat." She turned to Ollie. "Give Henry a dollar, would you?" Ollie put me in his shirt pocket and reached in his sports jacket for his wallet. He hesitated for an instant, then handed Henry a folded ten-dollar bill. That was an encouraging sign.

Carlos stayed in the car with Little Squeegee, while QTπ, Ollie, and I made our way into the store. Calista held the door for Henry, who inched forward, staggering under the weight of the cooler. Once inside, we were greeted by a middle-aged human wearing a black pencil skirt and white blouse who had sprayed herself with something that smelled like the digestive tract of sperm whales. She caught sight of QTπ and screeched with unrestrained happiness. The two hugged, squealed, puckered their mouths, and puffed at each other's cheeks. I suspected this wasn't the typical greeting between rappers and their admirers.

The woman said, "Darling, it is *so wonderful* to see you. We've all been *so excited*. You must tell me *everything!*" She grasped

QTπ's shoulders and studied her for a moment, smiling in disbe-lief. "You look positively *fabulous*," she said. "How do you *do* it? I must know your secret."

"Françoise, you are such a liar," QTπ said, delighted. "I'd like you to meet—"

"Henry, be careful," Françoise said. Henry had lurched into a display of shoes made by someone named Jimmy. His breath came in asthmatic gasps, his color had turned cadaverous, and a thin line of drool inched down the corner of his mouth. He seemed seconds from collapse.

Françoise glared at him. "Put down that cooler," she yelled, looking at him with disgust, "and go clean yourself up." She turned to QTπ and clenched her hands in frustration. "My father is such an embarrassment."

Henry dropped the cooler with a thud next to the display of Jimmy's shoes and staggered toward a rear door into the back room. Calista opened the cooler and started setting out trays of food on a large table next to a seating area.

"You've brought food," Françoise cried. "Let me see!"

"Just a little snack for the staff," QTπ said, gesturing dismis-sively toward a metal tray holding ten pounds of Belgian choco-lates. So far as I could tell, the staff consisted of Henry, who didn't strike me as hungry, and a wafer-thin young woman who had just come in from the back room and appeared to have successfully avoided eating for weeks.

"Oysters on the half-shell. My favorite. Oh, and look, dev-iled quail eggs. How did you know? And Belgian chocolates too?" She placed a hand over her heart and swooned. "QTπ, you are amazing. Monique, champagne for our guests. The good stuff."

She winked at QTπ. "We were saving it for Princess—oops, I can't say her name. MI-6 won't let us." Her eyes darted around the room, but seeing no one from MI-6, she leaned toward QTπ. "You know there are rumors about her and the home secretary." She buttoned her lips with her fingers.

"Françoise, this is my friend, Ollie—"

"What in the world do you have on your skirt?" Françoise said suddenly to Calista, who reddened and placed her hand over the yellow stain. "Henry did that to you, didn't he? That man. He's ruined your skirt. But you're in luck. We're having our huge spring sale, with unbelievable store-wide bargains. I've got the perfect skirt for you." She leaned forward and squinted, better to take in Calista carefully. "There's just no reason a woman as beautiful as yourself should have to put up with *that*," she said, wrinkling her nose at the yellow stain or, I suspected, at the skirt itself.

Calista appeared swayed by this line of reasoning, but then QTπ interjected, "Françoise, this is Ollie. Ollie Allyinphree."

Françoise, who hadn't noticed that Ollie and I were in the room, turned and regarded us with modest curiosity. "Yes," she said, eying his wrinkled khaki chinos, "it's nice to meet you." They shook hands. "And I see you've brought your, um, dog." She squinted at me, presumably to verify Ollie hadn't transported an errant sewer rat into her store.

"His name is Tex," Ollie said in a flat voice, taking me out of his shirt pocket. I faced Françoise and forced myself to wag and look friendly. "Do you mind if I set him down?" he asked.

Françoise glanced at QTπ and then turned to us. "Of course," she said. "I assume he's, you know . . ."

"Yes," Ollie said, "he's housebroken." Ollie caught my eye and shook his head ever so slightly. That was our first connection since we'd come into the boutique. Mostly, he'd been fixated on QTπ.

In the meantime, Monique, skirting the food table as if it had been piled with sewage, placed a *CLOSED* sign on the entrance to keep other customers at bay. Françoise directed QTπ and Calista to a maroon love seat, and I sat on Ollie's lap behind them in a straight-backed chair. Françoise pulled her desk chair to face the love seat. Monique left the room but returned shortly with a silver tray holding three filled champagne flutes. Then Françoise put on rhinestone-decorated reading glasses and took out a notepad and sterling silver fountain pen.

"Now, QTπ, tell me about your event. Is this another Junior League thingy? Everybody's raving about your performance at the Birdy Van Flutter cotillion. What's your group's new name? Oh yes, I remember. *The Cultured Pearls*." She gave QTπ a conspiratorial smile. "Birdy is so sweet and unassuming. Who would ever think she was heiress to the Van Flutter fortune? We made her ball gown for her, you know." Françoise leaned forward and lowered her voice. "It was a size sixteen, but we made it look like a size ten. I do wish Birdy would take off a few pounds. It would certainly make my job easier, if you know what I mean."

QTπ and Calista nodded to indicate they knew what Françoise meant.

"It's not for a benefit," QTπ said. "I'm taking Ollie to Las Vegas for the premier of my tour. I'm calling it my Ivy Rap tour. Ollie came up with the name." She turned and gazed at him adoringly. "So I need a dress for the cast party after the show. A very special dress."

Françoise turned and looked at Ollie with a modicum of genuine interest. "Hmm, of course you do. This handsome young man deserves something very special. Tell me what you have in mind."

"I'd like it to be above-the-knee, all white, elegant, simple, but also demur."

"Ah yes, I understand," Françoise said. "Something chaste, that reflects modesty and good breeding."

Calista made a choking sound and mumbled, "Until the regiment arrives." QTπ glared at her.

"Anything else?"

"I'd like it to be easy to remove," QTπ whispered. I glanced at Ollie, but he was staring vacantly at nothing and wasn't listening. Monique moved to refill his champagne flute.

"I see," Françoise said, looking at Ollie again. "Lucky man."

The next two hours passed at the pace of a Galapagos tortoise. I tried to snooze on Ollie's lap, while the contents of the champagne bottle beside our chair steadily dwindled. Our seating area faced the door of a large dressing room, and beside it stood a mobile clothing rack that held rejected dresses. Full-length mirrors covered every wall, illuminated by pinkish ceiling lights. Monique would bring out a dress for a group review, and after a preliminary screening, QTπ would retire to the dressing room with Calista to try it on. Finally, QTπ would model the candidate dress before Françoise, who would scrutinize it for irreparable faults: the material looked shiny, the hem was too long, the shade of white was too blue, the design was too flashy, the fabric had too many sequins, the dress made QTπ's bust look small, the dress made her bottom look big, the dress made her thighs look fat, the dress was too tight, the dress didn't hang well off her shoulders, the dress showed too much cleavage.

To me, and to Ollie I suspected, the dresses seemed mostly indistinguishable from each other. I tried to doze, but that didn't work, so I practiced computing cube roots, which was at least interesting. In the meantime, the champagne took over, and Ollie slumped ever lower in his chair. Finally . . . finally! QTπ's voice interrupted our near-comatose state. I opened my eyes and saw her standing at the dressing room doorway wearing a white thong, a lacy bra that cleverly cantilevered her breasts outward, and a spiky red pair of Jimmy's shoes. I glanced at Ollie, who had also awakened and was gaping at her. She blew him a kiss, and then her expression turned serious.

"Françoise, none of these is working for me. I'm ready to give up." Calista and Monique barged past her from the dressing room, looking distraught.

Françoise set her pen down and pushed back from her desk. She cupped her chin in her hand and gazed somberly out the window. "I have an idea," she said finally. "Monique, come here for a moment." Françoise whispered a few words in her ear.

Monique's face turned ashen. "Are you sure?" she said in a soft voice. "But we promised it to the duchess. She's been waiting months."

"I'm sure," Françoise said. "Go get it for her so she can try it on."

"Duchess?" QTπ said, still standing in the dressing room doorway. "What duchess?"

Françoise turned to her as Monique disappeared into the back room. "I do have one dress that *might* work for you. It was a custom order for . . . one of my special clients. She's not seen it yet, and if you like it, I think I can substitute a—well, let's just say a lesser garment for her. But, please, I don't want you to get your hopes up."

"Tell me about it," QTπ said excitedly, still standing in the doorway. It appeared to me her hopes were already in the stratosphere.

"My . . . client is also a size four. She's five feet eight, blonde, your body type—"

"Oh my God!" QTπ exclaimed. "I know who you're talking about—"

"Shhh," Françoise said, severely. "Word must never get out."

"Of course," QTπ said, properly chagrined. She clamped her lips together.

"The dress was designed for us by Salvatore Puccini, who—"

"Who died last month at his studio in Milan," Ollie interjected out of nowhere. I hadn't realized he was still conscious, much less listening. All faces turned to him.

"Yes," Françoise said, looking at him, clearly impressed. "A terrible loss to the fashion world. This was his last creation."

Monique emerged from the back room with Mr. Puccini's sartorial swansong suspended from a padded hanger. QTπ gasped and held both hands to her mouth. "That is so beautiful," she said. "I love it." To me, the dress looked much like the others. Accompanied by Monique and Calista, she retreated into the dressing room, leaving the door ajar. Ollie stared at the door, and at first, I assumed he was trying to resurrect the image of her in the white thong and lacy bra. But his anxiety seemed focused on the door itself, because he visibly relaxed when it drifted farther open. I decided he mostly was worried about the closed door blocking her scent. Interesting.

Ten minutes passed, and I heard exuberant squealing from the dressing room. Calista and Monique bustled out, smiling broadly and latching the door behind them. Françoise rose from her chair, and the three women stood silent, all eyes on the door. Monique had clenched her hands together at her chest, as if praying before the gate to heaven. Finally it opened, and QTπ swept into the room, beaming triumphantly. She twirled, an angel spreading her wings. Calista and Monique cheered, and Françoise applauded wildly.

"It's fabulous," Françoise said. "I can't believe it. I've never seen anything so beautiful. QTπ, you take my breath away." The three women hovered over QTπ, touching the arms of the dress, the shoulders, feeling the fabric, inspecting the stitching, viewing it from all directions. It appeared to be their consensus that, miraculously, the dress fit perfectly. The duchess was going to have to be burdened with a lesser garment.

After a few minutes QTπ returned to the dressing room with Calista in tow to change into her street clothes. Françoise turned to Ollie, who rose unsteadily to his feet. He set me down on the table next to the empty champagne bottle. "Ollie, this is such a wonderful present for your lady," she said, smiling warmly and touching his shoulder. "She's so deserving." I hadn't recalled any discussion between Ollie and QTπ about a present. Ollie frowned but reflexively reached for his wallet. "No need to pay now," Françoise said, laughing, as if any discussion of payment would be an unseemly intrusion into her budding relationship with a dear friend. "I'll just put your name on QTπ's account and send you the statement." She leaned over and kissed him on the cheek. Ollie, still looking puzzled, reached up and touched the spot.

A few minutes later, as Françoise escorted us to the front door, Ollie glanced back at the table still piled high with untouched food. "I guess we brought too much," he said.

Françoise laughed again. "Henry will box it up and take it to Captain Pattycake's Kitchen. The toddlers will love it."

While Carlos drove us home, I sat on Ollie's lap, with QTπ next to us holding Little Squeegee. With all of us bottled up in the car, QTπ's scent was again nearly overpowering. I felt like Ollie was about to be stampeded by a herd of wildebeest, and I wasn't sure how to protect him. There are limits to what a small dog can do. But at least I had a game plan: Ollie and I would fly to Las Vegas the following afternoon. We would visit his aunt and uncle for a few days, and then join QTπ at the end of the week for her show at that new casino. I figured Ollie could make it alone through her performance, and afterward, I would be there to protect him from her.

As if reading my mind, QTπ turned toward Ollie and said, "Baby, what time does your flight leave tomorrow?"

"One o'clock," he said. "Tex is going to stay here with a friend while I'm gone. She called me earlier today and volunteered to look after him." I snapped to attention, not sure I'd heard right. I was staying here with Regina? Oh no! Ollie would be alone in Las Vegas for an entire week with that awful woman?

"That's wonderful, baby," QTπ cooed. "We'll have lots of time alone in Las Vegas with no distractions." Little Squeegee leered at me and growled, but the sound was stifled by the thunder of enraged wildebeest.

# 18

# HOT
# WATER

*Wanda Wonders: Who was the dark-haired mystery dude spotted holding hands last night with celeb rapper QT-pi on the up-elevator at the Ritz-Carlton? Word on the street is they came down an hour later. Hey there, QT-pi, who's your new QT-guy? (Check out my fab WandaWonders T-shirts and so much more at wandawonders.com.)*

**The next morning** my head throbbed from Françoise's champagne. Tex sprawled on the bed watching me pack for my trip, and he, too, seemed out of sorts: moping, tail drooped, subdued. I was meeting Regina at nine at Bean So Long to drop him off with her, but I was moving in slow motion and needed to hurry.

The day was mottled gray again, gusty and unpredictable. I desperately needed advice from Hernando, but by the time I floundered out of bed, he'd already left for a college retreat and wasn't answering his cellphone. I had spent a sleepless night filled with wild dream fragments. My mind kept seeing QT$\pi$ looking up at me with dilated pupils, crying out "Baby, oh baby!" so loudly I was afraid guests in the next room would hear.

I needed to focus on my trip. I looked forward to reuniting with Uncle Joe and Aunt Harriet in Las Vegas, but I was apprehensive about spending two days alone with QT$\pi$ at that new casino. I hoped things wouldn't move too quickly between us, until we had a chance to know each other better.

I drove around for ten anxious minutes trying to park, almost plowing into two students at a crosswalk at Fayette and Church Streets before an empty spot opened up. I checked my watch, popped Tex into my shirt pocket, and raced the two blocks to Bean So Long. I was already eleven minutes late. At the entrance, I stopped to take a calming breath. I needed to act as if nothing had happened. I kept telling myself there was no reason to feel guilty, but it didn't help.

I entered the café, which had filled with the morning breakfast crowd, and heard, "Ollie, over here." I let my eyes adjust to the indoor light and saw Mr. Pettigrew chatting with Regina beside a two-top in the rear. Tex perked up his ears when he saw her. "Ollie, here," Mr. Pettigrew said, pulling the free chair away from the table. I sagged into it, still breathless after the rush from my car.

"My two favorite customers, and I didn't know you even knew each other," he said with a wide smile. "Say, I don't suppose you two are . . . ?" He raised his eyebrows.

"Oh no, nothing like that," Regina said. I saw her glance at me and quickly look away.

"Regina's taking care of Tex while I'm out of town," I said, noting Mr. Pettigrew's smile diminish.

"Sorry I'm late," I said, after we'd placed our order. "I had trouble parking." I plopped Tex on the table, and he loped over to her and perched beside her water glass. "It's nice of you to look after Tex for me. Too bad the casinos don't allow dogs."

Regina stroked his head with a fingertip. "Do you have any special instructions?" she asked. "Where does he usually sleep?"

"On a pillow on my bed, but on cold mornings, I'll find him under the covers, snuggled against my pajamas."

She looked at me and blushed slightly.

"What?" I said. "Is that a problem?"

"No, of course not. I was thinking that, well, I don't wear pajamas."

"You don't wear anything to bed?" I said, and there was that image of QT$\pi$ intruding into my head, again. I felt a little tingle of arousal. Regina gave a demur little shrug and looked down at Tex, now stretched out quietly on the table.

"He seems subdued today. You feeling okay, Tex?" She looked up and caught my eye.

"Last night he hardly touched his food," I said, trying to refocus, "even though I gave him some leftover duck, and I know he likes it." Regina had fixed duck confit for dinner at my place earlier in the week. That afternoon, we'd attended a lecture on the famous statue of Damdin Sükhbaatar on horseback in Ulan Bator. Nearly a century earlier, Sükhbaatar's horse had urinated on the statue's exact location, a symbolic marker of the 1921 Mongolian revolution. It had been a fascinating evening.

"That's worrisome," Regina said, still stroking Tex's head. "Did anything particular happen to him yesterday?" Just then a server brought our coffees. Regina took a paper bag from her backpack and set it on the table. Tex's ears perked but he didn't stand. "I baked some jelebi this morning," she said, extracting two orange pretzel-shaped pastries from the bag. "They're dipped in saffron syrup."

I took a bite and broke off a piece for Tex. It was crunchy with a sweet flavor. He sniffed at his piece but wasn't interested.

"I used to bake these for my dad," she said, studying Tex. "They're from an old Nepalese recipe." She looked up at me. "You were saying?"

I wasn't saying anything.

"Something's going on with you," Regina said, frowning.

"I'm just feeling a little distracted."

"I can tell. So what's making you distracted?"

"I . . . we, QT$\pi$ and I that is, went out together. For the first time."

"Oh, I see. I remember you saying you were going shopping with her." She smiled, but there was a bristly veneer in her voice. "Seems like an odd first date, don't you think?"

I was suddenly playing defensive. I fibbed. "She travels a lot, so mostly we use the phone."

Regina was no longer smiling. She thought for a moment and said, "I suppose she kept you out late?"

"No, it was just an afternoon date."

"And Tex went with you?"

"Tex and Calista, actually. And her driver."

"Who's Calista?"

"That's her assistant. She came with QT$\pi$ to my birthday party."

"I remember her. Skinny, dressed in black, frowned a lot." Regina leaned toward me with her palms on the table. "So your girlfriend brought along her assistant on your date?" I didn't know where this snappish tone was coming from, but a thread of panic started inching up my spine.

"She's not my girlfriend. I barely know her," I said in a futile gesture at sounding indignant. "She just needed a dress for her Las Vegas cast party. After her premier." I knew I was digging myself into a hole. Regina wasn't buying any of this. The hubbub in the coffee shop seemed to be swelling.

"I see. On your first date, QT$\pi$ took you to buy a dress. Sounds like she's really crazy about you. Did she let you pay for it too?"

God, how did she know that? I said, "It seemed like a nice thing to do." Truthfully, I couldn't remember why I'd paid for it. It just sort of happened.

"And afterward, I imagine you went out for dinner or cocktails?" I nodded, feeling a tremor in my fingers. I put them in my lap so Regina couldn't see.

"How nice. Where did you go?" she asked, her words nonchalant and seemingly half-interested. I tried to sound the same way.

"Nowhere particular. She just wanted to show me where she's staying."

"I bet she did. Did Tex go with you to see it too? So where is she staying?" I was trapped, and there was no escape. I couldn't face her, so I stared at the tabletop.

"In a suite at the Ritz-Carlton. Tex waited in the coffee shop with Calista." I looked up and saw Regina staring at my face. She didn't speak.

"How was it?" she said finally.

"How was what?"

Regina said nothing. She just looked at me, biting her lower lip.

"It was okay, I guess." I hoped she couldn't hear the desperation in my voice. I couldn't remember anything about QT$\pi$'s suite.

"I see," she said. We sat awkwardly for a minute. I started to pick up my coffee cup but decided to leave my hands in my lap.

"So you're spending the week with this woman in Las Vegas while I take care of Tex for you." Her voice had turned icy. There was nothing nonchalant about it.

I said, "I'll be mostly visiting my aunt and uncle. QT$\pi$ is flying in from Brazil on the morning of her concert. She sees a doctor there. Then afterward, I'm flying home and she's heading off to Los Angeles to meet with her accountant."

"Brazil? Is she ill? I hope it's not contagious."

"It's her plastic surgeon. She gets injections in her forehead. The serum is distilled from the venom of the golden lance head viper, which is only found on a coastal island there."

Regina didn't respond to this tidbit, so I tried a last-ditch diversion.

"My uncle is a professional Scrabble player. He's training for the world championship games. Scrabble has replaced poker at some of the big Las Vegas casinos."

"I need to get to work," Regina said, glancing at her smartphone. She stood and grabbed the strap of her backpack. Cradling Tex against her body with her free hand, she turned and faced me.

"Are you upset, Regina?" I asked pointlessly.

"Goodbye, Ollie," she said. "I hope the two of you have a wonderful time." She turned and walked quickly toward the exit. She had barely touched her coffee.

# 19

# CAST PARTY

*Dear Ming-huá,*

*Congratulations on your recent Nobel Prize. I know, of course, about your remarkable work on String Theory, although I confess to a bit of trouble picturing a thirteen-dimensional universe. With respect to your marriage proposal, I'm greatly honored, but I am now in a thrilling new relationship. My girlfriend and I are very unalike, but I know our differences are the key to a lasting relationship. I like to imagine how a skittery electron and its opposite proton are drawn together into a single stable neutron. To me, simple analogies are often the best way to understand human relationships.*

*Sincerely,*
*Oliphant*

**It was a few minutes before 3:00 a.m.,** and a tall Valkyrie named Skodra had just handed me another pewter flagon embossed with nude, large-breasted Norse women. A miniature dry-ice rendition of the Norse god Odin floated in the amber mead, looking a lot like Elvis. Skodra, who had earlier confessed that her real name was Candy, looked to be in her mid-twenties. She had a thick blonde braid down the middle of her back and wore a gray metallic breastplate with formidable pointed breasts. Except for her scandalously brief fur-trimmed skirt and thigh-high black boots, that was pretty much it in the attire department. The flickering light from the huge torches lining the side walls glimmered off her breastplate and dazzled me. I collapsed onto a bearskin-covered sofa, and she slid onto a stool beside me. We had been chatting about Old English poetry.

"You don't understand," Skodra said with earnest intensity. "You're confusing *syllables* with *positions*. If a verse has a string of unstressed syllables, it resolves into a single position." She hesitated to make sure I was following. "That's basically what Kaluza's Law says. It's simple, really. Oops, I gotta go," she said, before I could respond. "My supervisor's watching." She rose from her stool. "Nice talking to you, Ollie. Hope things work out for you and your girlfriend." She started to walk away but then turned toward me. "You might want to slow down on the mead."

I waved to her and leaned back on the sofa. The walls of the banquet room shimmered in the dim torchlight, and I could smell the huge roasting boar turning slowly on a spit in an open stone fire pit in the room's center. The smoke rose and vanished through a vent in the dark-timbered ceiling. As I watched, a bare-chested warrior wearing a horned metal helmet and fur loincloth hacked off a slab of meat with a heavy sword and bore it away on a large platter.

I squinted at my watch, but the room was too dim to make out the dial. I had been waiting for QT$\pi$ for at least an hour. The cast members had been dribbling in, and most seemed in a bad mood. Her Cultured Pearls premier had not gone well. Several of the thousand-dollar VIP ticket holders had shown up after the concert, swilled a flagon of mead, and then left. Two court jesters wearing purple velvet costumes with floppy hats now roamed the crowd, gamely juggling balls, but seemed unable to lighten the mood. I slurped some mead, blinked, and tried to collect my thoughts. There was a rushing in my ears, but I couldn't tell whether it came from the air-conditioning or inside my head.

My visit with Aunt Harriet and Uncle Joe had been a little disappointing. We hadn't had much time to talk, because they were about to leave on an expedition to the Australian Outback to band tree-kangaroos, but they seemed particularly interested and pleased to learn about Hernando. They were also pleased to hear about my Nigerian orphanage, but I left out the part about my sixty million dollars because they're both lifelong socialists who disdain capitalism and personal wealth. I told them about QT$\pi$, of course, but I didn't want to tell them *everything*, so instead, I focused on her huge following and best-selling albums, and how she traveled all over the world performing. I saw them exchange a glance when I told them she'd flown to Brazil to see her plastic surgeon, and while they were polite, I sensed they didn't totally approve of her.

Later, while Uncle Joe was studying for his Scrabble tournament, I tried to talk to Aunt Harriet about Regina, but I didn't get far. I didn't tell her about Regina being mad at my having sex with QT$\pi$. I didn't quite understand that myself; after all, it had been Regina's decision to have a platonic relationship, and she couldn't expect me to remain celibate forever. It's not like I'd cheated on her. So why did I feel so ashamed of myself? Whatever it was, I had been brooding all week.

A smattering of applause at the room's entrance interrupted my thoughts. I looked over and saw QT$\pi$ in the doorway, accompanied by a middle-aged, sallow-faced man in blue jeans and a velvet maroon blazer, carrying a vodka bottle. QT$\pi$ wore the white dress I'd bought her at Chez Charmante and looked extraordinarily sexy. I started to become aroused yet again, but also disoriented by the dizziness I always felt when she was nearby. Two warriors carrying platters of meat gaped at her open-mouthed, and it was obvious they were having the same reaction. I rose unsteadily to greet her and realized I desperately needed to use the bathroom. I took a detour to search for a men's room when Skodra, my Valkyrie friend, noticed my distress and led me without speaking down a corridor and past a bank of elevators. I pushed open the door into the men's room, and she patted my arm, gave me a tight, concerned smile, and turned away.

A few minutes later, better but still dizzy, I made my way back into the ballroom, which was heavy with the cloying smell of mead and roasted pork. QTπ spotted me at once and came over, still accompanied by the sallow-faced man with the vodka bottle, which I noticed was half-empty. He had sandy-blond hair and was visibly perspiring. "Here he is," she said to him and then turned to me. "We've been looking all over for you."

Before I could speak, the man stuck out his hand. "Good to meet you," he said, his speech slurred. "Rufus Goldfarb, but every-body calls me Ruthless." I stared at him, and he added, "That's because I'm a ruthless advocate for my clients." He laughed, giv-ing the impression I was the first person to hear his little joke. I decided he was quite drunk.

"Ruthless is my agent," QTπ said, sweeping her hair to one side. She also was struggling with her words. I supposed that made three of us. I found myself staring at her cleavage and forced myself to look at Mr. Goldfarb.

"QTπ tells me you're that guy who saved the Algerian orphans," he said. "You gotta love those orphans." He furrowed his brow. "How big did you say that commission was?" he added, recalling some nonexistent prior conversation.

"Sixty million dollars, but it wasn't Alger—"

"You shoulda called me," he said, shaking his head with somber regret. "I coulda got you eighty, easy. You have to watch those orphanages. They'll screw you every time. Okay, I'll leave you two alone. Good to meet you, kid." He turned away, still clutching the vodka bottle and wiping a bead of sweat off his upper lip with his free hand.

QTπ put her arm around my waist and leaned against me while we lurched our way to the sofa. I felt like we were walking through sand. "Goldfarb isn't his real name," she said. "He's Mormon and grew up in Salt Lake City, but he changed his name, you know, a status thing. He pretends he's from LA" My flagon still rested on the sofa table and had mysteriously been refilled. Seconds later the mystery was solved when Skodra came over carrying a tray with yet another flagon.

"Miss Pi, I thought you might like this," she said, handing the heavy metal vessel to QTπ, who accepted it and glanced suspiciously at its bubbling contents. Another Elvis writhed in agony in the foaming liquid. "My boyfriend's a huge fan. I can't wait to tell him I met you."

QTπ said nothing but sniffed the flagon's contents. She took a tentative sip. "Eww," she said grimacing, "what is this crap?"

"It's mead," Skodra said brightly. "In Old English, it's *meodu* and is made from fermented honey and flavored with hops, spices, and fruits." Misreading QTπ's silence as interest, she continued, "Mead plays an important role in Norse mythology. I'm sure you've heard of the Mead of Suttungr, the legendary drink that's said to be the source of poetic inspiration."

QTπ stared at her as if she had just stepped out of a flying saucer. "Get me some vodka, rocks, honey," she said, handing back the flagon. "The good stuff, you know, with the foreign name."

"Yes, ma'am," Skodra said politely. She caught my eye as she turned and walked toward the bar.

QTπ reached over and touched her fingertips to my lips. "Baby," she cooed, sliding over and turning to face me, "I need you to kiss me right now. I can't wait any longer." She threw her arms around my neck and pulled my face to hers. We kissed for a very long time, and I tasted garlic and felt her tongue rooting around in my mouth. Finally, we separated, and I gasped for breath. The room was careening starboard and making me queasy. She looked at me with an amused expression. "There's a lot more where that came from."

Skodra returned carrying a short, heavy glass of vodka. She set it on the sofa table with more force than seemed necessary and walked away without speaking. QTπ picked up the glass and gulped its contents. She turned back to me, and I was astonished to see tears in her eyes. "Baby, I'm so miserable," she blurted. I couldn't imagine what had happened in the previous thirty seconds to have caused such emotional torment.

"I'm sorry," I said. "I may not be the best kisser in the world, but I thought I'd done okay."

"It's not you, baby." Her face was inches from mine, and I could smell vodka on her breath. I wondered if cheap vodka smelled different from the good stuff with the foreign name. "This night has been a disaster," she said, sniffling. "Everybody hated my performance. I know you hated it too, didn't you, baby? Tell me the truth. I want you to be completely honest with me. I must know the absolute truth."

"No," I lied. "I loved your performance."

"Really and truly?" She leaned over, and we repeated our kissing experience. This time I focused on my technique, as best I could with the room careening.

"I fired Calista," she said when we finally disengaged.

"But I sat next to her at the concert, and she seemed fine," I said, shocked. I wiped my lips with my tongue.

"She's a lying, selfish bitch," QTπ said curtly. "This is all her fault." I said nothing. I wasn't sure what Calista's fault had been. "All this cultured pearl stuff. It didn't work. Nobody likes it. It was her idea. She made me do it." She lifted the glass of vodka and scowled when she found it empty. Irritated, she looked around for Skodra but didn't see her. "I should have trusted my instincts. Why oh why didn't I do that, baby?" she said, sobbing.

"Maybe you can go back to being QTπ and the Tarts," I suggested. That was the best I could come up with. My eyes wouldn't focus.

"You don't get it," she said, blowing her nose on a wadded-up cocktail napkin and stuffing it in her empty glass. "There isn't enough money. Not nearly enough. Ruthless says we're going broke." She began to wail loudly. A warrior carrying a huge broadsword looked at her, alarmed, glared at me, and raised his sword. Out of nowhere, Skodra appeared at his side and grabbed his arm. She whispered something in his ear, and he nodded and turned away.

I clenched my eyes shut and tried to concentrate. I needed to draw her out. "What *are* you going to do?" I asked, opening my eyes.

"Oh baby, oh baby," she said, shaking her head. I had never seen anyone so miserable. Choking, she buried her head in her hands. "Goose my knees to gut fat," she mumbled between sobs.

"Gut fat? What's wrong with your knees?"

"No," she said, raising her head. "Rufus . . . says I . . . need to . . . cut back."

"That doesn't sound so awful," I said. "There are several things you could—"

"WHAT!" she screamed. "Baby, I thought you loved me. Ohhhh, this is the worst night of my life." She started to sob again—loud, snorting honks.

"I do," I said, desperate to end her pain. I had to say something. "Of course I do." Her pain seemed to end immediately, and she looked at me adoringly. Okay, that worked.

"And I love you, too, baby," she said, wiping her eyes with another cocktail napkin. Her voice became subdued, and she took my hands. "Ollie," she said, leaning forward. My eyes drifted down again to her cleavage. "Let's get married. I want to be your wife. I want you to be my husband."

"Married?" I said. I felt like I was in a dream. My head throbbed. I heard screams and a loud roaring, like nothing I'd ever experienced. I saw people pointing upwards. There, a monstrous beast at least thirty feet long with a hideous head and glowing red eyes was slowly descending from the ceiling's dark upper reaches, its tail lashing violently. Its jaws held the body of a Norse warrior who was convulsed in agony, much like my foaming Elvis. "Married?" I said again. "Us?"

I heard a voice behind me. "Let's get out of here, you two. The fight's about to start."

"Fight?" I said. I turned around and squinted through the gloom at Mr. Goldfarb standing behind the sofa. Instead of the vodka bottle, he now carried a small leather briefcase.

He shouted over the din. "Once it starts, it gets real noisy in here. Some guy named Wolf comes in and kills Gretel. That's the dragon. She never wins. You ask me, it gets boring."

"Ruthless, we're getting married," QTπ said, clutching my arm against her breasts. "I've never been so happy."

"No kidding! That's great news. Congratulations, kid." Mr. Goldfarb reached over the back of the sofa and pumped my arm, all thoughts of Gretel and Wolf evidently forgotten.

"He," I said. "The dragon is a he. And his name's not Gretel."

"What?" he said, staring at me. Turning to QTπ, "When's the happy date, sweetheart?"

Still clutching my arm, QTπ leaned over and kissed me on the cheek. "Now, don't you think, baby? Let's do it now."

"Let's do it now," I said, trying to process the words amidst the chaos of the eighth-century saga unfolding around me. "Do what now?" People were screaming, and a small band of bare-chested Viking warriors with drawn swords had clustered on the floor underneath the descending monster. A huge warrior with a white polar bear skin draped over his shoulders led them, the bear's enormous head and black beady eyes making a gruesome helmet. The smell of roasting pork was making me feel nauseated. I gagged and felt bile rise in my throat.

"Easy, kid," Mr. Goldfarb said. "Let's get you out of here." I struggled to my feet but knocked over my mead, drenching my pants and socks. "Forget it," Mr. Goldfarb said, grabbing my arm. "They'll clean it up." QTπ took my other arm, and the three of us lurched slowly toward the exit. My pant legs stuck to my skin, and my shoes squished with each step.

"Where are we going?" I said, framing my words with difficulty.

"Why, we're going to get married, baby," QTπ replied happily.

As we reached the exit, I caught a glimpse of Skodra wiping up the spilled mead from the sofa table. She looked up and dropped her soaked towel on the table, watching me with a concerned frown.

The next minutes were a blur. I remember being led across the main floor of the casino, a football field-sized hall in which the Norse decor appeared to have morphed into an eclectic mix of Louis XIV and twenty-fifth century alien spacecraft. We threaded our way past hundreds of slot machines arranged into circular clusters, with multicolored neon tubes springing upward from the center of each cluster and gracefully arching outward like a cascade of fireworks. Giant video screens hung from the ceiling, some totaling the ever-increasing payouts, others enticing players with *Hot Slots!* and *Win! Win! Win!* I found the clanging bells and screeching sirens nightmarishly disturbing. About half of the slot machines had players seated on their stools. My watch said it was 4:35 a.m.

We pushed on. Beyond the slots, huge crystal chandeliers hovered over crescent-shaped blackjack tables, their green felt contrasting with maroon plush carpets and black leather upholstery. Valkyries carrying silver trays of stubby crystal glasses meandered among the tables, offering cocktails to glassy-eyed players. A monstrous rotating roulette wheel embedded in the ceiling spanned the blackjack tables. I felt another wave of nausea.

Finally, we reached an ornate gilded door at the far end of the casino floor. Above it, a large neon sign read *Eternal Bliss Wedding Chapel* in pink script lettering. Next to it, a miniature traffic light glowed red, and beside it a sign blinked *Do not enter. Sacred nuptials in progress.* A large, lighted menu stood to the left of the door, and in front of that a waist-high metal pole supporting a small loudspeaker.

"What are we doing here?" I asked QTπ, as she and Mr. Goldfarb studied the menu.

She turned and looked at me, surprised. "Baby, we're getting married! That's what you wanted, right?"

"It is?"

"Sure it is, kid," Mr. Goldfarb said, grasping my shoulder. "I heard you say it. This is your dream come true. You're a lucky man."

"I'm a lucky man," I said. I struggled to keep my eyes open. The drone of the slot machines reverberated in my head in unrelenting waves. I clasped my hands over my ears. The sound was driving me mad. It wouldn't stop, it wouldn't stop, it wouldn't stop. I wanted to scream.

"Baby," QTπ said as she studied the menu, "do you think we want the Heaven on Earth package or the Everlasting Passion package?"

"Hey, you need to be cutting back," Mr. Goldfarb said. "Why don't you go for Sailor's Delight? It's on sale this week."

QTπ shot him a reproachful glare and pushed the button below the loudspeaker. After a few seconds, a perky female voice answered.

"Welcome to Eternal Bliss," the voice said, "the only weddings on the Strip with a ninety-day warranty. Some exclusions apply. And *now*," the voice continued, in a tone of fervent happiness, "have you had a chance to look at our menu?"

"We have," QTπ said, squeezing my hand joyfully. "We'd like the Heaven on Earth package," she said, as Mr. Goldfarb sighed in resignation.

"An excellent choice," the voice said in the deferential tone of one skilled at addressing the newly affluent. "Heaven on Earth comes with many of our deluxe features at no extra charge. The package includes three live relatives, including father of the bride, best man, and bridesmaid. You can add a mother-in-law and ex-boyfriend for $59.95 each, and a Cirque de Soleil contortionist ring bearer for only $199.95. Deceased relatives are each ninety-nine dollars, but that includes the makeup required for our custom apparition look. We can also supply a flower child for $179.95. All flower children come with a reusable plastic bouquet. We use only trained and licensed little people."

"What do you think, baby?" QTπ said, biting her lip. "I think a flower child would be nice."

"Flower child?" I said. I hadn't been paying attention.

"Smart decision," the voice said. "Now, let me tell you about some of our specials. For this week only, we are selling white doves for half price. They're only $59.95 each, or ten for five hundred dollars. We guarantee their release at the casino entrance within six seconds of the last 'I do.' Sorry, no returns on doves."

"I'd think twenty or thirty doves would be adequate, don't you?" QTπ said to me.

"Can't you get by with ten doves?" Mr. Goldfarb said sourly. QTπ gave him an acid-filled look.

The discussion dragged on, but all I could think about was escaping from the slot machines. QTπ declined the armed guard, since there was no nearby jilted suitor, and we didn't need the chapel's prenup documents, since Mr. Goldfarb had brought his own. We completed the planning and were waiting for the traffic light to turn green when Mr. Goldfarb's cellphone rang. He excused himself and moved away a few feet. Holding one hand over an ear, he spoke for several minutes. Then, he ran back over to us just as the traffic light turned.

"Stop!" he yelled, as QTπ and I started into the chapel. I already had my Visa card out. "There's a change of plans. This is wonderful news."

QTπ looked at him blankly. "Ruthless, we're getting married. Can't this wait? What change of plans?" She gripped my arm tightly, as if to prevent me from fleeing.

"You've been asked to sing the national anthem next week at Fenway Park," Mr. Goldfarb said. "The Red Sox are playing the Yankees. It's the biggest game of the year."

"Well, that *is* good news, but can't we talk about it later? Ollie and I are anxious to complete our vows. Aren't we, baby?" She fixed me with an adoring gaze.

Mr. Goldfarb bounced on the balls of his feet from excitement. "You don't understand," he gasped. His face had turned crimson. "We'll have the wedding at Fenway Park. They'll let us do it during the seventh inning stretch. The whole country will be talking about it."

QTπ loosened her grip on my arm while she pondered this new information. "So how exactly would this work?"

"Okay," he said, holding his hand over his chest and struggling to breathe. "We'll announce that you're secretly engaged and that you and your mystery fiancé will share your happiness with the world during the seventh inning."

"So my fans will know I'm engaged, but they won't know who it is until the wedding?"

"The suspense will kill them. Every reporter in the country will be digging to find out who it is. Oh, this is just huge! This is just . . ." He left his thought hanging and squinted at her. "Who knows about you two, anyway? We can't have anybody spilling the beans."

QTπ frowned and looked at me. "Your birthday party," she said. "Everybody saw me there. Wait, if anybody asks, we'll say we're just friends. You've got women friends, right? Didn't I see you looking at that bartender girl?"

That bartender girl. My mind cleared, and I pictured Tex squealing at my birthday party when he recognized Regina at the bar table. I thought about Regina back in Boston at that moment, probably still asleep, lying nude with Tex snuggled up against her. Oh, God. I shut my eyes and tried to make sense of my life. Of my two lives. One was my exciting new alcohol-drenched life of casinos and hip hop and agents and all-night parties. And the other was my dull old contemplative life of libraries and coffee houses and walks with Tex in the dog park. That old life seemed to be quickly receding. It was times like this that I wished Tex and Hernando could be with me. "Yes, I've got a woman friend," I said. And then, remembering Regina's tight-lipped expression when she stalked out of Bean So Long, I added, "At least, I hope so."

"Then it's settled," Mr. Goldfarb said. "But you must not, repeat, you must not talk to each other or be seen together *at all* until the wedding. If you're discovered, it will ruin everything."

"Hold on," QTπ said, grabbing Mr. Goldfarb's arm. "I forgot about Calista. I fired her last night. She knows all about Ollie."

"Hire her back and give her a raise," he said. "You can fire her again after the wedding. Let's see. Kid, you've got a flight back to Boston, right? When does it leave?"

I looked at my watch. It was 5:15 a.m. "In about three hours. I left my suitcase at the hotel registration desk." I hoped I could sleep on the plane to clear my head.

"Good," he said. "You can take a Lyft to the airport. Remember, you can't say a word to anyone." We turned and started to retrace our steps across the casino floor, QTπ still gripping my arm. I glanced backward at the Eternal Bliss wedding chapel just as the voice from the loudspeaker called my name. The traffic light beside the door glowed green, and the lighted sign beckoned us. *Enter now, lovers!* it blinked.

# 20

# THE
# AWAKENING

**The Awakening began a week ago,** on the day Ollie left for Las Vegas. Although I'd been expecting it, I didn't at first recognize the signs. Regina and I had just returned from our morning walk, and while she showered upstairs, I wandered into the downstairs bathroom to my water bowl under the sink. It was empty. I had stared at it a few seconds when I heard Regina's footsteps. "You poor darling," she said, standing in the bathroom doorway in her robe. "Let me take care of that." Was that a clue something was up? Was this one of my new powers, or a simple coincidence? Had I unknowingly signaled Regina my water bowl needed filling? Who could say?

The Awakening is sneaky that way. It always comes on softly, like rising in the morning and discovering your dreams were coming true. But never *all* your dreams. The universe may have started listening to you, but it doesn't listen all that closely, and if you're not careful it will send you barking up the wrong tree.

Another odd thing about the Awakening is that each time it happens, I have to figure it out mostly, but not entirely, from scratch. I know it begins after about a year, and that I've never met another dog it happens to. I also know it will transform my life. The Awakening is a gift, a vaguely remembered but wondrous gift, something to be accepted and welcomed, but not scrutinized. So why does it come to me? That I will never know.

In any case, my water bowl experience raised my suspicions, and as the day wore on, I became aware of other changes. Like all dogs, I have trouble telling red from green. That day, however, I began to notice the green color of leaves and grass. The plastic fireplugs at the dog park looked red, and so did the package of strawberries on the kitchen counter. I didn't actually see the colors, but I sensed their greenness and redness. That's when I finally accepted what was going on.

It wasn't difficult to test my new powers. Regina hadn't slept well during the night, and so that morning she was dog-tired, and I could feel her radiating anxiety and worry as she awaited Ollie's return from Las Vegas. Her wine shop was closed on Sundays, so after lunch, still wearing her robe, she curled up to nap on the living room sofa. I hopped up beside her and tried to ease her mind by focusing on her and Ollie together. I pictured them strolling with me at Da Dog Run Run, chatting in Ollie's living room after a concert or lecture, laughing as they prepared dinner, practicing their sackbut duet, and so forth.

The effect was nearly immediate. As Regina lay half-dozing, I could feel her heartbeat slow and her breathing deepen. Her shoulder muscles softened and released, the arteries in her neck dilated, the blood flow to her extremities increased, and her core temperature and blood pressure dropped. It was as if the emotional connection between our species had suddenly strengthened a hundred-fold. I couldn't read Regina's conscious thoughts, but I had new insight into her emotional life. For sure, that was amazing, but it also meant my responsibility had doubled. Regina and Ollie were now a team, part and parcel of the same assignment. Unfortunately, their emotional lives seemed in total disarray, and at this point, I didn't know what I could do to straighten them out.

I lay there gnawing over my newly expanded awareness. Regina had constructed a barrier against emotional intimacy, and Ollie was on the wrong side of it. She believed her path to happiness was to hold Ollie at paw's length and treat him as a friend and nothing more. Her mind seemed closed to any other possibility. I felt like I could be chasing my tail by trying to bring them together.

Furthermore, my challenge with Regina was nothing compared with what I faced with Ollie. Ollie and I had lived together for a year, but until this morning, I hadn't truly understood his core issue: Ollie was a lonely and unfulfilled human who thought his salvation would be for Regina to be his lover. Never mind that neither he nor Regina was emotionally ready to make that commitment. Ollie's real problem was he didn't fit into his world. Ollie yearned to live in a universe ruled by logic and reason, where Nigerian email offers didn't beat the odds, where daily life was free of risks and unforeseen happenings. But such a world didn't exist. Instead, Ollie's world was irrational, unpredictable, and karma-filled, and Ollie was too uptight to adjust to that. No wonder he hadn't been able to find love and fulfillment. Ollie was a sweet man but also a misfit who lacked self-understanding.

My assignment, therefore, was to help Ollie seek out and embrace the wonder and beauty and mystery that surrounded him, to help him to take charge of his life, to have fun, and finally, to grow up and be an adult. Clearly, I had my work cut out for me!

I started to pant as I pondered my future. I know I'm not like other dogs, and that I have been charged with the most difficult missions. But I didn't know how those missions were selected. Understand I'm not complaining. I love my life. I love my humans and care about them, and I love doing good. I may be an old dog, evidently a very, very old dog, but I still know a trick or two. What I truly know is that I am in this world for an important reason, and that is all I am entitled to understand.

But first things first. If the Awakening had come only a week earlier, I could have tried to stop Ollie from going to Las Vegas. Now, I cringed at the thought of his spending a weekend with that awful rapper woman. Unfortunately, in his hormone-induced fog, Ollie couldn't see he was being manipulated by a charlatan who was only after his money. She had really muddied his water bowl. However, now Ollie was coming home, and she wasn't coming with him, so at least I had a chance he'd be able to shake off his infatuation and come to his senses.

I spent the morning trying to come up with a strategy but decided in the end that was a fool's errand. The best I could hope for was that Regina would tell Ollie her concerns about QT$\pi$ when he picked me up that afternoon after his flight landed. He might not be persuaded to drop her, but at least she could sow the seeds of doubt. Anyway, that was my hope.

An hour after our nap, Regina seemed a different woman: relaxed, collected, radiating resolve, her anger evaporated. For the first time in weeks, I felt the stirrings of hope. To tell the truth, I was proud of myself for pulling that off.

Unfortunately, my optimism didn't last long. Ollie showed up a few minutes before six, and at once, I knew something was wrong. I was flopped on the sofa, Regina in the kitchen, and when his car pulled into the driveway, the anxiety cloud was so intense I couldn't bark. I waited until I heard a timid rap on the door. Regina rushed in from the kitchen and, worried, I forced myself off the sofa to follow her. She checked herself in the front hall mirror and adjusted her blouse. Then she opened the door and stared at Ollie in disbelief, her hand still clinging to the doorknob. He was bent and red-eyed, like he had been locked in a basement. His shirt was a rat's nest of wrinkles and stains, and his pants smelled like fermented fruit. He struggled to steady himself, leaning forward, with one hand propped against the door frame. He radiated a confusion of casino smells, cigarette smoke, and the stench of QTπ's mating pheromone on his clothing. This did not bode well.

"Hello, Regina," he said, as they gave each other a perfunctory hug. He leaned over and picked me up. I licked his palm and he smiled weakly.

"Ollie, you okay?" Regina said, her brow creased with sudden worry. "What's wrong?"

He gave a small, twitchy nod. "I'm just a little tired." His eyes had the glazed look I remembered from Chez Charmante, his distress almost palpable. Mine too, probably. I had never seen him like this. What had happened to him in Las Vegas?

"Would you like to use the bathroom to wash up?" Regina asked. She tried to smile, but her face was tense, with a tight crease across her forehead. "How about I get you a nice glass of wine?"

"Maybe just water. I've been drinking too much this week. Way too much."

"Okay, sure," she said, and I sensed her self-confidence dissolving.

A few minutes later, they sat across from each other at the kitchen table. I sat on the tabletop watching them.

"How are your aunt and uncle?" she asked.

"Good. They're both good."

"I'm glad. What did you talk about with them?"

"Nothing much. My uncle was getting ready for a Scrabble tournament."

"That's interesting. Anything else?"

"Not really." Ollie stared down at the table.

Regina bit her lip. The mood in the room had turned bleak. After a moment, she spoke in a strained, nonchalant voice.

"So, you must have told them you were dating QT$\pi$." Ollie inclined his head in her general direction but said nothing. "What did you tell them about her?" I saw her hands tremble. Before he could answer, she continued, "Ollie, I need to say something to you." He looked up at her. "About when I left you at Bean So Long." Ollie still said nothing. Regina took a long, shaky breath and clenched her fingers. Her face was flushed. "I-I was pretty upset," she said, "and I know you must have been confused. I'm really sorry. But now, I want to tell you why I ran away. I—"

"I'm getting married," Ollie said in a monotone infused with self-pity.

"What? What did you say?" She stared at him.

"I'm getting married," he said again, speaking slowly, as if struggling to understand his own words. "QT$\pi$ and I are engaged." He looked down again at the table, avoiding her gaze. "That's good news, isn't it?"

Regina turned ashen and seemed to shrink into herself. I could sense her pulse rate and blood pressure plummet, and I thought she might faint. I felt my own heart pounding. Where was the Ollie I knew? Regina stared at him without speaking. She drew in a sharp breath as if air had been sucked out of the room. "Oh," she said.

"That's good news, isn't it?" he said again, pleading. He clenched and unclenched his hands and stretched them out on the tabletop. She opened her mouth, but no words came. She sat there, not speaking, looking at him. Both of us were in shock.

Finally, she spoke. "When?"

"In seven days, I think." He seemed ready to collapse from exhaustion. I could feel waves of confusion radiating from him.

"You're getting married this coming Sunday, you *think*?" She sounded like she had awakened to find herself in some bizarre theatre of the absurd. He gave a little jerky shrug but didn't speak. "Oh, Ollie," she said, as her eyes filled with tears. "Oh, Ollie." She started to cry.

"I thought you'd be pleased," he said stupidly, whimpering. He seemed suddenly very young. Regina pushed back her chair, rose, and retrieved a dish towel from the kitchen counter. She sat down again and wiped her eyes. Then she cleared her throat and looked at him.

"Do you love her?" she asked quietly. He just looked at her, again saying nothing. "I need to hear you say the words. Ollie, tell me if you love her."

"I guess so," he said in a mechanical voice, as if reading the script from a bad high school play. "We're getting married. In seven days." He had lost his mind, and I knew what was coming.

"I see," she said, a thin line of tears running down her cheek. "I guess there's nothing more to say."

They sat for a minute.

"I thought you'd be pleased," he said again. Finally, when she didn't respond, "I guess I should be going."

"Yes," she said, turning away from him. She picked me up, kissed me on my head, and handed me to him. He slipped me into his shirt pocket, which smelled of perspiration. She followed us to the front door. Ollie opened it and stepped out onto the porch, then turned and looked back at her. She stood in the doorway, silent, in shock. There were tear stains on her cream-colored blouse.

"Thank you for taking care of Tex," he said.

"Goodbye, Ollie," she said. She exhaled and turned into the house, closing the door behind her.

# 21

# LAST
# CHANCE

*Dear Oliphant,*

*A little knowledge is a dangerous thing. Positrons, not protons, are the opposites of electrons. Positrons and electrons feel a great attraction at first, but once merged, they destroy each other in a nanosecond. Nevertheless, I wish you the best of luck in your relationship with your opposite persona. I fear you are going to need it.*

*Sincerely,*
*Ming-huá*

**I had been responding** to marriage proposals all afternoon when Tex barked, hopped off my lap, and ran to the front door. It was after six, and I had to remind myself it was Wednesday. I was getting married in four days, but all I'd thought about since Las Vegas was Regina. "Goodbye, Ollie," she had said to me on Sunday when I left her standing on her porch, and the edge in her voice had cut like a hacksaw blade. I had lost Regina, and the thought was tearing me apart.

"It's probably Hernando," I called to Tex, who stood at the front door yipping and furiously wagging his tail. For the past three days, Tex had been listless and anxious, and this was the first time I'd seen him enthusiastic about anything. I followed him to the front hall and opened the door. It was still two hours until sundown, but the sky had turned an insipid gray.

At first, I didn't see anybody, but then I spied Hernando walking rapidly toward us from half a block away. I never understood how Tex did that, even allowing for his canine nose. Hernando spied me and waved furiously.

"Hey, Fighter, how're you doing?" he yelled to Tex as he bounded up my porch steps onto the stoop. "Oliphant, I have the most wonderful news!"

I gave a perfunctory nod, irritated by his ebullience, and he trailed me into the living room and sprawled out onto the sofa. Tex hopped up on his lap. "I'm starved," he said, looking toward the kitchen.

I swiveled my desk chair to face him and reminded myself that my sour mood wasn't his fault. "Where've you been?" I said. I hadn't seen him since returning to Boston.

"You look awful," he said in response. "You feel all right?"

Now my turn to ignore. "You didn't leave a note."

"I was with Fanny, at her house. It was very unexpected." He grinned, scarcely able to contain himself.

"Overnight? You mean you and she are . . ." I stared at him, unsure what to make of this news.

"She has a townhouse in Cambridge. Did you know her family owns Sabores Ricos? Here's something else. She's not a child, she's twenty-six. And do you know why she looks so young? You're not going to believe this, but before Boston she lived in..." He frowned, pursed his lips, and squinted at me suspiciously. "You already knew. You have guilt written all over your face."

"Knew what?" I raised my eyebrows but avoided his gaze.

"Oliphant, I am Hernando, your brother. How did you know? Tell me NOW."

Damn it to hell. I gave up and told him about my conversation with Fanny at Sabores Ricos and my promise to keep her secret. My confession deflated him, and he sat silent for a long minute.

"She should have told me the truth," he said quietly.

"She planned to tell you, but she needed to know if you had feelings for her. She wanted you to give her a chance, that's all. She knew that wouldn't happen if you thought she'd been stalking you."

Hernando pondered my explanation. "I suppose you're right," he said as the anger in his eyes waned. "I wouldn't have had anything to do with her." I sat back in my chair, relieved at my narrow escape, while Hernando's grin ramped back up to full brilliance. "I asked Fanny to marry me," he said, "and Oliphant, she said yes! Fanny is going to marry me." His voice quivered with excitement.

I sat up straight on the sofa. I hardly knew what to say. "But she told me you'd been rebuffing her."

Hernando took in a breath to calm himself. "While you were in Las Vegas, she came to see me after class to drop my seminar. For personal reasons, she said. She started out of my office, turned, and said she'd hoped to be my friend. There were tears in her eyes."

"She didn't want to be your friend, Hernando. She was in love with you."

"Oliphant, for all I knew, she was an eighteen-year-old freshman. But I couldn't get her out of my head—everything about her. I couldn't wait to see her in my seminars, and I lived for our tutoring sessions. But I was her teacher. I tried to mask my feelings, but she'd been driving me crazy all semester."

"So what did you do?"

"When she opened my office door to leave, I ran to her and put my hand on her arm. She turned, confused, and I spilled out my heart to her. She listened but didn't say anything. When my words ran dry, she looked at me with a dazed expression I couldn't read. She was biting her lip. I thought I'd made a terrible mistake."

"That was a risky move. So what happened next?"

"She stood there for the longest moment, saying nothing. I felt like running away. Finally, she stepped forward, hugged me, and pressed her cheek against my chest. Then she looked up at me, tears running down her face, and kissed me. I couldn't believe what was happening. I tasted her on my lips and felt her breath and the smell of her—"

"Okay, I get the idea," I said. This openness was a side of my brother I'd not seen. Hernando and I had identical DNA, so where did it come from?

"All I could say was, 'Fanny, I've wanted this for so long.' I could hardly speak. She said, 'You have no idea, Hernando, no idea at all.' And then, later that night, she told me the entire story of her life in Nicaragua. Now here I am a week later, engaged to be married."

He swallowed, and I handed him a tissue. He rose from the sofa and passed Tex to me. He said, "Oliphant, I'm going to fix us cocktails. This is the happiest day of my life." He seemed ready to burst like a piñata.

"Thanks, just water for me." He looked at me curiously and trotted into the kitchen. I heard the refrigerator door open and ice clinking.

I had to think this through. What if Fanny really had been a young freshman? If it had been me, I would have played it safe and kept my mouth shut. But then Fanny would have walked out of my office forever, leaving me miserable and heartbroken. I knew well that sick feeling, because it had been with me all week. Hernando was a risk-taker, and I wasn't. I had let Regina go and done nothing to stop her. That's why I didn't feel the same joy Hernando felt about my own engagement. QT$\pi$ was beautiful and famous and sexy, and I knew most men would give anything to be in my shoes, but at that moment, all I could think about was Regina.

Hernando returned from the kitchen, handed me a glass of water, and sat down on the sofa. Tex hopped back onto his lap.

"Have you picked a date?" I was desperate to move my thoughts off myself.

"Next month. We're being married in New Jersey. We'll camp there for a week."

"Why are you going camping in New Jersey?"

"The Princeton biosphere. That's where we took the little frogs I delivered. The biosphere is the closest thing to a rainforest we could find on short notice. Neither of us can take much time off from work."

I was dreading what came next, but I couldn't stall any longer. "Hernando, I'm engaged too. I'm getting married in four days."

Hernando snorted into his tequila and almost dropped his glass. He coughed, and I handed him my water. He took a swallow and looked at me without smiling.

"Who to?" he said, glancing at the pile of correspondence on my desk.

"My girlfriend, QT$\pi$. Who else?"

"The hip-hop singer who came to our birthday party? But you met her just a few weeks ago. She took you to Las Vegas, right? Did you introduce her to your aunt and uncle? What did they think of her?"

I felt like I was being interrogated. "There wasn't time," I said, trying to mask my irritation. "We were going to elope in Las Vegas, but we decided to wait until Sunday."

"What's special about Sunday?"

"We're getting married at Fenway Park."

"The baseball stadium? Why?" Yes, I was being interrogated.

"The Red Sox are playing the Yankees. It's the biggest game of the season."

"Oliphant, you're not a baseball fan. I've never heard you say anything about baseball."

"It's for QTπ. It'll be good for her career."

Hernando sipped his tequila, then set down his glass. He looked at me and spoke in measured words. "Oliphant, how well do you know this woman?"

"When I'm with her, it's hard to think of anything else." I knew I hadn't answered his question. His voice sounded like he was speaking from the next room.

"You look pale," he said, frowning. "What's going on with you?"

"I'm just a little tired."

"So what do the two of you talk about?"

Truthfully, QTπ and I didn't talk much at all. I always felt fogbound around her, so I had I trouble finding words. I guess it was the sex I found thrilling, but, of course, I wasn't about to bring that up. So I just sat there trying to figure out what to say.

Hernando looked at me expectantly. "I bet she's good in bed. That's it, isn't it?"

"Um . . . I suppose that could be a consideration," I said, feeling my face redden.

He laughed. "So what else is new? You know, Oliphant, you're not the first man to be entranced by a beautiful woman. But I'm guessing you must occasionally say a few words to each other? Or maybe not," he said, laughing again.

I tried to sound indignant. "We talk about her career, and her clothing, and she introduced me to Mr. Goldfarb, her agent."

"How often do you speak to her?"

"She's very busy. Mostly I speak to Calista, her assistant." I looked down at Tex to avoid Hernando's gaze.

"Oliphant, stop. Look at me," he said. "I want to get this straight. You're getting married in four days at Fenway Park to a rapper you've known for less than a month. A woman you seldom talk to, who's never met your family, who's made no effort to know your friends, and who shares none of your interests. Do I have that about right? So what is it you like about her besides her bedroom agility? Not that that isn't important. But does she have a sense of humor? Does she like animals? What books does she read? Does she floss? Tell me something, anything."

"Hernando, you don't know QT$\pi$ well enough to see her other qualities." And those qualities were . . . what? I scrunched up my face to try to clear the mist.

"Oliphant, are you high on something?"

"What? No, of course not," I said, trying again to summon up indignation.

He frowned and leaned forward in his chair. "So why do you

look so miserable? You're exhausted. You haven't smiled since I came in the door."

I didn't disagree, but I couldn't explain myself. I had to stop obsessing about Regina and focus on my future. But when I tried to think about QTπ, there was never anything specific. I just felt this desire to be with her. Except I wasn't feeling it then.

Hernando studied my face and spoke soberly. "Oliphant, this woman has you under some sort of spell. Can't you see that?"

I said, "Why can't you give me the benefit of the doubt? I'm not an idiot, you know." He gave a non-committal nod, and we sat for a long minute, saying nothing. Maybe I was an idiot.

"And what about Regina?" Hernando said. "What does she think about your getting married? You two are very close."

"I don't think she approves of QTπ," I said weakly. I really, really didn't want to talk about Regina, but I couldn't stave off Hernando anymore.

"When did she tell you that?"

"Last Sunday, when I picked up Tex at her house. I-I don't think we're going to be friends anymore."

"Why? What happened?" I swallowed and sank back in my chair. I struggled to control my voice. I was coming unglued. He didn't wait for me to answer. "Oliphant, how do you feel about not seeing Regina again?"

His question came like an electric jolt. I wanted to throw up. "I feel terrible," I said, my voice choking. "I've never felt so lonely. I haven't slept for three nights." My eyes filled with tears and, embarrassed, I turned my head toward the wall. Then I heard Tex whimper and felt him licking my palm. I glanced down and saw he'd pulled loose an old sock wedged between two seat cushions.

He looked up at me, pawed at it, and wagged his tail. "Not now, Tex," I said.

Hernando studied my face, stood, and said, "No more water for you, Oliphant. I'm getting you some tequila. We've got some talking to do." He returned a minute later and handed me a glass. I took a large swallow and felt its warmth in my stomach. I tried to relax and clear my head.

"Now, here's what I think," he said. I remembered he'd used the same words after reading Fanny's short story in his seminar. I tried to remember the story. It was about a woman who let her true love slip away because she lacked the courage to take a risk. "Regina is more than just your friend, Oliphant. You're head over heels in love with her. You've been pining away for months. Half the women you meet remind you of her."

I shook my head defiantly. "Hernando, I can't let myself think that. There's no point. Regina and I have talked about this. She can't handle romantic involvements, with me or anyone else." I hoped the tequila would kick in soon.

"People change, Oliphant. Suppose you're wrong? If Regina doesn't have feelings for you, why did she get so upset when you told her you were engaged to that rapper woman?"

Hernando's logic brought me up short. Was that possible? He continued, "Look at it this way. You might be correct about Regina, and if so, she's gone forever. But maybe you're not correct. Maybe she's heartsick too. You owe it to yourself to find out."

Unlikely perhaps, but a theoretical possibility. "I suppose I could call and tell her how I feel about her."

"How *do* you feel about her? Would you break your engagement to QT$\pi$ to keep her?"

"Yes, I would," I said without hesitation, surprising myself.

Hernando reached out and put his hand on my arm. "Then this is your last chance, Brother. Get your butt over to the phone and tell her you're coming over. You need to tell her how you feel about her. Now!"

Hernando was right: I had nothing to lose. I took a fresh swallow of tequila and set the glass on the table. With my heartbeat thumping in my ears, I picked up my desk phone and pushed Regina's speed-dial number. The phone rang five times with no answer. She didn't use voicemail. "Wait longer," Hernando said. "Give her a chance."

I waited three more rings, and the receiver finally picked up.

"Yes?" It was a male voice, tinged with impatience.

Startled, I said, "Hello, is Regina there?"

"Who's calling?"

"Ollie Allyinphree."

"Hold on, I'll get her." I waited, my hands quivering. I tried to calm myself.

Hernando looked at me quizzically. I put my hand over the mouthpiece. "Some guy answered," I whispered.

"Maybe she has a brother?"

On the telephone, a man's voice yelled in the background. "Regina, phone! Ollie Somebody. I'll meet you in the car." I heard him set the phone down.

A minute later I heard Regina's voice. "Hello?"

"Regina, it's me."

"Oh, Ollie. I'm surprised to hear from you." Her voice had a steely quality, the words stilted.

I said, "Who was that? What's going on?"

"It's Eli."

"How did he find you?" I blurted. "Do you want me to come get you?"

"No, Ollie, I'm fine. Really."

"But you left California to get away from him." There was a long silence, and I realized I was holding my breath.

"That was wrong of me. I shouldn't have done that."

"Regina, I can't believe this."

"He needs me, Ollie. I wasn't sure before, but now I know he loves me."

"He doesn't love you! He doesn't care about anybody but himself." I tried to think of something else to say, but I was too upset. Or desperate. Or confused. Hernando was watching me with a grim expression.

"Regina, please," I said finally, and tried to calm my voice. "Please. You're making a mistake."

"You don't get to talk to me that way, Ollie," she said, her words tight with suppressed fury. "Anyway, who are you to tell me *I'm* making a mistake? My only mistake was running away, and I'm not going to do that again."

"So what are you going to do?"

Another silence.

Finally, "We have to get on with our lives, Ollie. You've made your bed. You're getting married in four days, and that's what you should be thinking about. It's time we each do the right thing."

"But—"

"Ollie, I have to go. I really do. I'm sorry."

"What happened?" Hernando said, as I slowly placed the phone in its cradle. "What did she say?"

I didn't answer for a few seconds, then I looked up at him. "I fucked up, Hernando. I really fucked up."

## 22

# BIG DAY AT
# FENWAY PARK

*Dear Ollie,*

*I am very happy to hear of your marriage to QTπ. I know you love her and believe she is right for you. I do have a favor to ask. Eli has been to many of her concerts and has wanted to meet her for years. Before the game on Sunday, he wants to stop by her suite to introduce himself. Could you leave a suite pass for us at the ticket office? Unfortunately, we can't stay for the ceremony because we're meeting with a travel agent to plan a trip to Nepal to inspect my properties. Afterward, we're planning on moving to Las Vegas.*

*Sincerely,*
*Regina*

**I woke late Sunday morning,** let Tex out the back door, and waited for him on the stoop in my pajamas while I squinted in the glare and rubbed fatigue from my eyes. The little guy had kept waking me during the night with restless whimpers, so it appeared both of us were anxious. A few minutes later, I was in the kitchen spooning out scrambled eggs when the phone rang.

"Hey, kid, this is your big day," Mr. Goldfarb said with forced exuberance, before launching into an extended monologue. "I'll pick you up at eleven, so be ready. Gates open at noon and game's at one-thirty. We'll convene at a suite next to the Pavilion Club to sign papers. Be sure to bring your checkbook, charge cards, and latest bank statements so I can put QTπ on your accounts. Also any life insurance policies. QTπ will meet us at the suite after she sings the national anthem. Don't be late, and wear a suit and red tie, nothing too conservative or pointy-headed. I'll give you a Red Sox baseball cap for the ceremony. We'll have time to rehearse, but it's all standard stuff. You have two words to say. Think you can handle that? How many times you been married, anyway?"

"This is my first," I mumbled, as I searched for a notepad. I felt like I was moving in slow motion.

"No kidding. Well, how about that. Oh, almost forgot. Calista's picking up QTπ's wedding dress this morning at Chez Charmante. I hear it's a knockout, designed by some Italian guy. I told her for thirty Gs, it ought to be. Nice of you to buy it for her. I also left five suite passes at the will-call kiosk for your family and friends. Who'd you invite?"

I'd bought QTπ a wedding dress? Things were happening very quickly. I rubbed my eyes again and tried to remember the question. "My aunt and uncle can't come," I said. "They're on an expedition in Australia banding baby albino kangaroos. It's a rare species that—"

"Sorry to hear that. Kangaroos. No kidding. I've always liked those big reptiles. Anybody else?"

"My brother and his fiancé. And a friend wants to drop by with an . . . acquaintance, to get QTπ's autograph." I couldn't bring myself to elevate Eli to the status of fiancé.

"Okay, but tell them to be quick. We're gonna be busy."

We hung up, and I looked at Tex across from me on the kitchen table. He sniffed at his eggs and looked back. "I know, Tex. I'm not hungry either."

I'd never given much thought to weddings. However, I did remember a college roommate's wedding in the apothecary garden of a small monastery. The bride wore a blue gown and a crown of orange blossoms, and three musicians played Greensleeves on lutes during the processional. The betrothed stood in the garden beside a large stone sundial and spoke their vows in Latin, and afterward, we all drank spiced wine. The ceremony was touching and beautiful, so if anybody had asked, I'd likely have said I hoped someday to have a wedding like that. What I wouldn't have said is that I wanted to be married wearing a baseball cap in front of forty thousand strangers with another million watching on TV. Not that there was anything wrong with that, but I couldn't loop my mind around the picture.

I'd always assumed married life would be a predictable extension of bachelorhood, like fresh blossoms on a rose bush. But now the rose bush was about to be stripped out by the roots. I stared at my scrambled eggs, still half asleep, and had this feeling I was careening down the tracks on a runaway rail car. That was a more accurate metaphor than a rose bush.

I was sorry Aunt Harriet and Uncle Joe couldn't be with me. I'd tried to call them, but they'd already left for Australia. They'd done their best to raise me after my birth parents died, but I knew they'd never planned on children. Still, it would have been good to talk to them. At least I had Hernando. I was picking at my breakfast when he called.

"Oliphant, this is your big day!" Hernando's enthusiasm sounded as forced as Mr. Goldfarb's. How many more people were going to tell me this was my big day?

"Regina is going to be at the game," I said. "With that Eli guy."

"What! How did that happen?"

"He's a big fan of QT$\pi$ and wants to meet her." I explained the will-call suite pass.

"Is Regina coming to the suite with him?"

"I'm not sure."

"Are you sure you want to go through with this wedding?" he said, his voice somber.

"Hernando, why are you being so judgmental?" I felt like I was outside my body listening to myself. "I just wish you liked QT$\pi$," I heard myself say.

"Whether I like her or not doesn't matter. The point is, do you love her?" When I didn't answer he said, "Oliphant, I'm your brother. You know I'll support whatever you want."

"I get that QT$\pi$ and I are different from each other," I said. "But love is something that develops over time, despite outward differences. You and I have talked about that."

"Right. Then Fanny and I'll see you at the stadium."

At precisely eleven a horn honked, and Mr. Goldfarb's car-service limo pulled into the driveway. I slipped Tex into the pocket of my white dress shirt, checked myself out in the hall mirror, and stepped onto the front porch. My big day had begun.

The drive to Fenway Park was pretty much a blur. I sat in the rear behind a partition and held Tex in my lap while Mr. Goldfarb chatted up front with the driver. I had no desire to meet Eli, and I didn't believe for a second Regina would want to live in Las Vegas. I sat back, stared out the window, and let my thoughts settle. I needed to be positive, to focus on my future, to get with the program. Regina had chosen another man and was probably going to marry him. It was time to accept that and stop fretting about her. QT$\pi$ was a beautiful woman who wanted me, and marrying her was my only sensible decision. We could work out our differences.

I set Tex on the seat beside me, leaned forward, clasped my hands between my knees, and tried to relax. We passed a small city park bordered by two tiny lakes, and as traffic swelled near the stadium, our car slowed to a peristaltic crawl. The driver finally surrendered at Boylston and Jersey, a block from the stadium. Mr. Goldfarb and I stepped onto the curb into a maelstrom of frenzied high schoolers. Jaywalking fans crowded the street, sidestepping street vendors hawking programs and souvenirs. Uniformed officers did their whistle-blowing traffic dance. Occasional arrogant-looking Yankee fans strutted down the street wearing blue-and-white baseball caps.

We elbowed our way down the block to the ticket office, where serpentine lines of ticket holders snaked through turnstiles. Everywhere were white jerseys with red numbers, and red jerseys with white numbers. The odd numbers outnumbered the evens. I saw Ted Williams's number nine and Jackie Robinson's forty-two, which about exhausted my knowledge of baseball uniform numbers. The air crackled with energy. I tried to embrace the spirit of the forty thousand people surrounding me, but I felt too much like an outsider.

Finally, we made it up the escalators to our suite. Mr. Goldfarb opened the door and stepped aside to let me in, and as I walked past, he gripped my arm. "Snap out of it, kid," he said. He was beginning to irritate me. I glared at him and said nothing until he let go of my arm.

The suite was small, designed for business meetings, with whitewashed concrete block walls and red indoor/outdoor carpeting. It was a tired place that vaguely smelled of mildew and cigarette smoke. A whiteboard was screwed to one wall, with sun-bleached team photos and posters fastened to the others, along with a large wall-mounted television tuned to a pre-game show. Two windows faced an employee parking lot, but there was no view of the field. I wondered if the suite was one of Mr. Goldfarb's economy moves.

An interior door to a tiny adjoining room stood open, and through it, I saw Calista laying out QTπ's wedding gown in its vinyl cover on a banquet table. Françoise from Chez Charmante was assisting her, and they both looked up and greeted me with perfunctory nods. QTπ hadn't arrived yet, and I assumed she was down by the playing field getting ready to sing the national anthem. One side of the suite had a built-in laminate-topped bar, and behind it, two men about my age wearing Red Sox base-ball caps were setting out cellophane-wrapped sandwiches, foil bags of potato chips, and a tray of weary-looking vegetables. Mr. Goldfarb spied the bar and beelined to it.

"Can I get you something?" he called, reaching for a vodka bottle and plastic cup. "It'll take the edge off."

"Thanks, maybe some water."

Just then the door to the outside corridor opened, and Hernando and Fanny entered. Hernando, my best man, had on his guerrilla dress uniform, with black beret, short-sleeved fatigues in jungle camouflage colors, and leggings tucked into gleaming black boots. He wore a ceremonial bandolier with sterling silver ammunition cartridges and matching dress grenades. Hernando waved a greeting, and Fanny came over and hugged me.

"How're you doing, Ollie?" she said, with a tight, worried smile. "Feeling okay?"

"Great. This is my big day," I said, with unnoticed sarcasm. I couldn't push out of my head how Regina had dropped me. Had I merely been somebody she could hang out with for a few months? Maybe she hadn't been truthful about fleeing that actor. Maybe she had been counting the days until he could join her.

The corridor PA system interrupted my thoughts. *"And now, to honor America, please join two-time Grammy nominee, QTπ, as she sings 'The Star-Spangled Banner.'"* Everybody stood and faced the room's TV monitor. The bar servers held their baseball caps over their hearts. The TV camera focused on QTπ, who stepped up to a microphone, smiled radiantly and bowed deeply. Then it cut away to fans waving tiny American flags and to close-ups of respectful, sober-faced players. After a brief piano introduction, QTπ started singing, her amplified voice low and throaty and rich with reverberation. She sang the anthem as a slow, traditional ballad, devoid of vocal twirls and pirouettes, and all went smoothly until her voice caught on "the land of the freeee," and squeaked like an injured chipmunk. She partly compensated for this flub by projecting the home-of-the-brave finale with great power, after which a huge cheer arose from the stands, followed immediately by the window-rattling scream of Air Force fighter jets racing over the stadium. The game between the Boston Red Sox and the New York Yankees was underway.

"Okay, kid, let's take a look at those bank statements," Mr. Goldfarb said as the TV monitor switched back to the playing field. He directed me to a small table in the back corner of the room, opened his briefcase, and pulled out a calculator and notepad. I handed him the manila folder I'd been carrying. He studied the statements for a few minutes. "Not bad, not bad at all," he said. Then he frowned. "But wait, how do you get access to the principal?" I explained there were legal restrictions. "Says who," he said, "the Algerians? Gimme a break. I'll get my lawyer to fix that. Shouldn't be a problem."

"But I don't need to get access—"

"Listen, Ollie, you're going to be married," he said, fixing me with a severe gaze. This was the first time he'd used my name. He set the bank statements on the table and crossed his arms. "It's time to think about your wife and *her* needs. It's not just about you anymore."

He was right that I hadn't been thinking about QT$\pi$ and her needs. Or anything else, actually. My head was filled with cotton. "Okay, whatever," I said.

"That's my boy." He started filling out the forms, while I sat silent. I extracted Tex from my coat pocket and placed him on the table. He sat watching me as Mr. Goldfarb wrote. I looked at the TV monitor, which was now showing the game, but I couldn't concentrate on the play.

A few minutes later a hush fell over the room as the door opened again. An attendant entered and held the door as QT$\pi$ followed, looking flushed. She still wore her national anthem outfit: white jump suit, tall platform heels, and a sequined white jacket with a large American flag on the back. One of the servers rushed up and handed her a plastic champagne flute.

"What is this shit?" she said to him, glaring at the contents.

"It's champagne, Miss Pi. You know, to celebrate."

QT$\pi$ clenched her lips. "Bring me some vodka. Rocks, no lime. Just vodka."

Calista emerged from the adjoining room and sidled up to us. "I thought that went very well," she said unconvincingly. "You looked beautiful, and I don't think anyone noticed that little slip."

"I looked like crap," QTπ said. "Why in God's name did you have me wear white? I looked like a fat ghost." She scowled in disgust.

"Françoise is here," Calista said, tight-lipped. "We need to get you changed. The photographer is waiting." The two of them retreated into the adjacent room and closed the door. QTπ hadn't noticed me sitting in the corner, and I felt a spasm of guilt for not going to her to be supportive. I wasn't thinking straight.

"Back to work," Mr. Goldfarb said. "Read me this account number, kid." He handed me one of the bank statements. I tried to read off the eleven-digit number but kept making mistakes. The number ended in an odd digit, and I wondered if banks used prime numbers to identify their accounts. To test my hypothesis, I divided the number by three. That didn't work. I knew five wouldn't work, so I tried seven. Not that either. Primes were a possibility. Mr. Goldfarb stared at me in disbelief, snatched the statement, and started transcribing the number himself. I reached over to pat Tex, who licked my hand and stood with his tail tucked between his legs. I looked away and noticed Hernando and Fanny watching me from across the room. I caught their gaze, and they came over to my table.

"Hey, Oliphant," Hernando said. "Let's take a break. We'll go explore the stadium for a few minutes." Fanny smiled at me and held out her hand. I stood as Mr. Goldfarb looked up from his form.

"What's going on?" he said. "We're not finished here."

I scowled at him. "You'll have to wait," I said, slipping Tex into my pocket. "I'll be back." Fanny gave me a gentle look and, taking my arm, led me out into the corridor, saying nothing.

They could tell I didn't want to talk. We wandered around the Big Concourse, watching fans line up to buy Monster Dogs, Fenway Franks, kettle corn, chicken tenders, cotton candy, double-burgers, doughnuts, soft-serve ice cream, sausage pizza slices, and nachos. The sight of the food made me feel vaguely nauseated, but when we came across a small stand with no customers selling *healthy options,* I bought a gluten-free pretzel from the bored attendant and pinched off a small piece for Tex. He sniffed it but seemed no hungrier than I was, so I gave the pretzel to Hernando.

After about twenty minutes we returned, and, feeling calmer, I found Mr. Goldfarb leaning against the bar, drink in hand, watching the game with the two servers and the photographer. The Yankees led three to two, top of the third. "Let's finish this up," he said, waving me impatiently toward the corner table. "We've still got lots to do."

I sat down as the door to the adjoining room opened and Françoise emerged. "Here comes the bride!" she announced triumphantly, as if introducing royalty. She looked over at the television. "Somebody mute that damn thing." The servers looked like they'd been stabbed in the throat, but one of them dutifully obeyed. A few seconds later, QTπ swept into the room wearing her full bridal regalia. Calista followed closely, holding the long, carefully folded train in her outstretched arms. QTπ beamed radiantly, her sour mood transformed by her dazzling Italian-designed wedding gown. I started to stand but became dizzy and had to sit down again. She stepped to the center of the room and twirled to showcase her perfection, nearly yanking the train out of Calista's hands. She stopped and glared at her assistant, whom she evidently blamed for the intractable physics of the situation.

The photographer disengaged himself from the now-silent television. He took QT$\pi$'s arm and escorted her to a corner of the room where he had set up a neutral backdrop flanked by large bouquets of fresh hydrangeas. I rose to join them, but he gestured for me to stay put. "I've got to set things up," he called. "It'll be a while."

QT$\pi$ looked up and noticed me for the first time. "Baby," she cried, rushing over to me, Calista and the wedding train in tow. "Where've you been? I've looked everywhere." To express her thwarted passion, she lightly touched a fingertip to her lips and then to mine. "I don't want to smudge my lipstick. There'll be time for that later," she said, laughing while Mr. Goldfarb smiled approvingly at this chaste display of pre-marital devotion.

QT$\pi$ posed amongst the hydrangeas while the photographer fiddled with his tripod and bulky camera. Françoise and Calista began arranging the lengthy train in a graceful curve at QT$\pi$'s feet but encountered a crisis when it turned out to be too long to fit the available space. "Damn Italians," Calista muttered as if everyone on the Italian peninsula from Leonardo da Vinci onward was to blame for this design flaw. The photographer quickly solved the problem by rearranging the bouquets and sliding the tripod farther out from the corner.

While Mr. Goldfarb continued with paperwork, I stroked Tex and gazed absently at the television. Just then a Red Sox batter hit a long double to right field, and runners scored from second and third. I heard a muted rumble from the crowd, and the screen said the Red Sox were up by one, with one out and a man on second. It was the bottom of the third inning. The crowd noise increased, and I looked over to see QT$\pi$ and Calista gaping at the open doorway to the corridor. Françoise walked in from the dressing area and froze. "Oh my, oh my," she said. A towering, backlit figure wearing a large Western hat over black curly hair stood in the open doorway. I had to squint to make out his features. He had that square-jawed outdoorsy look of men in 1960s cigarette commercials and was wearing a burgundy cravat with gold brocade waistcoat and lizard cowboy boots. A diamond horseshoe pin sparkled on his lapel.

Eli had arrived.

# 23

# DOG
# FIGHT

**"Can I help you?"** Mr. Goldfarb said, walking up to Eli. "This is a private party."

"I'm expected," the man said, looking down at him dismissively. He was at least six inches taller than Mr. Goldfarb, three inches taller than me. "I'm here for QTπ." His eyes roamed the room, ignoring the men, and then zeroed in on the three women standing speechless by the hydrangeas. The mouth twitched slightly, the hint of a grin. He straightened, shoulders back, walked over to them, and removed his hat. "Ladies," he said in a practiced drawl, bowing slightly and extending his hand to QTπ. "I'm Eli."

She accepted his offering as if being addressed by the Pope and gave what appeared to be a slight curtsy. "Hello, I'm QTπ," she simpered, still grasping his hand.

"I know who you are, Miss Pi. I know all about you."

"Oh my," Françoise said again.

"I've been wanting to meet you for years," Eli said. "I'm a great admirer."

"I just *love* talking to my admirers," QTπ said, leaning toward him and speaking in a throaty whisper. She dropped her free hand to her side and surreptitiously fluttered her fingers at Calista and Françoise, who took the hint and vanished.

Mr. Goldfarb had returned to the bar, so I left Tex on the table and stood, trying to decide whether to introduce myself. I looked at Eli and was pleased to see his boot heels were at least two inches high. Ha, three inches down to one inch. At that moment I felt pretty much the same way Mina Harker's husband must have felt when he looked at Count Dracula. Nevertheless, I'd decided to force myself to be polite when Tex barked. I glanced back at the doorway and saw Regina standing there, looking confused. She was heart-wrenchingly beautiful. I set Tex on the floor, and as he ran to greet her, I changed direction to follow. Everything was happening too quickly again.

"Hi," I gasped, discovering I'd been forgetting to breathe. Eli and QTπ had disappeared. And so had Fenway Park, Boston, and the Western Hemisphere. There was nothing in the universe except Regina standing before me. I wanted to throw my arms around her.

She leaned over to pet Tex, who now seemed to echo her confusion, displaying none of the effervescence her presence usually provoked. "Hello, Oliphant, it's nice to see you," she said stiffly, standing up and reaching out to shake my hand with a clammy palm. Her cheeks were pale. I glanced at Eli, who evidently hadn't noticed her.

"You feeling okay?" I said.

"Yes, I feel fine. Congratulations on your marriage, Ollie. I'm sorry Eli and I can't stay. We have to meet our travel agent for our trip to Nepal."

"Come sit down," I said, gesturing to the table where Mr. Goldfarb and I had been working. Regina sat facing me with her back to QTπ, who was now in earnest conversation with Eli. QTπ's hand was on his arm, and I saw her glance at Regina and me and whisper something. He turned and looked at us, then whispered to QTπ, who smiled knowingly. I knew I should have been bothered by his flirting with my fiancée, but in fact, I didn't care. I tried to think of something to say to Regina.

"So you're really quitting the wine store?"

"Yes, and then we're moving to Las Vegas. I don't know the city, but Eli says we'll be very happy there."

Her voice had the flat, steely tone I remembered from our phone call, and she looked down at the table as she spoke. I shut my eyes in an effort to unfog my thoughts. We sat in silence, and I overheard QTπ laugh and say, "I love Las Vegas too. Have you been to Valhalla yet? It just opened, you know." I couldn't hear what Eli said, except for "Lamborghini," and saw Calista and Françoise look up. They stood discreetly in the doorway of the dressing room within earshot.

Regina twisted in her chair and gave Eli a mechanical little wave, but he didn't see her, so she turned back toward me. "Eli says there's no reason for me to have left him," she said in the same flat voice. "He told me about the trouble he'd gone through to find me, and how that proves how much he loves me." To me, that didn't prove anything, but before I could challenge this absurd perception, I saw Calista walk up to QTπ and Eli.

"What is it, Calista?" QTπ said, frost in her voice.

"I'm sorry to interrupt, but it's getting close to the seventh inning, and we've got to snap a few photos of the bride and groom.

The photographer has everything ready to go." She glanced over and gestured for me to join them.

I pushed my chair back just as QT$\pi$ gave a loud shriek. Her face had turned fiery, and she stood rigid, staring at the floor. There, Tex perched atop her meticulously displayed wedding train, looking up at her with wagging tail. Next to him on the embroidered silk was a large bright-yellow stain. Françoise gasped and stood open-mouthed as the stain slowly diffused over the exquisite hand-stitched fabric of her customer's Italian masterpiece.

"What the hell," QT$\pi$ screamed at Tex. "You've ruined it. You've ruined my goddamn wedding." She turned and glared at me. "This is your fault!" she shouted, shoving her finger toward me. "We're getting rid of that damned dog. Right after the wedding, out he goes." She yanked on the train, and Tex tumbled off onto the floor.

"What! No!" I yelled, jumping to my feet and knocking over my chair. Regina also jumped up, speechless.

"There's no need to wait," Eli said, stepping forward. "I'll take care of this right now." He moved quickly to confront Tex, who had already regained his balance and was crouched, his tail rigid, ears back, his eyes focused on his attacker. "I've never been able to stand these little runt mongrels," he said as he raised his right boot six inches above the carpet, aimed, and stomped down hard. But Tex barked and feinted to the right.

"Stop!" I yelled and kicked my chair out of the way. Regina yelled also and started toward Tex. I followed, but the table and upturned chair slowed me down.

"Get the little son of a bitch," QT$\pi$ yelled, a technically correct but likely fortuitous observation about Tex's ancestry. Eli stomped again, but this time Tex smoothly feinted to the left, turned, and dived under a fold of the wedding train.

"Get him, get him," QTπ cried.

"Where'd the little rat go? I don't see him," Eli shouted, his face crimson. I didn't see him either. Regina stood in the center of the room, stunned.

"There, he's over there!" QTπ grabbed Eli's arm and pointed at the floor toward the far end of her train, near the dumbfounded photographer. Tex was standing again on the train. He barked twice, as if daring Eli to attack. QTπ yanked on the train to dislodge him, but there was too much slack.

Eli took three steps toward Tex and again raised his boot.

"Get him!" QTπ said.

"No," Françoise screamed, "not on the dress!"

"Tex, look out!" I yelled.

Our warnings came in time. With Eli and QTπ in pursuit, Tex bolted through the legs of the tripod into the center of the room. The photographer tried to move out of their path, but QTπ lost her balance when her wedding train caught on the tripod's adjustment knobs and knocked it over.

"Hey, that's an expensive camera," the photographer said. "You break it, you bought it."

"Fuck off," QTπ said, as she struggled up from the floor.

By then, I was panicked and desperately trying to reach Tex, but Regina got to him first and shoved Eli out of the way. "Tex, come!" she said, and Tex yipped and jumped into her outstretched hands. She clutched him to her chest. I was still a few feet away but could see his body quiver, seemingly with excitement, not fear. He gave Regina a quick lick but never lost his focus on Eli, who had regained his footing and turned to her, his face contorted with rage.

"Give him to me," Eli said. "Give him to me right now." He towered above her, his face still crimson.

Regina ignored him and hugged Tex more tightly. Then she looked up at him. "I never want to see you again," she said in a furious tone. There was nothing flat about her voice now. She was back!

Eli looked at her in disbelief. "Oh, you are making such a big mistake." He reached over and grabbed her arm. She cried out and flinched as he raised his other hand.

Something inside me snapped, and the cloud in my head dissipated. I felt a deep, overwhelming rage, with tears stinging my eyes. I grabbed Eli's vest and yanked him around to me. I felt myself choking with hatred. "You cretin," I screamed in his face, probably the first time I'd ever called anybody that. "Get your lousy, fucking hands off her," I added. Eli let go of Regina's arm and looked at me, mystified. I was shocked to see fear in his eyes. I couldn't imagine what he saw in my eyes. Regina stepped back a few feet.

"Hey, ease up, buddy," he said. "This isn't any of your business."

"You are so wrong," I said. "You need to leave her alone and get out *now!*"

Just then Hernando arrived at my side from across the room. He stood ramrod straight, the silver ammunition cartridges on his bandolier gleaming in the sunlight from the windows. "Let me help," he said, grabbing Eli's lapel and yanking him forward until their faces were inches apart. Eli swallowed and stood motionless while Hernando stared at him, unblinking. "My brother told you to leave."

Eli's eyes darted between the two of us. He started to protest, when QTπ rushed over and grabbed his arm. "Eli, are you okay?" she said, giving Hernando a contemptuous glare. "Did that man hurt you?"

"I'm okay," Eli said, his shoulders sagging, his voice hinting at mortal injury.

"Oh my God, Eli, what did they do to you?" QTπ said, placing the flat of her hand on his chest to ease his pain. He reached up and put his palm over her hand.

I turned to Regina who, still shaking, had cradled Tex to her chest with ferocious intensity. "I'm so sorry," I said to her, not completely sure what I was apologizing for.

She gripped my arm. "Ollie, I've got to get out of here. This is too much. We'll talk." She hurried through the door, still holding Tex. The room fell eerily still. QTπ stood hugging Eli, her wedding train splayed out on the floor behind her. Several footprints on the hand-stitched silk now accompanied the yellow stain. Françoise stared at them in despair. Calista stood in the doorway, her arms crossed. I looked around the room, exhaled, and turned to Hernando and Fanny standing beside me.

"I'm out of here too," I said. I started to follow Regina when Mr. Goldfarb stepped forward from the bar counter.

"Hey, folks," he said, "let's all calm down. We've got a wedding coming up. This is a stressful time, but we need to pull ourselves together and—"

"For God's sake, shut up," I said, glaring at him like I was ready to rip out his tongue, which I was.

QT$\pi$ started crying. "What am I going to do?" she bawled as I started toward the exit. Twin ugly streams of tears and black mascara edged down her face, highlighting the very years she'd tried to conceal. Eli cradled her in his arms, and she sobbed into his chest.

"Go ahead, she's all yours," I said to him, as I opened the door to the corridor. I could hear my voice quiver with contempt. "You two deserve each other."

"What did I do?" he said, incredulous that trying to stomp on the tiny dog his fiancée adored and then threatening to strike her could in any way be held against him.

Mr. Goldfarb turned to Eli and QT$\pi$. "Now hold on," he said, with an air of desperation. "We've got a problem to solve. There are forty thousand people out there expecting a wedding, and one way or the other, we've got to give them one." He looked at the two of them clinging to each other, and his face brightened. "I've got an idea," he said. I stared at him in disgust, and on my way out the door, muttered something about slimy weasels, but I didn't think he heard me.

Outside in the corridor, I looked for Regina but didn't see her. I hurried to the down escalator. The corridor was deserted, except for a small cluster of women in line at the women's restroom. I was about to take the escalator down to the stadium exit when I remembered I'd left behind my checkbook statements and financial records. "Damn it to hell," I said in a voice that would have attracted notice had the corridor not been nearly empty. I trotted back to the suite and pushed open the door just as Hernando and Fanny were leaving.

"Nice going, Brother," Hernando whispered, squeezing my shoulder. Fanny beamed at me. "We'll talk later," he added. I slipped into the room and saw Eli, QTπ, and Mr. Goldfarb sitting at the table at the back. The wedding train was piled on the floor beside QTπ, looking like a dirty wadded bed sheet. I spotted my papers on the bar counter and crept toward them, hoping nobody would notice me.

"That's a wonderful suggestion," I heard QTπ say, "but we've just met." She smiled coyly at Eli and placed her hand over his. QTπ seemed to have a remarkable ability to extract herself on short notice from the dark pit of emotional trauma.

"Look, this is just for show," Mr. Goldfarb said, "so don't get carried away. We gotta get through this ceremony. You don't like each other, you get divorced afterward. Happens all the time."

"I feel like I've known you forever," Eli said to her, shaking his head in wonderment. I shook my head in disbelief.

"Great," Mr. Goldfarb said. "Then it's settled. Fifty-fifty split. I'll fill out the papers. Now, I need you both to get ready. We're running out of time." He turned toward the doorway of the adjoining room where Calista and Françoise stood silently, looking ill. "Hey, Calista," he called, gesturing toward QTπ. "Get her cleaned up, will you?"

Calista didn't respond. She stood in the dressing room doorway, biting her lower lip, her gaze fixed on QTπ. Then she turned to Mr. Goldfarb. "Clean her up yourself," she said. "I'm out of here too." She abruptly turned on her heel and headed toward the door just as I reached it. "Bitch," she muttered as the two of us stepped out into the corridor. Once the door closed behind us, she stopped and exhaled, her face flushed. Then to my amazement she turned and hugged me.

"Good luck, Ollie," she said with a brittle smile. "You dodged a fastball today."

I said, "What're you going to do now, Calista?"

She shrugged. "I dunno. Something will turn up." She started to walk away and then stopped and faced me again. "Ollie, you're a good man. I hope you know that." Then leaving me standing beside the doorway, she walked briskly toward the escalator.

The corridor was still deserted, so I just stood, overwhelmed and unsure what to do next. In the prior five minutes, my life had changed direction completely, but toward what I didn't know. I still didn't get why I'd so misjudged QT$\pi$, but Calista was right: I'd dodged a fastball. I found myself smiling and realized I was proud of myself. I'm not a particular fan of baseball metaphors, but I'd just stepped up to the plate, and it felt really good.

I saw Regina come out of the women's restroom. She smiled weakly, still clutching Tex, and I walked over to her. "Hi," I said, feeling suddenly nervous.

"You okay?" she said.

"I think so. You?"

"I'm a little shell-shocked. I guess I'm not going to Nepal after all," she said with a mirthless half-smile. She looked down at the floor for a moment and then looked up. "Ollie," she said, "I feel badly about all this. I've mistreated you, and I've said things I shouldn't have." Her voice caught, and she struggled to contain herself.

I tried to laugh. "I was going to say the same thing. Regina, I'm so sorry."

"I guess we've got a lot to talk about." She smiled grimly. "But not today."

"No, definitely not today," I said.

"Here, you hold Tex," she said, passing him to me. I cradled him against my chest. He gave me a lick and a tail wag and seemed surprisingly calm. "He saved us, you know," she said, reaching over and stroking his head. Her fingertips brushed the top of my hand. "He knew exactly what he was doing."

I nodded and blinked, feeling tears well up. Regina caught my eye. "Ollie, I don't understand what happened to either of us," she said with a sober smile. She placed her hand on my arm. "But it's over now. And we're still going to be friends, right?"

"I very much hope so." I don't know why I said that, because it was only half true. The whole truth was that I desperately wanted to kiss her. Instead, I placed my hand over her hand. She glanced down and I moved my hand away. I couldn't take much more of this; I needed to know where we were headed.

"I guess we've proved Professor Von Hindenberg's theory," she said.

I looked at her blankly. "Lucretia Von Hindenberg, from the college? What theory?"

"From her book about platonic friendship between the sexes."

"Platonic friendship?" It was beginning to come back to me. Hernando had talked about that.

"What you and I have. About how romantic entanglements end in disaster. How passion and sex are a barrier to intimacy." I was pretty dubious about this theory, but I got where she was coming from; her relationship with Eli had certainly been disastrous. Also, I was one to talk.

"Professor Von Hindenberg is lecturing this Wednesday," Regina said, seeming to read my thoughts. "Why don't we go hear her?"

I gave a non-committal shrug, which I intended to mean maybe. "Do you feel like doing anything now?"

"Ollie, I'm pretty wiped from, well, all this." She out-stretched her hands, still quivering, palms up. "What did you have in mind?"

"There's a poetry reading at Damned Spot this afternoon, but I'm pretty tired, too, so—"

"You mean the poems of Ferdinand Laholli?"

"You know them?" I said. Regina was constantly surprising me.

"I do," she said, "though I'm told they're better in the original Albanian." She smiled at me. "Yes, that I could handle."

We started toward the escalator when I had a thought. "Regina, are you sure you want to cancel your trip to Nepal?"

She stopped and turned to me. "I'm sure they'll let me return the tickets. Why?"

I smiled and held her gaze. "I thought you might change your mind if you had a different traveling companion and his small dog."

"You'd go with me?" she said, brightening. "Oh, Ollie, that would be wonderful, but I didn't think you liked to travel."

"I've read about Kathmandu for years. Yes, I'd love to go with you and see it in person. If I could bring Tex, of course." She laughed, but before she could say anything, a red-faced fan raced by, breathing hard and almost colliding with us.

"Sorry," he gasped as he thundered past and galloped down the escalator. He yelled to us over his shoulder. "Two outs, bases loaded. This is an unbelievable game! Historic. Hurry or you'll miss it."

"Remind me who's playing," I said to Regina, and she grinned at me. We followed him down the escalator but turned toward the exit. Once outside the stadium, we walked on nearly deserted sidewalks toward the Kenmore Station subway stop. The afternoon sun had warmed the air, so I took off my suit coat and loosened my tie. The day was peaceful, the stillness punctuated by occasional bursts of crowd noise from the stadium, like waves crashing. A few minutes later, we heard the muffled reverberations of Mendelssohn's wedding recessional.

"I've always liked the wedding march," Regina remarked, taking my arm. "It was played at Victoria's wedding to Prince Frederick William of Prussia in January 1858. That's when it became famous."

"Really?" I said. "I didn't know that. Tell me more."

# 24

# PROFESSOR VON HINDENBERG'S THEORY

*Dear Valued Customer:*

*We regret that because of high demand, we are currently unable to fill your order for the Lucretia Von Hindenberg book,* Hands Off: Conquering the Scourge of Romance. *We do have in stock the author's popular earlier work,* Crafting the Perfect Suicide Note, *available in our newly expanded Existential Despair section (between Ruined Marriage and Childhood Trauma). Sorry, no returns.*

*Sincerely,*
*F. Truman Carver,*

**"Let me put it to you this way,"** the professor said to us. "How many of you have been in a romantic relationship that ended badly, leaving you miserable and desperate?" Every hand in the lecture hall went up, Regina's, I thought, with particular conviction. I guessed Professor Von Hindenberg was in her seventies but surprisingly energetic. She paced back and forth across the stage, her arms outstretched as if to embrace the multitude of miserable and desperate souls sitting before her.

"And for how many of you did that relationship begin with a kiss—not a peck-on-the-cheek kiss, but a kiss of passion? Let me be frank: a kiss of *carnal* passion?" She stopped and her eyes took in the audience.

Regina raised her arm, and belatedly I did too, although the two of us had never so much as held hands. In the three days since our near-marriage disasters about all we'd said was how relieved we were to be free from "those people." But free for what?

"The kiss," Professor Von Hindenberg sneered, as if speaking of dog excrement, "is the bellwether of impending disaster." As she spoke, the iconic 1939 smooch between Clark Gable and Vivien Leigh flashed behind her on a huge video screen. The audience murmured recognition, but I was unsure what impending disaster the professor had in mind. However, she was a step ahead of me.

"Reflect upon the act of kissing," she said somberly, as she turned toward the screen and then, grimacing at its savage display of animal desire, quickly back to us.

"The clumsy pressing together of lips, with the possibility of bruising the mouth.

"The exchange of bacteria and viruses – leading to likely illness and possible death.

"The transfer of decayed food remnants to another's mouth, not to mention the stench of bad breath and dyspepsia."

It seemed to me there was arguably another side to her case, but the surrounding nods suggested I held the minority view.

"Do you remember what Rhett Butler said to Scarlet O'Hara?" the professor asked. 'You need kissing badly. You should be kissed, and often.' She paused to let us ponder the moral depravity of Rhett's words.

"Is it any wonder," she continued, drawing herself straight, her shoulders held back with fierce determination, her voice a steel file, "that these disgusting, carnal practices are promulgated throughout our culture? The arts—music, literature, poetry—tell us not only to succumb to our base instincts but, God in heaven, *to celebrate them!*"

I looked around the room and recognized several English professors from the college. Two senior poets sitting near us evidently had celebrated base instincts and were whispering to each other with worried expressions. Professor Von Hindenberg fixed a severe gaze on them.

"If you doubt me," she said, her rising tone daring anyone in the audience to doubt her, "then listen to these words by Brazilian poet Olavo Bilac, written more than a century ago, and consider their message of depravity." She opened a small book and began to read, her amplified words reverberating off the walls of the auditorium in a dark, ominous rumble.

> *Naked, but for love modesty is unfit,*
> *On my mouth I pressed hers.*
> *And, in carnal trembling, she said:*
> *—Lower, my love, I want your kiss!*
>
> *In the brute unconsciousness of desire*
> *Frenetic, my mouth obeyed,*
> *And her breasts, so rigid I bit,*
> *Making them stir in sweet uprising.*
>
> *In sighs of infinite enjoyment*
> *She told me, still almost shouting:*
> *—Lower, my love!—in a frenzy.*

*In her belly I laid my mouth*
*—Lower, my love!—she said, crazy,*
*Moralists, forgive! I obeyed...*

The audience reacted with shocked silence as Professor Von Hindenberg closed the book. Well, almost everyone. A young couple two rows in front of us stood, their faces flushed, and raced hand in hand from the auditorium, apparently unpersuaded by the virtues of platonic friendship. I glanced over at Regina, half-hoping her response might be like theirs, but her rapt attention told me there was no such luck.

"Well, what do you think?" she said, after we returned home. We sat on the sofa in my living room eating chocolate truffles. I built a fire, turned on the stereo, and opened a bottle of sparkling rosé. Regina took a truffle from a plate on the coffee table and broke off a tiny piece for Tex, who was stretched out on the arm of the sofa, and handed the rest to me. A Nepal travel brochure, marked up with yellow Post-it notes, sat on the coffee table.

I swallowed the truffle and collected my thoughts. "That was a much bigger audience than I expected," I said. "I didn't realize there'd be so much interest in her book."

"It's on the bestseller lists," she replied, glancing at *Hands Off: Conquering the Scourge of Romance* on the coffee table. After the lecture, I stood in line with her for fifteen minutes because she wanted to buy it. For now, I was prepared to play along, but soon, I needed to know if platonic friendship was Regina's long-term goal or if she was just running scared. That was going to be a difficult conversation.

"So, did you like the professor's method?" Regina said,

evidently unwilling to let me off the hook.

"I'm not sure, but I'm willing to give it a try," I said without enthusiasm. I knew the idea that physical passion is a barrier to intimacy dated from the Greeks, but the new twist was the professor's recipe for coping with it.

Regina relaxed and exhaled, and I realized she had been holding her breath. She leaned forward, took a healthy swallow, and set her wineglass on the coffee table. Turning to me, she said with a hopeful expression, "How about now? This can be our first practice session."

"Okay, you go first." I wasn't sure what she had in mind.

She retrieved her book bag off the floor and extracted a notepad from the lecture. She looked at her notes while I sat silently, and then up at me. "Okay, step number one. Tell me if there are things about me you find attractive? Anything at all." Her voice had a worried tone, as if she half-expected I might come up empty-handed. "Of course there are," I said. "I like your sense of humor, that you love animals, that you enjoy Tibetan throat singing." I gestured in the direction of the stereo speakers, from which came the near-subsonic drone of Tibetan monks who had learned to mimic the mating calls of sperm whales.

"No, I don't mean those kinds of things," she said, frowning slightly. "I mean, physically. Are there things about my *body* you find attractive, that could provoke carnal desire? I mean theoretically, of course, not that you would ever—"

"You mean like your face? You have a pretty face." I smiled as I remembered the first time I had seen her image on my computer screen. "Actually, I think it's the prettiest face I know," I blurted without thinking.

She stiffened at this disclosure, but I couldn't tell whether she was pleased or discomfited. Then she smiled back at me and spoke sternly. "Ollie, I think we're supposed to be specific. What about my face do you like specifically?" She turned her head so I could inspect it from different angles.

I was in dangerous territory. I loved Regina's smile, and the wrinkles around her mouth when she laughed, and her intelligent, thoughtful eyes, and the graceful curve of her chin, and the soft glow of her skin when she blushed. And that was just for starters. But I needed to be cautious. "Your ears," I said. "I think your ears are attractive."

"My ears?" she said, furrowing her brow. "Really? Well okay, now step number two. According to Professor Von Hindenberg, you should touch my ears carefully and describe exactly what they feel like." She turned to face me, scooping her hair to the side, her cheeks slightly flushed with that soft glow I liked.

I took my hands and very slowly and lightly stroked her ears, starting from above, just at her hairline, and then inching my fingers around the back curve of each ear, penetrating ever so slightly into the opening with my thumb, and then squeezing her delicate lobes between my thumb and index finger. I continued moving my fingers slowly down the smooth skin on her neck. She shut her eyes, presumably to analyze the sensation more objectively. Her body quivered as my fingertips moved down her neck to her shoulders.

My task completed, I realized I, too, had been holding my breath. I tried to breathe normally and struggled to come up with a description of my experience. "I thought that was very informative," I said, stalling. Touching Regina's ears felt electrifying, like nothing I'd ever experienced, but I didn't want to disappoint her.

I inhaled, tried to relax, and blathered on. "In humans, the outer visible ear, or *pinna*, is called the *auricle,* and is mostly cartilage." I glanced at Tex, who was still perched on the sofa arm, and saw him watching us, his tail motionless.

"Yes, good," Regina said. "Cartilage. That's all ears are. See, there's nothing erotic about cartilage."

I continued. "Like other vertebrates, we have a pair of ears placed symmetrically on the sides of our head. That's what gives us the ability to know the direction of…" My mind went blank. Regina was watching me with a studiousness that didn't seem warranted by the minuscule profundity of my analysis. "Maybe I should try it again?" I said.

"No, my turn," she said, swallowing. She took another sip of rosé, and I did likewise. A large sip. "I particularly like your chin," she said, as she set down her wineglass and inspected my face. "Now shut your eyes." I did as instructed, and a moment later felt her fingertips touch my face. My skin tingled as if from a mild electric shock. She held her hands still for a moment and then slid them downwards, lightly brushing my cheeks. She curled her thumbs under my chin. I felt her fingers slide slowly over my lips, barely touching the skin. The heat of my breath reflected off her fingertips. I could feel my heart beating rapidly.

"I'm not sure this is working," I stammered, opening my eyes. I was beginning to suspect Professor Von Hindenberg had never actually tried her method on another person.

"It is more difficult than I expected," Regina replied in a weak voice. "Maybe we just need more practice. Let's try again. So what else do you find pretty about me? How about something below my head?"

"Your ankles are nice," I said, frantically seeking a calming, neutral body part.

"Okay, let's try those," she said with an amused smile. "I'll shut my eyes and concentrate." So we went back and forth several times. We tried toes, hands, knees, and elbows, but Professor Von Hindenberg's method clearly required more practice than we'd anticipated.

"It's getting warm in here, don't you think?" Regina said after a few minutes, when we paused to rest. She refilled our wineglasses and reached for a truffle, breaking off a tiny piece for Tex. Her face was flushed, and I was having trouble catching my breath. We were still sitting side by side on the sofa, and I felt our arms brush. Regina flinched and pulled away. "Oh, sorry," she said. "I need to take this off." She leaned forward and struggled to remove her blue cardigan. I helped her wrestle it off her shoulders. She folded it and set it on the coffee table. She unbuttoned the top two buttons of her white blouse and picked an issue of *Ancient Asian Fonts* off the coffee table to fan herself.

"That's better," she said after a moment. She returned the magazine to its resting place and sank back into the sofa. We sat for a minute, trying to calm ourselves while we listened to sperm whale mating calls. Regina seemed lost in thought. Her neck was long and graceful, and the curve of her breasts pushed against the fabric of her blouse. I couldn't take my eyes off her.

Finally she took a breath, exhaled, and sat upright. "Okay, let's try one more time. Your turn again. Ollie, tell me something else you find pretty about me." She closed her eyes and sat there expectantly.

I looked at her and felt my face redden, hoping she wouldn't be able to read my thoughts, which had turned decidedly non-platonic. I was glad Professor Von Hindenberg wasn't in the room watching. I searched for some body part we hadn't yet covered. "I'm sure your navel is pretty," I said. I had never seen Regina's navel, but I figured I was on safe ground. But then I realized I didn't want to be on safe ground. I was tired of always being on safe ground.

"Regina, I've changed my mind," I said. "Open your eyes, okay?" She looked puzzled but followed my instruction. I took my right hand and very slowly moved it to her left breast. She gasped when I touched her, but didn't push my hand away, so I held it there, cupping her breast, and I could feel her heart racing. Or maybe that was my heart. All thoughts of Professor Von Hindenberg's method had vanished. She sat quietly and watched me intently.

Holding her gaze, I removed my hand from her breast, reached out and slowly unfastened the remaining buttons of her blouse. I slipped it off her shoulders and folded it on the coffee table. Underneath, she wore a delicate lace-trimmed bra. She was painfully beautiful. With my eyes never leaving her face, I pulled her toward me, reached behind her, and unfastened her bra. The straps slipped over her shoulders, and it fell to her lap. She draped the bra on the sofa arm. Then she turned back toward me, her breasts revealed, her chest slowly rising and falling. She folded her hands loosely in her lap and trembled slightly. She smiled at me and bit her lower lip. At that instant, she seemed so vulnerable and courageous in the flickering firelight, I wanted to take care of her forever.

I reached out my right hand and again cradled her breast. The skin was soft and flawless, her nipple erect against my palm.

I caressed it with my fingertips. Then I leaned my head over and shut my eyes and embraced her. I put my mouth over her breast and felt her nipple with my tongue. She moaned softly and pulled my head against her chest, her fingers stroking my hair. I wanted her to hold me there so I could feel her heart beating and the warmth of her body.

Instead, she gently pushed me away.

"Ollie, I need to ask you something," she said in a soft, shaky voice. "I'm sorry, but I really do."

"Now?"

She nodded and folded her arms, covering her breasts.

"I know my timing isn't the best." That seemed to be the understatement of the decade. I propped myself upright. "Okay," she said, taking a deep breath, "here goes." She looked at me with a grim smile. Not again, I thought, fearing the worst. I couldn't go through that again.

"Ollie, I need to know why you decided to . . . touch me there. I thought we'd never do that. For me, it's a big step and I'm scared. This changes everything."

I searched for words, and my voice was also trembly. "I don't want a faint heart, Regina. I hoped you'd understand. I was terrified you wouldn't."

She nodded. "But I need to know what this . . . *development* means to you. What are you thinking right now? About us, you know, being more than friends?"

I wasn't sure what I was thinking right then. I don't think I was thinking anything. I suppose I must have looked confused, because now she spoke with an edge of desperation.

"Ollie, I want to know if you'll let me in?"

Let her in? I struggled to find something to say. I didn't know what she meant. "Do you mean *in* as an adverb meaning to be enclosed by—"

"Ollie, stop! Don't do that now. I need you to answer." She sat upright, clutching her arms to her chest, her lower lip aquiver.

I forced myself to ponder her question. I remembered sitting at my computer, answering her inquiries about my medical history and not wanting our conversation to end. I remembered my heart hammering when she spilled wine on me at my birthday party, and showing her Uncle Gus's book, and playing "Olly Olly In Free" with Tex. I thought about our concerts and lectures and poetry readings and eating duck confit at her home on a balmy spring evening and walking in the dog park. And I recalled her despair when I returned from Las Vegas and told her I was engaged.

"I want us to be much more than friends," I said finally, in a definite voice. I felt my face flush and a sudden chill. My words seemed to gather momentum. "I've wanted that for a long time. I want to be with you. Yes, I'll let you in. I want you in my life and in my thoughts, and I don't want you to ever leave. That's what I'm thinking, right now." I stopped speaking, but then realized there was more I needed to say. "You make me happy, Regina. You make me happier than I've ever been."

She exhaled, and her eyes filled with tears. She squeezed my hands, saying nothing. I thought about Fawn and her small-dog phobia, and $QT\pi$ and Mr. Goldfarb and my thousands of marriage proposals.

"I love you, Regina." The words tumbled out of me. "I love you so much," I said, and then realized what had just happened. "I've never meant that before with anyone else."

I leaned over and put my arms around her and drew her to me. Her eyes glistened in the firelight. I took her head in my hands, and we kissed, our tongues brushing, and then we held each other without speaking. When I opened my eyes, I saw Tex, who had moved to a decorative pillow on the other end of the sofa. His head was turned toward a spot on the wall, his eyes half closed, focused on nothing. His tiny chest expanded and contracted in slow, serious breaths. He seemed lost in thought. I took Regina's hand, and without speaking, we stood and slowly climbed the stairs to the second floor. She had loosely buttoned her blouse but left her bra on the coffee table. Tex turned and watched us walk up the stairs but made no effort to follow.

Regina stopped in the upstairs bathroom, and I walked down the hallway to my bedroom. I took off my clothes, folded them on a straight-backed chair, pulled back the bedspread, and crawled under the sheet. It was nearly dusk, and the setting sun infused the room with long sepia shadows. A faucet ran, and then a minute later the bathroom door opened, and I heard Regina's footsteps pad down the hall. I looked up and saw her standing in the doorway, wearing nothing, her arms limply hanging by her side. She had combed her hair in the bathroom and swept it back over her shoulders. I could tell by the shy, nervous way she smiled that she wanted to cover herself with her hands, but she didn't. She just stood there silently and let me look at her pale, lovely body. Then, still without speaking, she moved to the bed and slid beside me under the sheet. I think we both were relieved at the cover it provided. I wasn't completely sure what to do next, so I tried stroking her shoulders and arms with my fingertips. Then she placed her palm over my hand and gently guided me while I explored her body.

Our lovemaking was desperate and over too quickly. Afterward, we lay there, breathing hard, Regina on her side, her head on my chest, one arm wrapped around me, one leg draped over my leg. The house was very still, with a slight breeze through the open screened windows. The sun had set finally, and darkness gradually enveloped the room. I lay there motionless, listening to the two of us breathe, and tried to resurrect every word, every movement, every feeling of the evening.

And then Regina began to cry. Her body quivered with soft, quiet sobs, and I felt her warm tears fall on my chest and slowly roll down my side. I held her, saying nothing, until finally her breathing deepened and she settled into sleep. The last thing I remember before I drifted off was that I wanted to cry too, but no tears would come.

# 25

# NEPAL
# AIR

*Dear Ollie,*

*Thank you very, very much for recommending Calista to be my new store manager. She's a perfect fit for Chez Charmante, and I couldn't be more pleased! I so enjoyed seeing you and Regina and that adorable little dog last week and to hear about your upcoming Nepal vacation. I'm sure Regina and I will become dearest friends! As a tiny expression of my affection, I hope you will enjoy this antique pet carrier for your journey. Birdy Van Flutter's great-grandparents, Violet and Squeaky, had it made in London for their Yorkie, Cabot, for their return voyage on the Titanic. As great good fortune would have it, Squeaky had purchased a first-class ticket for Cabot, thus entitling him to one of the last spots on their lifeboat. Bon voyage!*

*Fondly,*
*Françoise*

**On the first leg** of our flight to Kathmandu, Regina and I took a red-eye from Boston to Istanbul on Turkish Airlines. We splurged and sat in business class, and Tex came along in his antique pet carrier, which Regina tucked in front of her feet. Tex sat on a purple satin cushion inside the carrier's soft, leather-trimmed fabric sides and positioned himself so he could see out the mesh front. Despite his opulent accommodations, he whimpered quietly, so after takeoff, we surreptitiously let him out to join us. That appeared to improve his spirits a bit, but he still seemed morose, with droopy tail and his nose planted on my lap. When the flight attendant checked seat belts, Regina hid him in a cup holder on her armrest, covered with an airline magazine.

I gazed out the window at the glow of Boston fading behind us. Ahead, the vast dark expanse of the Atlantic Ocean stretched to the horizon. The moon hung low in the east, a misty yellow crescent, and I could see dim lights far below from ocean freighters marking the shipping lanes like giant floating streetlamps. As I stretched out in the dimly lit cabin with Tex curled on my lap and Regina nestled against me, her head resting on my shoulder, I couldn't remember feeling happier.

We landed in the afternoon in Istanbul and had a four-hour layover before boarding our Nepal Air flight to Kathmandu. We found a convenient pet relief area for Tex and then browsed the duty-free shops and ate an early supper of braised lamb with peanuts and roasted quince at a restaurant on the international departure floor. Over Turkish coffee ice cream and an almond liqueur, we reviewed our travel schedule.

Our plan, once we landed in Kathmandu, was to spend two days checking out Regina's properties inherited from her great-great-grandfather. These had been managed by a large trust company, and the head of the company, a Mr. Souchong, was to meet us at the airport. Afterward, we had three unscheduled days for sightseeing. I especially wanted to tour my Uncle Gus's museum, which housed artifacts of his life and works and reportedly had the best account of his trek up Mount Machhapuchhre, where he had vanished. I felt like I should pay my respects to his memory in the city he loved and had spent his final years.

The check-in line at the Nepal Airlines counter was long, and we inched forward for twenty-five minutes before our turn came up. That's when we learned Tex would have to travel to Kathmandu in the cargo hold.

Regina protested. "Can't he just stay with us? He's a very small dog, and we'll keep him in his carrier."

"It's a new regulation, ma'am," the ticket agent replied in nearly accent-free English. He was a thin, middle-aged man with a narrow, pinched brow and an airline name tag pinned to his black vest identifying him as a Mr. Chaudhary. "We had a bad experience last year on this same flight. A passenger's poodle twirled up and down the aisle on his rear legs, bumping into flight attendants and causing them to slosh their beverages."

I said, "Why would the airline impose such a restriction because of a single incident?"

"The European Union forced the rule on us, sir," Mr. Chaudhary replied wearily. "They're clamping down because of safety concerns. It's been a hard year for us, what with that and the poodle incident." He sighed with frustration at the thought of the European Union's safety-obsessed bureaucrats.

"What kind of safety concerns?" Regina asked, gripping my arm. "Were there any, you know, *crashes*?"

"A few, ma'am," he replied, taking a deep interest in his computer screen.

"Like, for instance, how many would that be?" Regina is nothing if not persistent.

He sighed again. "Ma'am, we've had thirty-two crashes but not many recently."

"And fatalities?" Regina sucked in her breath and increased

the pressure on my arm ten-fold.

"In total, only about seven hundred," he replied, his tone suggesting such a paltry number was not worth pursuing. "But we've made great strides in the past two years." I glanced at Regina, whose face had turned ashen. With her free arm, she clutched Tex's pet carrier to her chest. "Now we sacrifice goats to appease Akash Bhairab, the airline's Flight Safety God," Mr. Chaudhary said with a hopeful smile. "We put two baby goats on every flight, so we'll have them ready in case we run into mechanical problems."

I stared at him in disbelief.

"We've also improved our crew training. As of this year, we require our flight attendants to have PhD degrees. And every flight has a veterinary technician on board." Noting my puzzled expression, he added, "For the goats."

Regina looked at me. "So what should we do?"

"I don't think we have any choice," I said. I turned to Mr. Chaudhary. "Tell me about the cargo hold."

He smiled, evidently relieved at being asked a question with a good answer. "It's very comfortable for the animals. It's pressurized and heated and not at all crowded." He tapped a few keys on his computer and studied the screen. "On this flight, we'll be carrying only your dog and a cat."

"What about the goats?" I said.

"Oh, they're considered airline mascots, so they get to travel with the passengers." I shrugged at Regina, who reluctantly placed Tex's carrier on the ticket counter. Mr. Chaudhary looked at it with dismay. "Ms. Malbec," he said, "I'm afraid pets have to travel in the airline's own cages. They clip onto fixtures in the cargo hold so they don't jar loose with turbulence. They're quite comfortable and safe. I'll bring one out for your dog." He turned and walked quickly though an employees-only door behind the ticket counter. Regina looked at me with pained resignation.

"It'll be all right," I said, trying to sound more confident than I felt. "It's only for a few hours, and he'll sleep the whole way." I opened the top flap to Tex's carrier and handed him to Regina, who still seemed dubious.

Mr. Chaudhary returned carrying a small metal cage. He handed me a brass padlock and a key. "Here you are, sir," he said. "You can put your dog in the cage, verify that his water bottle is full, and then lock it. You have the only key, so please don't lose it. We'll give your pet back to you at the baggage claim in Kathmandu." Seeing the worried look on Regina's face, he added, "There's really nothing to worry about, ma'am. He'll be fine. We do this all the time."

Regina handed Tex to me, opened Françoise's antique pet carrier, and took out the satin cushion, which she positioned in the airline's cage. Then she opened her purse and took out a bag of homemade dog biscuits. "In case he gets hungry," she said, as she placed a large dog biscuit in the cage beside the satin cushion. We exchanged smooches with Tex, and I set him in the cage. He perched on his cushion next to his dog biscuit and looked at us with a dispirited tail wag. I had never seen him act quite so anxious. I hoped he wouldn't be too lonely during the seven-hour flight.

Our plane was an older Boeing 757 with well-worn, gray fabric upholstery. The flight was full, mostly with Western tourists. A boisterous group of German backpackers boarded ahead of us, and a chatty, retired Australian couple from Melbourne stood in line behind us on the ramp. Our seat assignments were in the front section, and Regina sat on the aisle so she could pat Rashmi and Sabita, the two baby goats. Once everybody was seated and the overhead bins closed, they bounded up and down the aisle in matching brightly colored diapers, greeting passengers. We buckled our seat belts as a flight attendant stood in front of our row and spoke into a handset.

"Dearest passengers, good evening. I am Rohini, your air hostess." She appeared to be in her forties, with dark hair pulled back and a cream-colored blouse with a wide scarlet-and-blue scarf.

Regina leaned over to me and whispered, "Those are the Nepalese flag colors." Rohini smiled at her and placed her hand over her handset.

"Very good," she said. "I'm always pleased to find passengers interested in the vexillology of the Nepalese flag. The crimson red is the color of the rhododendron, our national flower, and the blue border signifies peace. Our flag combines two triangular pennants. Nepal is the only country whose flag is not a quadrilateral polygon."

Regina reached over and squeezed my hand. Rohini straightened and spoke again into the handset. "Dearest passengers, may I have your attention for a few announcements." She narrowed her eyes and squinted down the aisle. "You, *sir*, in 9C, put down your newspaper and give me your full attention. Thank you." She continued. "Our Boeing 757 has many safety features, but I'm not going to bore you by talking about them. I'm sure all of you already know how to fasten your seat belt. We're not flying over water, so you can forget about your flotation seat cushion. And should there be a catastrophic drop in cabin pressure, well, frankly, it's pointless to spend your remaining seconds messing with the air mask.

"I highly recommend you read our complimentary in-flight magazine. I know you'll be interested in learning about the C-Com R665 software upgrade to our multi-core navigation system. I wrote the article myself. And be sure not to miss the fascinating review of the hydrodynamic wind patterns over the Himalayas. If you have any problems understanding the equations, press your call button, and I'll be glad to explain them. Now, please sit back and enjoy your flight. I'll be around in a few minutes to serve our famous yak jerky and signature 'K2' cocktails. We call them that because their survival rate is only seventy-five percent. Haha, just kidding, but please don't feed any to Rashmi and Sabita."

Regina yawned and hugged my arm. "I'm exhausted," she said, "especially with Hernando's and Fanny's wedding coming up. It's going to be frantic next month. So much to do." I yawned too. It had been a very long week. After their wedding, the new-lyweds planned to move to Nicaragua to open a school for young poets and writers. Fanny's trust would provide most of the fund-ing, and I was giving them whatever else they needed as their wedding present. I hadn't seen much of Hernando since Fenway Park. His seminar had ended for the semester, and he and Fanny had been researching their new book, *Tragedy Beneath the Streets of Boston: The Lost Souls of the MTA*. Yale University Press had already expressed interest in it.

"I'm going to miss my brother," I said, "but I'm glad he's found his soulmate."

Regina looked at me without speaking. "Do you think you and I are soulmates too?" she said finally, assessing my face.

I pondered the question. "Theoretically, I suppose it depends on your definition of soulmate."

She said, "There's the conventional definition as a person with whom one forms an immediate, unprecedented connection."

"Agreed, but there's another consideration, and that's the *duration* of the connection. Why don't we give it thirty or forty years, and then we'll reassess." She grinned and leaned against me, still holding my hand, and rested her head against my arm. I shut my eyes, feeling jet-lagged after our long Istanbul flight. I already missed Tex and wished he could have been snoozing on my lap. I hoped he was comfortable down in the cargo hold.

We landed at Kathmandu's Tribhuvan Airport early the next morning, our scheduled seven a.m. arrival delayed twenty minutes by a snow leopard who wandered onto the runway and forced our plane to circle until she finished nursing her cub. While circling, turbulent air caused the plane to lurch, and the wings tilted sharply for a few seconds before straightening. There were alarmed cries from passengers, and the baby goats started bleating. I felt my pulse racing and reached over and squeezed Regina's hand. After a few seconds, when normalcy had returned, she exhaled, reached up, and pressed the flight attendant call button.

"What will happen to Rashmi and Sabita after we land?" she asked, when Rohini appeared.

"They'll be permanently reassigned to this flight, until we experience a mechanical problem, or somebody buys them."

"They're for sale?" Regina asked, surprised.

"Not exactly," Rohini said. "If a passenger buys them, they go to an animal rights organization, which gives them to families in rural villages. Unfortunately, female goats are very expensive, so we don't place many that way."

"How expensive?" I said, reaching for my wallet.

"Two hundred US dollars each."

I handed Rohini my Visa card. "I'd like to buy Rashmi and Sabita," I said. Regina raised an eyebrow, and I took the hint. "And also the baby goats for your next ten flights." I was beginning to appreciate the possibilities of my Nigerian trust fund.

# 26

# HE LEFT ME
# IN SILENCE...

**After landing,** we lumbered down the airplane steps with our carry-on bags and Tex's empty carrier and filed across the asphalt to the international terminal. Baggage carts, mobile stairs, white vans and buses, and cargo storage containers cluttered the tarmac. We watched while a small truck towing two empty luggage carts pulled up alongside our plane's cargo door. I took a deep breath of the gritty air and smelled the faint odor of aviation fuel. The weather was mild, with scattered wispy clouds, and through the morning haze I could see a ridge of mountains on the horizon. Regina stopped and squinted at the distant peaks.

"Can you see your Uncle Gus's mountain from here? I forget its name." She shaded her eyes with her hand.

"Mount Machhapuchhre. It's about a hundred miles northwest of here. Those are just foothills. Machhapuchhre is nearly twenty-three thousand feet."

Inside the red brick terminal, an official steered us to a long line of glassy-eyed passengers waiting to clear immigration and customs. We passed the time in line watching an interesting

282 • POCKET DOG

documentary on a TV monitor about Nepal's stinging nettle, which grows in the Himalayan foothills and has the longest fiber strands of any plant. After twenty-one hours of traveling, I felt groggy and more than ready for a shower.

We cleared immigration and moved on to baggage claim on the lower level to pick up Tex and our suitcases before heading to customs. The area was noisy and crowded with passengers from our flight. I looked around for a gate agent carrying Tex's cage, but the bags hadn't arrived yet. At the foot of the escalator, an older, distinguished-looking Chinese gentleman in a dark wool suit and red necktie approached us carrying a slim black leather briefcase.

"You are Miss Malbec," he said cordially to Regina, bowing slightly. "I am Souchong. Welcome to Nepal." He steered us toward an empty bench in a waiting area next to baggage claim, and after introductions, he turned to me. "Mr. Allyinphree, is this your first visit to Kathmandu? I'm guessing Gustav Allyinphree must be your ancestor. I'm sure you want to visit his museum."

"He was my great-great-uncle," I said.

"And who better than Miss Malbec to show it to you? But first, we will drive you to your hotel to freshen up. I have many properties to show today so we'll need to start soon." He turned to Regina. "In deference to Mr. Allyinphree, let us begin by inspecting your museum."

Regina gave him a puzzled look. "*My* museum? I didn't know I owned a museum."

I was puzzled too. "You're saying Regina, Miss Malbec, owns my great-great-uncle's museum?"

"Yes. I'm surprised you didn't know that."

Regina looked at me. "Then that must mean our two ancestors knew each other."

Mr. Souchong smiled. "Of course. I assumed that's why you came to Nepal together."

She said, "My great-great-grandfather was a businessman. It never occurred to me there might be a connection with Gustav Allyinphree."

Mr. Souchong laughed. "Oh my, the men were best friends. Your great-great-grandfather was Allyinphree's guide, and after the accident on the mountain, inherited his estate. Miss Malbec, your ancestor used that bequest to open the museum. I'm surprised you didn't know this." Then he frowned at a thought. "But if you didn't know about your shared history, what brings the two of you together to Kathmandu? Karma, perhaps? Such things happen in Nepal, you know," he added, smiling.

"Not exactly karma, Mr. Souchong," Regina said, glancing at me and putting her arm around my waist. "Our little dog brought us together. Ollie and I first met because of Tex." So Tex had become *our* little dog. I liked that. I watched a gate agent carry a largish pet cage through a door from an off-limits area. He set it on a chair, and a middle-aged blonde woman from our flight handed him a key from her purse. The agent opened the cage, and the woman lifted out a large yellow tabby. She kissed it on the head, laughed, and exchanged a few words with the gate agent, who returned to the back area. It wouldn't be long now.

Mr. Souchong smiled knowingly. "So your dog brought you together? That is a wonderful story. Then it appears your families have actually shared two dogs. Surely that cannot be coincidental."

"Two dogs?" Regina said blankly. "Who's the second dog?"

Mr. Souchong seemed startled by the question. "Why Darwin, Gustav Allyinphree's Dalmatian. Your ancestor cared for him throughout the remainder of his life. His body has been preserved at the museum for over a century. Except for his spots, of course. They vanished the day of the incident on the mountain."

I started to speak, just as the gate agent I'd seen earlier approached. He said, "Excuse me, sir, are you Mr. Allyinphree?" He carried Tex's cage and had a worried frown.

I peered into the empty cage. "Where's Tex?" I said. Something was wrong. The gate agent swallowed and silently held out the cage to me. "Where's our dog?" I insisted again, taking the cage. "I want him now."

Regina reached over and clutched my arm. "What's happened?" she said. "Is Tex okay?"

The gate agent's expression told me I wasn't going to like his answer. "I don't know, ma'am," he replied. "The padlock is still in place, and you have the key. Your dog couldn't get out."

The key. I held the cage under one arm and reached into my pocket and felt the brass key given to me in Istanbul. I inserted it into the padlock and clicked open the cage's front lid. There was nothing inside but the velvet cushion from Françoise's carrier and a water bottle attached to the side wall. The water bottle was about half full. I could barely breathe. "Have you searched the area?" I said, knowing he most likely had. I couldn't believe what was happening. "Could Tex still be in the cargo hold? He's got to be somewhere." I clutched the empty cage to my chest.

The gate agent lowered his head and said, "I am so sorry, sir. We've looked everywhere. I will file a report. I don't know what else to do."

I clenched my fists and felt myself redden. "No, you need to search again. Dogs don't vanish into air."

"Excuse me," Mr. Souchong said, stepping forward and facing the gate agent. He frowned and said, "May I have a word?"

The agent looked up at him and paled. "Mr. Souchong. I'm so sorry, sir. I didn't know you were here." He clutched his arms to his side and bowed as if seeking absolution.

"What is your name, please?" Mr. Souchong's voice had acquired a commanding edge that reminded me of Hernando's.

"Sanjiv Gautam, sir."

"Thank you, Mr. Gautam. Kindly escort me to the office of my brother-in-law. Immediately. I fear we haven't much time." Evidently, Mr. Souchong and his brother-in-law were a known presence in Nepalese airport circles.

"Of course, sir," the agent said, bowing again. Ignoring Regina and me, he turned and started toward a door that said Airport Security, nearly colliding with the woman with the yellow tabby. It hissed and arched its back, and she nearly dropped it.

Mr. Souchong followed the gate agent for a few steps, but then stopped and turned to Regina. "My brother-in-law is the general manager of Tribuhaven Airport. I'll have him gather the flight crew, baggage handlers, anyone who could have had access to your dog. Somebody must have known how to open the padlock. We'll get to the bottom of this." He pressed his lips into a tight smile, turned, and followed the gate agent out through the airport security door.

Regina and I retrieved our suitcases and sank onto the bench outside baggage claim. This couldn't be happening. The area had mostly cleared, as passengers from our flight migrated to customs with their luggage. I forced myself to focus on Mr. Souchong's lock-picking theory. I couldn't buy it. A thief would have grabbed the entire cage rather than bother with the lock. And why would anyone want to steal Tex in the first place?

"This is like before," Regina said, interrupting my thoughts. "We found Tex in a locked cage at the kennel. Mrs. Knightsbridge thought somebody had picked the lock, but that didn't seem plausible. And now it's happened again, except that he's disappeared."

I was too jet lagged to think clearly. Regina hugged my arm, her face pale with streaks of tears. I squeezed her hand and propped my feet up on a suitcase. There was nothing to do now but wait. My eyes felt leaden, so I closed them, and the next thing I remember was Regina nudging my shoulder. Mr. Souchong stood before us, and we both rose to face him. He wasn't smiling. I rubbed the fatigue from my eyes with the back of my hand. Baggage claim was nearly deserted, and the area had grown quiet.

"Miss Malbec, Mr. Allyinphree," he said, "We have not found your dog yet, but I have some information." He went on to explain that the baggage handlers in Istanbul remembered seeing only two pets on our flight, that both of their water bottles had been full, and their cages had been securely latched in the cargo hold. The baggage handlers in Kathmandu reported that there was no dog in Tex's cage when they removed it from the airplane. They also said that Tex's water bottle was about half full, which struck them as odd, since there would be no need to fill the bottle at all if shipping an empty cage.

"So I conclude," Mr. Souchong said, "that your dog disappeared while the aircraft was in flight, but after he drank half the bottle of water. Given your pet's tiny size, I conclude that was near the end of the flight, possibly even while the aircraft was approaching the Kathmandu airport."

Neither of us spoke for a moment, then Regina said, "If Tex somehow got out of his cage, is there any way he could have escaped from the cargo hold?"

"Unlikely. Pet cages are stored in the Boeing 757's heated aft hold. The hold's door is elevated, and a small dog could never reach it. I, myself, checked the side moldings and wall liners with a flashlight to see if there was any place an animal could hide. There was nothing."

I felt myself flush. "So our dog vanished for no reason?" Regina looked up and caught my eye. I took a deep breath to settle down.

"I'm sure there is a logical explanation," Mr. Souchong said quietly, "but I don't know what it is. I am so sorry." I sank down on the bench seat, Regina beside me, but Mr. Souchong remained standing.

We sat silently for a moment, and then Regina said, "Ollie, we know Tex and the kennel founder's puppy were discovered one hundred fifty years apart in the same locked cage." I turned to look at her, to see where she was going. "And we know the founder's puppy was a Dalmatian, like Darwin, your Uncle Gus's dog."

I stared at her. "Seriously? You think Uncle Gus may have bought Darwin from Chateau Dom Pedigree?"

"The kennel records don't say, but it's possible."

"Miss Malbec," Mr. Souchong said, "you have made a very good point. I suggest we go directly to your museum. It seems likely there is a connection between your missing dog and Gustav Allyinphree's dog."

"But we don't know what we're looking for," I said.

"No, but we might learn about the connection between the two animals. I'm afraid we'll learn nothing if we remain here." He reached into his suit jacket and took out a cellphone. "I'll notify our driver to take us to the museum. He'll deliver your luggage to your hotel."

"We better take this with us," Regina said wearily, lifting Françoise's antique pet carrier from atop a suitcase. "I hope we need it." I looked at the empty carrier and pictured Tex's anxious face at the Istanbul airport when Regina checked his water bowl and placed a dog biscuit in his cage. I prayed that hadn't been the last time we'd see him.

# 27

# ASK NOT FOR WHOM
# THE DOG BARKS

**Mr. Souchong's limo** turned south out of the airport exit onto Ring Road. It was a ten-kilometer drive to the museum, near the Kathmandu Old Town. I stared out the side window as our car turned west onto Madan Bhandari Road and passed a block-long complex with a large, red-tiled, pagoda-like entrance. I glanced over at Tex's empty dog crate on the seat between Regina and me. The excitement I'd felt as our flight landed had been displaced by despair. I didn't want to be in Nepal at all. What I really, really wanted was to be back in Boston with Regina and my little dog. I swallowed and fought back tears.

I heard Mr. Souchong say, "That is Nepal's international conference center," but I didn't look up. We passed several sports fields, and the pace of activity ballooned as we neared the city center and edged past souvenir stands, religious sculptures, prayer flags strung on wires, and open-air bazaars with sari-clad Hindu women selling spinach, mustard, fresh coriander, and garden cress. Rickshaws, motorcycles, and backpack-hefting European trekkers clogged the streets and sidewalks. The drive was taking forever. I glanced at Regina, whose hands were folded in her lap, her eyes closed. We swerved to avoid a sleeping cow.

Regina's museum turned out to be a two-story rectangular white building with a long covered porch two blocks from Durbar Square, the large plaza facing Kathmandu's old royal palace. We pulled to the curb, and the museum's director, a Mrs. Shrestha, greeted us. She was a short thin woman, about sixty, dressed in a dark Western business suit. She gestured toward a small crowd of women with young children gathered on the porch outside the museum entrance. "They're waiting for the museum to open," she said. "It's like this every day. We open in forty-five minutes." She smiled and exchanged a glance with Mr. Souchong. "But for you we open now, Miss Malbec. It's your museum."

Regina blushed. "Then let's go see the exhibit now."

Mrs. Shrestha escorted us into the building, deserted except for our group and a handful of employees. She explained how Uncle Gus's dog had been preserved by a taxidermist, and how for decades the display had been a favorite of Kathmandu children. She led us down a corridor past a gift shop, a small theater, and a room featuring Uncle Gus's scholarly writings. I glanced through the door and saw a display case containing his famous book on extinct Polynesian languages.

At the end of the corridor, Mrs. Shrestha stood aside while we entered a windowless room devoted to the ill-fated expedition up Mount Machhapuchhre. The left wall displayed a large color photograph of the mountain, taken in late afternoon summer. It showed a barren peak jutting out of a narrow mountain ridge glowing red in the setting sun, a giant, luminous shark's fin cruising the crest of the Himalayas.

We stood to let our eyes adjust to the indoor light and then moved to a wall of early black-and-white photographs. I stopped to inspect the embossed leather shoulder harness used to carry Darwin up parts of the mountain while Regina studied a large lithograph of her long-dead ancestor, made just before the fateful expedition. In the lithograph, her great-great-grandfather faces the camera. Uncle Gus's arm rests on his shoulder, and Darwin sits at their feet. Uncle Gus seems lost in thought, perhaps contemplating a mathematical abstraction, but Regina's ancestor grins at the camera, evidently excited about their forthcoming adventure.

"He seems like a kindly man," she murmured as I joined her. Mr. Souchong and Mrs. Shrestha stood silently behind us, and I felt like we were standing in a temple.

"Our archives suggest they were Buddhists," Mrs. Shrestha said, moving beside us while we studied the faded image. "They were close friends and well known in Kathmandu."

"Let's go see Darwin now," I said, feeling a rising impatience that we were wasting time. "I'm not seeing anything yet that takes us closer to Tex."

Mrs. Shrestha escorted us to the rear of the room, where a large acrylic enclosure rested on an ornate wooden stand flanked by two carved Buddhas. A brass plate engraved *Darwin* and *1868-1887* was attached to the stand. Inside the enclosure, the dog's preserved body sat on its haunches on a brown sisal mat, with ears flopped down and a longish tail curled to the side. It was an elderly Dalmatian, with dark-rimmed eyes, black nose, and white muzzle. The grayish hair on the flanks had thinned, and I could see the faint bleached outline of once-dark spots. The body was so lifelike it wasn't hard to picture Darwin rising, hopping off the stand and joining us. His head was cocked slightly to one side, his mouth closed with a sober countenance that reminded me of Tex. Despite their size disparity, the resemblance in the two dogs' faces gave me goose bumps.

"The dog was nineteen when it died," Mrs. Shrestha explained. "The enclosure is sealed and filled with dry nitrogen gas to protect the body from humidity and oxidation, and we open it a few times a year to inspect for deterioration. After so many decades, the body is very fragile."

I looked at Darwin's body for a minute and returned to the lithograph of him taken before the trek up the mountain. Below that image was a smaller picture of the dog with Regina's great-great-grandfather, taken just after their return. Regina's ancestor looked exhausted, obviously devastated by the tragedy. I studied his morose eyes and wondered if he had felt guilty for the loss of his friend. I was sure feeling that way about losing Tex.

The earlier photo showed a cluster of three black spots on the right side of the dog's neck, just above the shoulder blade. I walked back to the display case and saw the faded outline of the same spots on Darwin's preserved body. I couldn't reconcile the circumstances that linked Tex, Regina, and me to these one-hundred-fifty-year-old events: Darwin and Tex both found in the same locked cage; Tex's disappearance from another locked cage; Regina and me having ancestors who were best friends. But the facts spoke for themselves. I caught Regina's eye and shrugged. We stood silently, and I found myself biting my lower lip.

"You doing okay?" she asked.

"What I'm worried about is whether Tex is okay. I couldn't stand it if, you know . . ."

"Yes, I do know, but let's not think about that."

"How can I not?" I snapped. "I let them put him in the cargo hold. Why did I do that, Regina?"

"Ollie, stop it. You couldn't know what was going to happen." She gripped my arm, and I tried to calm down.

I said, "Do you remember how dispirited Tex seemed when we put him in that cage at the Istanbul airport? Maybe he was trying to tell us something, and we didn't pick up on it."

She gave me a patient look. "Ollie, I don't see how we could have missed anything."

"Darwin was a handsome dog," Mrs. Shrestha said as the three of us convened before the sealed enclosure. "It's amazing how well preserved he is after all these years."

I studied the dog's body. "I see a little deterioration, though." I pointed to dark flakes on the mat below the dog's head. "It looks like some small pieces have fallen off."

"May I see?" Mrs. Shrestha stepped forward, frowned, and peered through the acrylic. "If there had been any deterioration, my staff should have told me about it." She removed a large key ring from her handbag and inserted a small brass key into a hinged panel on the side of the enclosure. It swiveled open with a sigh from the pressurized interior, and she peered inside at the small pieces.

"These look like crumbs." She retrieved the largest piece and inspected it. "I don't know what this is," she said, peering at a dime-sized chunk of some brown material, her brow furrowed. "It's not supposed to be in there."

She handed it to Regina, who looked down at it and gasped. Her face had turned pale. It was the dog biscuit from Tex's cage. "Ollie, he ate half of it," she said, handing it to me, her voice catching. "I put it in his cage at the airport because I didn't want him to be hungry." I stared at the fragment of dog biscuit in my palm, then turned to Regina. I knew what it meant. Mr. Souchong looked over from the doorway and came to us.

"He left it here for us," I said, my voice choking. "He wanted us to see it." My chest constricted, and I struggled to breathe. "It means he's alive." I had more to say but didn't know if I could get the words out. Mr. Souchong looked at me curiously. I tried to gather myself. "He's saying goodbye to us."

And then something happened I never expected: I stood there and cried like a two-year-old, right in front of Mr. Souchong and Mrs. Shrestha. I clamped my mouth shut but couldn't stop. Tears streamed down my cheeks. Noisy sobs welled up from some buried, stunted place, and I couldn't choke them off.

"Oh, Ollie," Regina said, and reached out to hug me.

I shut my eyes and buried my face in her shoulder. I felt her hair against my cheek and her arms around me, warm and loving, and I saw myself back in Boston on our first night together, Regina asleep beside me and the room cloaked in darkness. I remembered a quiet breeze rustling the curtains on the bedroom windows facing the rear alley, and how the room seemed chilly. Regina had given a little start, which awakened me, and I yawned, pulled the thin blanket up over our chins and lay on my back, listening to the nighttime sounds of crickets and tree frogs. The bedsheets still held the earthy odors of perspiration and lovemaking. Regina had draped her arm over my chest, and her leg was intertwined with mine, and I felt her breasts press against my side. I held very still so I wouldn't wake her. Then she shifted slightly, and her leg moved, and I felt her toes stroke the top of my foot.

She murmured something I couldn't understand, and a few seconds later, I felt Tex gently pushing against me under the covers. His wet nose brushed my palm, so I stretched my hand open and felt his tongue licking my fingers, like he had done when I first met him. I sensed again a familiar reassuring warmth radiating up my arm. Then Tex stopped, and with a soft thump, hopped off the bed.

With a start, I opened my eyes and was back in the museum, my chest aching. My eyes felt puffy, and my nose dribbled. "Oh my God," I said, sniffling. "That isn't what happened. Tex was never there. He was downstairs on the sofa the entire time." Regina pulled back from me, and I felt my heart pounding. "He just said goodbye to me."

"Ollie?" Regina said, as if unsure it was really me she was talking to. Mr. Souchong and Mrs. Shrestha watched me, puzzled. I coughed and cleared my throat. Mrs. Shrestha had evidently found a drinking fountain because she now offered me a plastic cup of water. I took a sip and returned it.

"I'm okay now," I said. "Thank you." Mr. Souchong stood beside her, calmly stroking his chin. Then he handed me a handkerchief from his breast pocket.

"Mr. Allyinphree," he said, gazing at the ceiling while I dabbed at my face. He could have been talking about trash pickup at one of Regina's office buildings. "I am not sure I agree with your theory that your dog is not coming back."

Still sniffling, I returned Mr. Souchong's handkerchief and struggled to compose my words. I took Regina's hand. She had streaks of tears down her cheeks, too, and I felt an impulse to lean over and kiss them. "Why else would he have left his dog biscuit for us?" I said, hoping Mr. Souchong would overlook the fact he was being questioned by a blubbering fool.

"Because he wanted to tell you he was safe. Anything you infer beyond that is speculation."

"It's more than that," I blurted, "but I can't fit the pieces together."

"Ah," he said, smiling, "just like a person from the West. I have the greatest admiration for your people." I had the impression Mr. Souchong was lumping together the inhabitants of Europe, Australia, and both Americas. I sensed a 'but' coming.

"But I believe a failing of your people is your intolerance of ambiguity. Your great-great-uncle was lost on our most sacred mountain. All that has happened to both of you derives from his disappearance. Do you understand what that means, Mr. Allyinphree?"

"I'm beginning to, Mr. Souchong, but do you really believe a Hindu god lives on Mount Machhapuchhre?"

He smiled at me. "Don't you? Your famous kinsman believed so, and that is why he made his journey there. He was a wise man." Turning to Regina, he added, "And so was your great-great-grandfather, Miss Malbec."

"I'm sorry," I said, before she could respond, "but I'm finding all of this very troubling." I saw Regina look up and raise her eyebrows slightly, as if I were embarrassing her.

Mr. Souchong continued. "I appreciate that, Mr. Allyinphree, and yet here you are, standing in a city that has been a spiritual center for the human race for more than two thousand years." He stopped speaking to assess my reaction, but finding none, he added, "Perhaps it might help to reflect on the events that led you here." Smiling soberly, he turned his head to Regina and then back to me. "I don't know whether your little dog will ever return," he said. "None of us can know that. That is the best you can hope for.

"Please excuse me now," he added, glancing at his watch. "I have a few financial matters to discuss with Mrs. Shrestha. Perhaps tomorrow we can discuss our plans?" Bowing slightly, he shook hands with Regina and me. Mrs. Shrestha said goodbye to us, and the two of them walked into the corridor.

We stood silently for a moment, and then Regina sighed and looked at me, her gaze weighted with exhaustion. "He's right," she said, rubbing an eye. "We can't know if Tex is ever coming back, but I want to think he is."

I sighed too. "I wish I could be more philosophical about all of this, but right now I feel despair, like a parent who has just lost his child." I instantly regretted my words. I wasn't feeling despair. It was self-pity.

"No, Ollie, you're being melodramatic." Regina leaned toward me and kissed my cheek. "This is nothing like that. This isn't even close. It's more like . . . a baby bird that fledges and flies away. Or a child who grows up and leaves home for college." She studied my face.

"Okay, but you've got it backward."

"What do you mean?"

"The baby bird part. Tex didn't outgrow us."

She didn't speak.  Finally, she said, "I get your point, but don't you still wonder where he's gone?"

I shrugged. It was a question without an answer. We turned toward the corridor. I knew Mr. Souchong was wrong. Tex had just said his final goodbye to me, and I needed to accept that. In time, Regina would, too, but that was a conversation for another day. I stopped and looked down at her pale, distraught face. She caught my eye, expecting me to speak, but before I could say anything, she grasped my arm, something else on her mind.

"Ollie," she said, "can you imagine how terribly bittersweet it must feel to have your baby grow up and leave home for college?" Her question took me by surprise, but I was glad she'd changed the subject. She fixed her brown eyes on me and smiled, a loving, gawky smile. I felt a profound weariness but forced myself to consider her question.

"Yes," I said finally, "I'd like to have that feeling."

I turned to look again at my great-great-uncle's dog. Then we walked silently down the corridor toward the museum exit and out into the luminous shadows of the Nepalese sun. We stood outside the entrance for a moment without speaking, taking in the city. It sparkled, vibrant and alive, and the air was infused with the scents of incense and spices. Two bespectacled Buddhist monks in crimson robes walked past and nodded politely. We heard horns beeping and the staccato barks of motorcycles. Across the street a large brown monkey scampered up a wire-draped telephone pole. We watched him hang one-armed from a narrow wooden crossbar, pivot his body around a tangle of wires and ceramic insulators, and leap in a single fluid motion onto the low roof of an adjacent building.

"I wonder if he came from up there?" Regina said, gesturing toward the distant Monkey Temple, the ancient stupa that overlooks the city. "Manjushri, the bodhisattva of wisdom and learning, is said to have created that hill." I followed her gaze and saw the planet Venus suspended above the Temple. It glowed in the reflected sunlight, a benevolent celestial eye watching over the peaceful valley. Regina reached out and took my arm. A blue mist had settled over the snow-shrouded mountains, and the world seemed a kaleidoscope of colors and possibilities.

# EPILOGUE

**Anastassia Andropova,** twenty-seven, sits alone in her tiny Anchorage apartment on a frigid January morning, her thoughts on her family in Saint Petersburg. Outside, a bruising arctic wind blows, and during the night, six inches of heavy snow added to the eighteen already there. Anastassia has not seen her mother and her younger sister in two years. She does a mental calculation and decides, if frugal, she should be able to visit them in August.

She dresses, and as she does every morning, makes her bed and toasts a bagel. She takes a plastic container of cream cheese from her refrigerator and looks at her wristwatch. In forty-five minutes she must catch her bus to work.

Anastassia sets her laptop computer on her small kitchen table, opens a browser, and studies the for-sale postings from an online California kennel. She has visited this site several times, but the beautiful purebred puppies are beyond her means. This morning, however, she sees a button labeled CLEARANCE and clicks on it. The image of a female puppy appears, and below it, a description:

*A large, long-haired domestic blend with black spots, generous of spirit, cuddly and warm-hearted, perfect for those lonely winter nights. (Interview required.)*

Oddly, her computer's cursor seems drawn toward the web page's ORDER NOW button, as if by magnetic attraction.

# ACKNOWLEDGMENTS

**The author is indebted** to many colleagues, friends, and fellow writers, starting with Michelle Herman and Lee Abbott, who decades ago encouraged me to audit their Ohio State English creative writing courses. *Pocket Dog's* Tex was born as an overnight classroom exercise, and then the poor creature languished for years before finally coming back to life. B.K. Loren was instrumental in his revival, as were Frank Huyler, Minrose Gwin, Diane Thomas, Sandy Dickerson, my patient and long-suffering wife, Carole, my developmental editor, Heather Shaw, and the other talented folks at Boyle & Dalton.

**It was stormy and dark** the night of Jim's birth. The wind howled out of the western plains, and tree branches flailed like enraged birds against the windows of the small Missouri hospital.

"My God," his father said when the nurse handed his infant son to him for the first time. His hands trembled and his voice was tinged with apprehension. In the next room, Jim's mother sobbed softly, her body convulsed with pain. "Do you suppose that baby's normal?"

At Princeton, Jim was an erratic student, easily bored, who spent his time daydreaming and arguing with his professors. Nevertheless, he is now quite unsympathetic to those students who act the same way he did, seeing them as lazy and unfocused.

Jim's few remaining friends believe he is well-organized and compulsive, but in truth Jim leads a chaotic life devoid of self-discipline. He prefers hanging out with buddies, swilling margaritas, and watching *Airplane* on Netflix to grown-up dinner parties with napkin rings and assigned table seating. This preference was a source of great concern to his ex-wife.

Today Jim lives on 110 cactus-ridden acres in Santa Fe, New Mexico, with three dogs, six chickens, a very tolerant spouse, and a friendly courtyard bull snake named Beatrice.